My sweetest darling Nina,

I have been waiting for a long time now to hear from you, but your letter has not arrived. Is it possible that you haven't written to me? I can't believe that, not when I've told you so many times how I feel about you, what you mean to me, and how wonderful our future together is going to be. I won't allow anyone to come between us!

Perhaps you don't realize I'm serious. But you'll know that I am just as soon as I hold you in my arms and you look into my loving eyes. Soon, even before we meet, you'll have proof that your own Secret Lover has dedicated his life to his Melanie.

Oh, sweet angel of love, how ecstatic I am just to think about you, to picture your lovely face, to whisper your name, and to know that one day soon you will whisper mine. I am yours forever.

Until we meet . . .

Other books in the **Take One for Murder** series:

#1 Take One for Murder
#2 Death of a Golden Girl
#3 Dying for Stardom

Take One for Murder

Eileen Fulton's
LIGHTS, CAMERA, DEATH

IVY BOOKS • NEW YORK

To Merrill Lemmon,
who made this book possible
just by being himself.

Many thanks to Lewis Morgan for his
invaluable help with this manuscript.

Ivy Books
Published by Ballantine Books

Produced by Butterfield Press, Inc.
133 Fifth Avenue
New York, New York 10003

Copyright © 1988 by Butterfield Press, Inc. & Eileen Fulton

All rights reserved under International and Pan-American Copyright Conventions. Published in the United States by Ballantine Books, a division of Random House, Inc., New York, and simultaneously in Canada by Random House of Canada Limited, Toronto.

All the characters in this book are fictitious and any resemblance to actual persons living or dead is purely coincidental.

Back cover photograph: Tom Gates

Library of Congress Catalog Card Number: 88-91140

ISBN 0-8041-0203-1

Manufactured in the United States of America

First Edition: October 1988

Chapter One

"Hilda! It's almost time."

"I know it, Harold. I'm moving as fast as I can. You can't let eggs just stand, they get like rocks."

As he switched on the television set in the living room, Harold Hotchley heard the water suddenly gush full force from the kitchen tap and then just as suddenly go off. That was Hilda's habit, to give the sink a final cleansing tidal wave after she finished washing dishes.

As the images swam up into view, Hilda bustled into the living room carrying an iron in one hand and the ironing board with the other.

"Why don't you let me carry that for you, honey?"

"What am I, a cripple or something?"

"Honey, at your age, you ought to let me—"

"Never mind my age, I'm doin' just fine. It's exercise keeps you going. And speaking of exercise, you need more of it. Don't want to turn into one of them couch potatoes, just 'cause you retired."

"*Ssh*. It's starting!"

"I don't need to listen to the commercials, Harold. Now you pay attention to me. Just 'cause you spent thirty-eight years walking around this town delivering mail don't mean you can just sit back with your feet up.

Your body's used to exercise and it's going to be hurting if you don't keep it moving! You hear me, Harold?"

"Yes, honey, I hear you."

"Well? What are you going to do about it?"

"I guess you're right."

"'Course I'm right, that's not the point. You got any ideas?"

"Well . . ."

Harold reached for his pipe and began to fill it thoughtfully while Hilda set up the ironing board, plugged in the iron, and started to sprinkle her clean laundry. She was used to waiting for Harold's answers. Maybe he wasn't the swiftest man in Las Cruces, New Mexico, but he surely was the lovingest.

"I did have an idea . . ."

"Oh, my stars, look at how they've got her dressed today! I don't like that color on her at all, do you? Makes her look like she's got the pip."

Hilda's hands continued to sprinkle and fold laundry, but her eyes were glued to the television screen, where Angela Dolan was playing out the resolution of the previous day's cliff-hanging final scene in *The Turning Seasons*. Hilda had been a faithful viewer of the long-running daily soap opera since the first episode was aired, and she considered herself an expert on all aspects of the trials and tribulations of every single character on the show.

"Arthur Murdock, you are the lowest snake ever to crawl out of the jungle," Angela hissed from the screen as her character, Victoria Allender, confronted her current nemesis. "If I had a gun in my hand, I'd use it on you and no court would ever convict me!"

"Pretty corny lines," Hilda commented.

"And she's overacting like crazy," Harold added.

They lapsed into fascinated silence as Angela played out the brief scene, ending it with a torrent of scorn. "Just the thought of you gives me terminal migraine!" Angela/Victoria ended, flinging the line over her shoulder as she threw herself down onto a sofa, clutching her temples.

"Now I know *that's* wrong," Hilda said, starting to iron a napkin. "That business about rubbing her head—what do you call that, Harold?"

"Indicating, honey. She's indicating."

"That's it, indicating. She's indicating to beat the band. You'd think she'd know better."

"She usually does, honey. Victoria's having an off day," Harold said, giving Angela Dolan an excuse for a below-par moment. Ever since Harold had tried out for and won a tiny part in the Las Cruces Players' production of *Our Town*, Hilda considered him an authority on matters theatrical. The fact that he usually wound up selling tickets or ushering had no effect on her opinion of his theatrical knowledge. And when it came to indicating, Harold could spot it a mile away.

"How would you do that, Harold? Let the audience know you have a headache without rubbing your head?"

"Lots of ways, honey." He blew a cloud of smoke toward the screen and considered the ways.

"Just tell me one, Harold."

"Well, you could just sort of close your eyes halfway, maybe not even that much, like the light was too strong."

"Show me."

Harold obliged, and Hilda agreed. It was definitely a sign of a headache.

"That's good, Harold, that's really good. You ought to go back to the Players and try out for something again. They're doing *Bus Stop* next. You remember that one? Marilyn Monroe was in the movie. Some say it was her best. Anyway, there's sure to be something in that for you."

"I don't know, honey . . ."

"Sure there is. We'll get the play out of the library tomorrow. You'll see."

"Matter of fact, I was thinking about it, if it'd count as exercise. You think it would?"

"*Ssh*. It's starting again. Oh, here comes my babydoll! I bet she's nowhere as mean as she lets on."

3

The Hotchleys fell silent again as the drama's arch villainess, Melanie Prescott, came on to hatch yet another plot in her insatiable climb to power in the corporate world. Without taking her eyes from the screen for longer than a moment, Hilda finished ironing six napkins and two of Harold's shirts while the scheming Melanie made mincemeat of two business competitors and turned her attention to her new love interest, the dashing and debonair Norman Chandler. When the next commercial break arrived, Hilda released a deep sigh of satisfaction.

"I don't know how she does it," Hilda observed, "but that Nina McFall can do the *meanest* things, and still I'm kind of on her side. Is there a name for that, Harold, some theater term?"

"I guess there is, honey. I guess it's . . . likeability, that's what it is."

"If you say so, Harold. But whatever it is, she's got a wagonload of it."

"She's still your favorite, isn't she, honey?"

"Yep. Has been since the first day she came on the show."

"Must be a couple of years back."

"Five years and ten months, going on eleven. When she first came on, I didn't think they were planning to have this Melanie take over the show, because all she was supposed to do was get Montgomery Cromwell's job away from him, unintentionally of course, but when she found out that Montgomery's secretary, Gloria Payne, was having an affair with Tilden Webster, she knew the Webster account was going to be up for grabs and so she maneuvered to get the boss's first wife, Martha Howard, right where she'd overhear everything on the day the new accountant, Victor Murchison, audited Clarence Wooster's books and discovered how much money he'd been spending on that snip Letitia Venable! *Then*, when . . ."

Harold concentrated on his smoke rings.

* * *

"I don't know why you watch that crap, Judy."

"Maybe I like suffering."

"Whose, theirs or mine?"

"Just shut up, Dick. This isn't costing you anything."

"It's costing my sanity to listen to it."

She turned her cold gaze on him for a moment and decided to take a risk. "Then don't listen to it. You're not supposed to be at home this time of day anyway. Wives are supposed to be at home. Husbands are supposed to be at work! Earning money! Remember money, Dick?"

"Who could forget, with you around? You invented spending."

"I remember when there was something to spend!"

"I remember when there was something left to buy!"

Having reached their customary midmorning standoff, the Olcotts lapsed into their customary post-midmorning standoff sulk.

"Jesus, I don't believe it! What's the name of this garbage?"

"This *garbage* is called *The Turning Seasons*. The same name it went by yesterday."

He stood behind the sofa where she lay stretched out, watching intently. They listened for a moment, and then he couldn't resist aping the dialogue.

"'Oh, Arthur! You give me terminal migraine. You're the slimiest snake in the jungle.' God, does somebody get paid for writing that kind of stuff?"

"Yeah, somebody gets paid for writing it. And the actors get paid for acting it. And the director gets paid for directing it. And the producers get paid for—"

"Okay, just put a cork in it. I think this stuff is turning your brain soft."

"Listen, Dick, lots of people watch soap operas! All kinds of people."

"Sure they do."

"That's right, they do! They did a study, it was in the paper. College professors even watch, and truck drivers, and doctors. Not just little old ladies with bad feet. All kinds of people watch!"

"So who cares who watches it?"

No response.

On the little screen, Melanie Prescott opened the door of her apartment to admit a devilishly handsome man.

"Who's he? Somebody new?"

"Yeah," Judy said, mesmerized by the extreme close-up as the camera gave viewers an idea of what it would be like to get very close to Norman Chandler. "Melanie just started dating this guy. I think she's going to wind up in the sack with him."

"So who is he?"

"Rex Reynolds."

"She just called him Norman."

Judy fidgeted impatiently; she almost missed what Norman just whispered into Melanie's ear. "Norman is the character, Dick, the *character*. The *actor* is Rex Reynolds."

"Never heard of him."

"You will."

"What's that supposed to mean?"

"Oh for Pete's sake, now I don't know what she said to him!"

As the image of Melanie Prescott wrapped in Norman Chandler's arms slowly faded and the music swelled, Dorothy Wooten reached for the phone and waited, still gazing at the screen. At the first ring, she snatched up the receiver with one hand and turned the volume down to zero with the other.

"I could die, could *you* die?" No greeting was necessary for this daily ritual. "I *told* you she was going to go after him. . . . Yeah, he does look a little bit like that one she was mixed up with a few weeks ago, what was his name, Leonard something? . . . Anyway, who cares about him? This guy is something else. He's over the rainbow! Did you see those *lips?* And the *eyes?* Any time he's sick of Melanie Prescott, he can come knock on Dottie Wooten's door, and he won't have to knock twice, believe me! Oh, here's that stupid diet bread commerical again. They sure run that thing into the ground, don't they? And it's no good anyway, I tried it once. Ate the whole damn loaf and didn't lose a pound. . . . It's like chewing on air—you have to put too much jelly on it to get any flavor. Sure, look at that one dancing around with the stupid loaf of bread. She probably never weighed more than ninety-three pounds in her life, a lot she knows from diets. . . . Yeah . . . Yeah . . . Anyway, who cares about Victoria? She's such a pill. Always the same thing with her, telling everybody off and putting everybody in their place. I'd like to hear Arthur or Peter Kingston turn around and tell *her* off, for a change. . . . Yeah, probably never happen. Anyway, who cares about them? I can't *wait* to find out what's going to happen with Melanie and Norman. You think they're going to do it? How soon? I want to see the shoulders on that man . . . Yeah, that, too . . . Hey, that's great! That's a wonderful idea! You ought to write them a letter about it, no kidding. . . . Sure they do, I sent a letter once and I know they read it because I got an answer. . . . Come on, you got to do it. Look, come on over later and I'll help you put it together. . . . Sure, what else have I got to do? And listen, stop at the corner and pick up a snack, okay? My treat. Anything you like. . . . Yeah, good, the ones with fudge on the top."

Chapter Two

A casual visitor to Meyer Studios on the west side of Manhattan that day in May would have thought that things were not going particularly smoothly. A more astute person would have known that something seemed to be wrong. And a really keen observer would have run for cover.

On *The Turning Seasons*, several of the principal actors were assembled on the set of the Allender living room where Angela Dolan, as wealthy widowed socialite Victoria Allender, was having trouble getting through the next to last scene of the day. It was a fairly simple scene: Victoria had to chew out Peter Kingston for interfering with the life of his daugher, Buffy, who was in the throes of breaking her engagement to Victoria's nephew, Gregg Thomas.

"Peter Kingston, if I ever again become aware that you are interfering in the lives of these young people," Victoria was to tell Peter, "I might not be able to restrain myself from telling Buffy why her mother abandoned her seventeen years ago!" Tight close-up on Victoria's face, tight close-up on Peter's face, medium two-shot of Victoria and Peter for his rejoinder: "You can't threaten me!" Dissolve to long shot of Buffy and Gregg in the Allender rose garden, dissolve to tight close-up of

Melanie Prescott eavesdropping on the young couple from behind the drooping branches of a weeping willow. Slow fade as a calculating smirk appears on Melanie's face.

"If I ever again become afraid that . . . oh, Christ!" Angela said, flubbing the line for the third time. Ordinarily Angela could paraphrase herself out of just about any flub she uttered, hang onto the sense of the intended line, and finish with a smooth delivery of the proper cue for the actor with the next line. But today she seemed wholly dependent on total recall of her exact words, a facility that had never been her strong suit.

"If you ever become aware that . . . I think I'm going to *scream!*" Angela's usually cool composure was nowhere in evidence as she pounded herself on the brow with the heel of her hand and stamped to the edge of the set to look at the script again. Noel Winston, as Buffy's interfering father, was puzzled and somewhat embarrassed for Angela. Robin Tally and Bob Valentine, in position only a few feet away on the garden set, exchanged mystified glances. And Nina McFall, peering through the graceful branches of the willow tree, wondered if she should step in and see if she could offer any assistance. No, she decided, whatever's bugging Angela is none of my business. Let Bellamy handle it.

Bellamy Carter, the pompous but talented assistant director whom Helen Meyer had fired the previous December for less than solid reasons, had recently been rehired and was treading a very narrow line in an effort to resolidify his position among cast and crew.

"Angela, love," Bellamy said soothingly, "don't worry about the words." Nina was very glad the writers weren't around to hear that particular piece of direction. "All you need is the sense of the thing. Just order this piece of garbage to leave the young folks alone or else you'll tell young Buffy the truth about her dear old mum. Don't worry about the words, don't worry about the timing, don't worry about anything. Ready now, love?"

Angela nodded quickly, but she projected desperation rather than confidence as they began again.

"Peter Kingston . . . you listen to what I have to say. And listen hard. *Very* hard." From her vantage point, Nina watched in fascination as poor Noel realized he wasn't going to get his cue according to the script. "You just keep your meddling hands off those two children or I'll go to young Buffy and tell her you-know-what about dear old you-know-who!"

". . . Was that a threat?" Noel said with what Nina considered wonderful presence of mind. The altered line was a believable response to the words Angela delivered, and in fact helped her spontaneous paraphrasing sound better in retrospect. Nice save, Noel, Nina thought as the camera taped the long shoot of the young lovers. Then she eased into a classic Melanie Prescott sneer for the close-up through the willow branches.

"Cut. That's it. Terrific, gang. Let's move into the final scene." Bellamy must have been exasperated with Angela, but to his credit he looked and sounded totally thrilled with her performance. He'd probably work out his frustrations later by arguing with his cab driver, slamming his apartment door, shouting at his mother on the phone, and throwing things at his cat.

Nina was pretty exasperated herself, for a number of reasons. She'd expended far too much energy over the past several weeks dickering with the manager of her building for a new apartment, and only the day before had finally come to terms. She was due to meet him at five o'clock to sign the agreement, and it was unsettling for her to realize that she still had reservations about her decision to move. She loved the comfort of her luxurious white-peach-and-chrome art deco apartment, and she'd lived there for only a few years, so why invite trouble by flirting with the endless problems of moving and decorating a new place? Was the extra space really worth the inevitable headaches? On the other hand, this was undoubtedly the chance of a lifetime. . . .

Nina wallowed uncharacteristically in a pit of indecision and felt the familiar throbbing start up again across her forehead. But she forced all thoughts of her apartment shift to the back of her mind. There was still one more scene to get on tape before the day ended, and it would be a doozy.

She walked quickly away from the willow tree and into the next set, Melanie Prescott's living room. En route, Nina removed the topcoat she'd put on for the garden shot over her costume for the bedroom scene, which was nothing more than a filmy pale pink peignoir that seemed to reveal more than it concealed. The whistles and good-natured but smarmy remarks from the crew were testimony that the costume was well chosen. In it, Melanie was to tempt Norman Chandler into forgetting his wife. Considering the decolletage, Nina could probably have gotten any man to forget his name.

As the lights came on to their present levels and the camera rolled into position, Nina stretched out on the sofa, feeling Melanie's mood and objectives settle over her. She was somewhat uneasy about this scene, not because it was a seduction scene—she'd played enough of those to remove any self-consciousness—but because Rex Reynolds was so incredibly attractive.

Nina had played opposite a large assortment of attractive men in her career, but this was the first time she'd ever come up against one who reminded her so strongly of the only really important man in her life—Detective Lieutenant Dino Rossi of the New York City Police Department. Both men were in their mid- to late thirties, both were over six feet tall, both were powerfully built, both had thick black hair, and both had mouths of intense sensuality. The difference, and it was one she had to force herself to focus on, was that Dino's goodness shone through his eyes like a beacon, whereas the basic quality that was apparent in Rex's eyes was quite another matter. Nina wasn't sure what it was, but it was definitely not goodness.

The scene began. Melanie was waiting for Norman Chandler to walk into the trap she'd set, planning to seduce him and destroy not only his marriage but his career as well. There was a knock on the door, and she smiled knowingly to herself. Enter the victim. She called out, "Who is it?" and he answered, "Melanie, I have to see you." She arose from the bed, quickly checked her hair and figure in the mirror that hung near the door, and put her hand on the knob. "Just a moment, Norman," she said, unbuttoning her peignoir to reveal the silken curves beneath the matching nightgown.

Then Melanie opened the door and the camera picked up her look of surprise and pleasure, artfully mixed with a measure of confusion. "Norman! I had no idea! What a surprise to see you. But you don't look well. Is anything the matter?"

Rex Reynolds stepped into the room, exactly hitting his mark so that the special light above the doorway would pick up the noble brow, the broad cheekbones, the full mouth. Rex had come on the show only a few weeks earlier, but from the way his fan mail was increasing, the producers of TTS knew they had a winner and had instructed the writers to build his part accordingly.

"Melanie, I couldn't sleep. I had to see you."

"Say no more, I understand," Melanie murmured, taking one of his hands in hers and bringing it to her cheek. "Come in, we have to talk. Would you like something to drink?"

He followed her into the room, his eyes wandering over the lines of her luscious body. "Whatever you're having."

"Brandy and soda, I think." Nina threw him a slight glance that said, in effect, *Make the drinks and don't waste a moment because I can't wait to get my hands on you.*

Watching the scene from the control room, producer Horst Krueger said to his secretary, "How does she do that? If we had to spend time dialoguing all the thoughts Nina can pack into one look, we'd never be able to stick to the half-hour format."

"That's what you pay her for," Myrna Rowan answered. "And that's why she gets more damned fan mail than anyone else on the show." Keeping track of TTA fan mail was one of Myrna's endless and least favorite tasks, but she realized it was essential to know not only the amount of fan mail each cast member received, but also the general content so the scriptwriters could soft-pedal unpopular themes and plotlines and build up the more successful ones.

Within moments, Melanie Prescott had Norman Chandler next to her on the sofa, pouring out his problems and drinking in her allure along with her brandy. When Melanie set down her drink and took Norman's face in both her hands, drawing his mouth close to hers, even the most hardened and cynical members of the technical crew were mesmerized.

The scene ended with Rex taking Melanie into his arms for a long and particularly intimate kiss, with the camera carefully picking up the soft lamplight that glowed from the open bedroom door in the background.

"Cut! If that doesn't bring them back to their sets for the follow-up, nothing will," Bellamy Carter said. "Beautiful job, Nina. Perfect, Rex."

"Do you think it was all right?" Rex said. "I thought I was a little off. If you want to do it again, no problem," he said lightly but with a meaningful look at the sparsely clad Nina.

"Forget it, you dirty young man," she teased him. "I don't care if your lower plate was slipping and your toupee was at half-mast, I'm finished for the day. Got to run, guys."

Robin Tally caught up with Nina as she hurried along the corridor leading to the dressing rooms. "For a while it looked as though we were going to be here all evening. Poor Angela!"

"She certainly was off her stride today. Something serious must have happened."

"Don't you know?"

"Don't I know what? I've been very preoccupied lately. What have I missed?"

"She's stewing over her fan mail. It's been slipping like crazy. Myrna posted last week's numbers right after lunch. It's a wonder Angela didn't blow all her scenes."

"I didn't realize she was slipping so much."

"It's been going on for weeks. She's really worried. How could you not have been aware of it?"

"It's a personal thing. I've been thinking about taking a different apartment, and it's become an obsession."

Robin studied her friend's face closely. "You do look a little frazzled, hon. Just around the edges, nothing the camera's going to pick up. But maybe you could use a little extra sleep one of these nights. Or would that interfere with matters *italiano*?"

Nina gave the grinning Robin a long and cool look. "What I could use is a vacation," she said. "A nice long rest, far from this nuthouse. And for your information, *nothing* interferes with my foreign relations. Nothing and no one."

"Just don't let Dino Rossi see your scenes with Sexy Rexy," Robin said lightly. "His eyes might turn greener than yours."

Nina laughed. "I don't think Dino ever watches *The Turning Seasons*. He's just not the soap-opera type."

"You never know. Judging from the letters I've been getting lately, there isn't any such thing as a soap-opera type anymore. Maybe there never was."

"I think you're right. Listen, toots, I want to see Angela for a minute, and then I really have to step on it or I'm going to be late for an appointment."

"Oh? Meeting Dino?"

"Robin, I don't have *appointments* with Dino, I have *dates* with him. This is a business meeting with the people who run my building. I told you, I'm thinking about taking another apartment."

"You're unbelievable! You have an apartment some people would kill for, and you're thinking about moving?"

"I know, it's crazy. Don't confuse me further—I'll see you tomorrow."

As Nina changed from Melanie's seduction outfit into her own clothing, her eye fell on a huge stack of mail, some addressed to Nina McFall and some to Melanie Prescott, and she thought about Robin's comments on soap-opera fans. It amazed her that she received so much mail from men. Some of it consisted of straightforward compliments and requests for photographs, and some included suggestions about the twists and turns of the plot. But an increasing amount was on a personal level, sometimes startlingly personal. What disturbed Nina weren't the wild and wacky proposals of marriage or the strong protestations of undying adoration, but the deeply brooding letters that made her feel she was being watched in a frighteningly intense way.

"Come on, McFall," she told herself, "stop fretting about some weirdo types you're never going to meet and get your mind back to the real world."

But despite her own advice, she picked up a handful of envelopes and leafed through them, noting the variety of postmarks and the different types of handwriting. What a strange business, she thought. People from all over the country watch a television show every day to find out what's happening to a group of characters who are totally fictional. Yet the fans get so involved with these characters that a lot of them take the time and trouble to sit down and write letters about them. Sometimes they write letters *to* them, as though the characters continued to exist after the show is over. As though they had lives of their own.

The habit of imagining what was happening to Melanie Prescott between shows was a basic actor's technique that Nina herself had always found very useful. It wasn't enough for her to know her lines and Melanie's motivations; she also had to be totally familiar with everything Melanie Prescott did and said, from the profoundly important to the totally trivial. The more Nina knew about Melanie, the more convincing she was before the cameras, and the more the fans seemed to appreciate the detailed texture of her portrayal.

"Dear Miss McFall," one letter began. "Words can't express how much I enjoy your thrilling portrayal of . . ." It was a Type A letter; straight applause all the way through.

"Dear Nina. The way you always see to it that

Melanie gets what she wants is an inspiration to me. I try to think about how Melanie runs her life and goes after what she wants . . ." Type B, from someone who didn't make a sharp distinction between the actress and the character.

"Dear Melanie. You really stink . . ." Type C, unaware that the character is not a real person.

"Dear Melanie. Don't have an affair with Norman Chandler! Whatever you do, don't trust him for a minute! He's out to take your job away from you, he doesn't love you at all. Can't you see that?" Type D, swept away by the more turgid aspects of suffering and love.

"Dear Melanie, you bitch . . ." Type E, too deeply affected by the ruthless aspects of the Prescott persona.

"Dear (bleep!)" Type F took out his or her aggressions on distant strangers. Particularly devoted to uncivilized language.

"Darling. Just the sight of your beautiful face on the screen makes me sigh with love for you. How I long to meet you and say what's in my heart and tell you . . ." Type G, emotionally unstable.

Nina sighed. The deeply personal letters always affected her the most profoundly, even those that reflected a dark nature. She knew there were actors who didn't spend much time with such correspondence, and that it was even considered chic by some to express cynicism at fan letters. But she was unfailingly touched by the people behind the messages, just as they were touched by the performer behind the character.

Of course, there were also the types of letters she'd prefer not to receive, the ones that hinted at a true psychological imbalance. Thankfully, those weren't too plentiful, but they tended to arrive in sudden spurts, sometimes going on for weeks, even months, and then stopping as abruptly as they began, as though the writer had suddenly been silenced. Or satisfied.

Nina found herself riffling through the stack of letters, looking for a particular handwriting that had become very familiar to her lately. There it was. She pulled it out of the pile and sat at her dressing table looking at the unopened letter.

This particular correspondent, a man, had been writing to Nina regularly for nearly three months. His first two or three letters were Type A expressions of admiration, and she had put them on the pile to be answered with form letters that included standard responses of appreciation. But then his letters had grown more impassioned, and he'd begun to use "Nina" and "Melanie" interchangeably—and to express a determination to be taken seriously.

She'd told herself she wasn't going to open any more of his letters, but the fascination proved irresistible.

"Dearest Nina. You mean more to me than anyone else ever has in my entire life. Today I saw a beautiful flower, a lilac in bloom, and I smelled its sweet scent and felt that you were as close to my lonely heart as one day I will be close to your beautiful face. Oh, Melanie, you are my angel of pure love, and I will do anything you ask. I am your Secret Lover now and forever. Faithfully."

Nina refolded the letter and began to slip it back into its envelope when she noticed there was something else inside—a tiny sprig of lilac blossom, crushed and withered. She held it to her nose for a moment, but the delicate fragrance was gone.

This man is really getting to me, she told herself, wondering if what she suspected was true—that he'd been sending her gifts as well as love letters. She often received presents from fans, but they always came in boxes with return addresses and notes included.

Except for the earrings. About a month earlier she'd received the first of what proved to be several pairs of earrings, all sent anonymously. Most of the gifts Nina received were sent on to hospitals or, in the case of perishable items such as flowers or food, shared with other members of the cast. But the earrings were a different matter. They were all quite attractive pieces of costume jewelry, and Nina had them tucked away in a drawer in her dressing table. She didn't plan to wear them, but she couldn't quite bring herself to give them away.

One day it would all become clear, she supposed. Or, more likely, the letters and gifts would simply stop coming, and that would be the end of it. Well, so much for imponderables. Right now it was time to go and try to soothe Angela's injured ego.

Outside Angela's closed dressing-room door, Nina paused for a second, then knocked gently.

"Who's there?" Angela responded after a moment during which Nina heard sniffling and the rustle of facial tissues.

"It's Nina, Angela. May I come in?"

For a while it seemed that Angela was thinking it over. But just as Nina was about to knock again the door opened, and she saw that Angela had been trying unsuccessfully to repair her mascara.

"Hello, Angela. I thought you might like a little company."

Angela shrugged unconvincingly and turned back into her dressing room. "As long as you didn't come to gloat," she muttered.

Oh Lord, Nina thought, this is going to be harder than I thought. "Now really, would I do a thing like that?"

"Why not? *I* would, if I got the kind of mail you've been getting!"

"Well, I can't gloat over that—it's not my doing." Angela looked quizzical, and Nina continued her line of reasoning. "I mean, if anyone should gloat, it's the writers. That's what the fan mail is in response to, the plotline and the scenes."

"Maybe . . ."

"No maybe about it. You should read some of those letters—they're full of comments and advice on what Melanie should do and whether or not to trust Norman. You have to admit, Dave and Sally have come up with a sizzler of a plotline."

"Yes, they certainly have. And our dear producers

have come up with a sizzler of a hunk for you to act it with, haven't they?"

Careful, Nina told herself, Angela is spoiling for a fight and the subject matter isn't important.

"I guess they have. He's pretty good, isn't he? Have you noticed how he hits his marks? The guy never looks down; I don't know how he does it."

"With a face and a build like that, he could trip all over his own feet and bump into the camera and they'd still want to see more. You know, Nina, it's pretty cheeky of you to come in here and carry on like this!"

Forget it, Nina, you can't win this time, just get out of here. "Angela, you sound so angry. I just don't know what you're getting at. I just thought . . ."

"You 'just don't know'! You 'just thought'! You *just thought* you'd come in and lord it over me oh so sweetly, oh so delicately about your *ton* of fan mail and the sexy leading men they keep finding for you to play with! With the kind of dialogue they write for you and a gorgeous hunk to curl up with, even Godzilla would get fan mail!"

"You're right, Angela, you're absolutely right," Nina soothed. "TTS needs more variety, and more excitement for your character. And I'm going to go tell that to Helen Meyer right now! See you tomorrow!"

By the time Angela recovered from her surprise at the unexpected agreement, Nina was back in her own dressing room, gathering up her things. Ready to leave, she surveyed her image in the mirror.

For the upcoming appointment with the Primrose Towers management, she'd selected a two-toned light gray wool dress with an unconstructed jacket of gray-green. Her shoes were dark gray leather pumps and her jewelry was limited to a single strand of pearls. Her hair had been a major challenge; to minimize the stunningly sexy effect it inevitably created, she'd swept the burnished red mass into a moderately severe French twist. At least she didn't look as though she was going to a cocktail party. To promote an additional note of tough-mindedness, instead of a purse she was carrying a very businesslike black leather attaché case. She hoped it would help create the impression that although she was a major name on the most successful soap opera ever to make its way into American homes, she was no air-brain to be taken advantage of in a business transaction. She knew the moment would come when she'd have to haggle with the managing agent over the price of the penthouse, and she intended to be much less Nina McFall and much more Melanie Prescott.

Satisfied with the effect, she flicked out the lights, locked her dressing room behind her, and set off down the corridor. Despite the impromptu visit with Angela, she still had plenty of time. Too much, in fact. It wouldn't do any good to be early. Actually, a slightly late arrival would be more in keeping with her planned crowded-schedule, no-nonsense mood.

Most of the cast had already departed for the day, and the studio was settling down for the evening. As she approached the production offices a burst of garbled conversation drew her attention. It was coming from the big boss's office. Nina wondered what new crisis had caused Helen Meyer to hold a late-afternoon meeting and promptly decided it was better not to know.

Nevertheless, Nina's steps slowed considerably when she realized she was hearing her name being uttered over and over again, as though someone were trying to set it to music.

"Nina McFall, Nina McFall, *Nina McFall!*" The voice went on, rising in intensity and clarity to the point where Nina realized it was Helen Meyer herself, and she was obviously in a rotten mood.

Nina summoned all her willpower in the determination to resist the impulse to knock on the door and find out why her name was being bandied about so relentlessly.

It's better not to know.

But you want to know.

It's probably none of my business.

None of your business! It's your name, isn't it? Your career might be at stake.

I doubt that.

You know how Helen tries to blame you for everything that goes wrong around here.

"Nina McFall, Nina McFall, Nina McFall, *Nina McFall!*"

You'd better find out, sweetie. It won't take long.

So instead of knocking on the door, Nina simply barged in and asked, "Somebody want to see me?" before even looking to see who was in the room.

"Not really, Nina," Helen answered sourly. Nina's glance told her Helen was in one of her major snits. "We were talking about problems that don't concern you." "We" proved to be Helen's two producers, Horst Krueger and Ken Frost, the writing team of Dave Gelber and Sally Burman, and two newly hired publicists, Ferde Ungar and his assistant, Doris Kinling.

"In that case, I beg your pardon. I could have sworn I heard my name pronounced thirty or forty times."

"It has nothing to do with you," Helen insisted. The producers were looking in exasperation at each other, the writers were gazing at the ceiling as if for divine intervention, and the publicists were studying the floor in acute discomfort.

"I see. You were talking about some other Nina McFall."

"Oh, for God's sake, Helen, don't be so mysterious," Horst Krueger said. The others managed to express agreement with a variety of mute expressions and attitudes that Nina noted as an excellent minicourse in body English.

"All right, Horst, since you're so anxious to talk, go ahead and talk," Helen said, granting regal permission.

"It's very simple, Nina," Horst began. "You heard your name being repeated over and over because we were tallying this week's fan mail."

Nina was genuinely puzzled.

"I thought that was Myrna's job."

"Normally it is, but the load has gotten so heavy she can't do it alone anymore. And the lion's share of the mail is for you. You usually get a nice steady stream of letters, of course, but for the last couple of weeks it's become an avalanche. Not only letters, but packages."

Nina didn't feel this was exactly the best moment to deliver the opinions she'd uttered to Angela on the spur of the moment.

"Well, I mentioned in an interview somewhere that I was trying to learn how to bake bread, and it got into the story and people started sending me all kinds of recipes and things." They looked skeptical, especially Helen. "Things like baking pans. And rolling pins. There were even several sacks of special flour."

"You really have some loyal group of fans out there," said the younger of the two publicists, Doris Kinling, grinning broadly. "Good thing you didn't tell the interviewer you had a hankering to make your own wine, or the mailroom would be full of grapes."

"May I ask a question?" Nina said, and proceeded to do so without waiting for permission. "Why this high-level meeting to discuss a mailroom problem that's obviously going to be very short-lived?"

"Your actor's ego is running overtime, as usual," Helen answered, beginning in a low tone but building rapidly. "Mailroom congestion was only a fleeting topic. The purpose of this meeting is to discuss our ratings. We are not here to discuss fan mail, nor are we here to swap recipes. And when you barged in so rudely, I had just asked this distinguished and *high-priced* assemblage to explain why our ratings are sagging again, especially when one of our *players* . . ." she infused the carefully selected word with a particularly nasty tone, ". . . is so incredibly popular that the mere mention of a whimsical desire to knead sourdough is enough to tie up our mailroom six ways from next Sunday!" Helen was on the edge of spluttering, a sure sign that she was only syllables away from saying things everyone would be sorry to hear.

"And now that we have satisfied Miss McFall's burning desire to know why her name was uttered, perhaps we can return to the more urgent topic of boosting our ratings back up where they belong. And where I *insist* they remain."

A short but uncomfortable silence ensued. Helen went on. "Now, I'm not unreasonable. I don't expect miracles. But we've all seen the statistics and the demographics, and I do expect that by the start of the week I will have on my desk a plan to recapture many, oh so very, very many, of our former viewers who seem to have found choicer company on other channels. Otherwise, I too will be tempted to follow their example and seek choicer company. Are there any comments?"

By the time Helen reached that unanswerable final question Nina had finished edging her way toward the door. She glanced at her watch and realized that at least she'd solved one problem—she no longer had to worry about being early for her appointment.

As Nina crossed the deserted main rehearsal hall on her way to the exit, her mind was filled with thoughts about her contemplated move. What should she do? Stay in her present apartment because it was the comfortable and easy thing to do, or admit that she wanted the penthouse desperately and grab it? There would be the hell of packing and moving, the agony of dealing with the contractors she'd have to hire to rearrange the space to her liking, and the frustration of making professional decorators understand that she wanted to recreate her old apartment, but on a different scale. . . .

So what? The result would be a splendid layout with a bigger kitchen, two full bathrooms, a spacious terrace, and a second bedroom. She could afford it, and it was what she wanted, and it was her choice, so there! Who could possibly challenge that reasoning?

"A second bedroom?" Robin said minutes later, turning to Nina with a sly expression as they stood on the curb waiting for taxis. "You wouldn't be planning to expand your household, would you?"

"Don't be silly, Robin. A guest room is always useful to—"

"Honey, try it on the other foot. This is *Robin*, remember? I know you well enough to see the little wheels going around, and that whirring noise tells me you're thinking how handy it will be to have somewhere to house Dino's son one day. One day soon, I bet."

"You're on a fishing expedition, cutie-pie. The chief reason I'm considering taking the penthouse is because of the terrace. It'll be great for sunbathing, and I can do some gardening. That's the one thing about living in New York that I really miss."

"Gardening? You want to get back to the soil?"

Robin gazed at Nina shrewdly for a moment through narrowed eyes. "Somehow, Nina, the picture of you with a package of seeds in one hand and a trowel in the other, toiling over the freshly spaded earth while the honest sweat of a simple laborer pours down your aching back, doesn't quite jibe with the Nina I know—the toast of the tubes, with a taste for designer clothing, art-deco furniture, and hunky Italian detectives, not to mention gourmet food and fine wines."

"People do have varied interests, you know," Nina said lamely as Robin stepped into a cab, realizing how hollow it sounded, even to herself. What if she did entertain thoughts of setting up housekeeping with Dino and his son? Was it a crime to be prepared in case she and Dino ever saw eye to eye on the subject? Of course it wasn't. Then why be so secretive about it? At least the part about gardening was true—anyway, the gardening she had in mind was done a little differently from Robin's exaggerated description. Terrace gardening was done in raised planters, without kneeling down. You did it wearing the snappiest little outfits from Bloomie's, and it took about twenty minutes a day. Maybe fifteen.

Another cab rolled to a stop, and Nina gave the address of the Primrose Towers management office. It was definitely time to trade up.

She tried to imagine what Dino's reaction to the penthouse idea would be, and wondered for a fleeting moment why she hadn't discussed it with him in advance. She knew he didn't like surprises, but this wasn't something silly like an unexpected birthday party or an unplanned night on the town. This was—different.

Nina spent the rest of the taxi ride imagining how Peter's room would look in a medium blue, with a nice masculine plaid carpet.

Chapter Three

After the meeting with the building management, Nina returned to her apartment and headed straight for the bar, knees shaking. The next day was Friday, and she wished she was written out of the show and had a day off. She mixed herself a vodka gimlet and took it to the sofa where she stretched out and surveyed her home. Already it looked hostile, somehow, as though it resented what she'd committed herself to.

"All *right*," she told the walls, "what's done is done. Don't look at me that way!"

Then she giggled to herself. If anyone heard her, they'd think she'd gone bananas. "Talking to the walls" was an expression that meant talking to yourself. But Nina was actually addressing the walls, apologizing to them for the coming betrayal.

For she'd done it. She'd signed an agreement to take the penthouse. So far, not a soul except the managing agent knew about it. Yet her apartment, her faithful old apartment, knew. And so she had to explain.

"You have to understand," she said quietly but earnestly, "nothing lasts forever. It doesn't mean I don't love you—it's been wonderful here, but the time has come to move on."

Then she burst out laughing at the sight of Chessy,

her beloved adopted stray tomcat, who'd wandered out of the bedroom at the sound of her voice. Now he sat on the threshold of the living room, looking at her speculatively. Obviously his mistress had gone wacko.

"Come here, you old tiger," Nina said, patting the sofa cushion invitingly. "I have something to tell you."

Chessy jumped smoothly up onto the sofa and burrowed his head into Nina's lap, his outboard motor already warming up.

"You'll never guess what's going to happen, Chessy," Nina said, stroking him under the chin. "We're going to move. Mama's gone and taken a new apartment. What do you think about that?"

Chessy was interested, but noncommittal. He needed more information before forming an opinion.

"Wait'll you hear about it. It's much bigger, almost twice as large as this place, with a second bedroom and bath, and a *much* bigger kitchen, and best of all, a terrace! You'll be able to go outside whenever you want to! Won't that be terrific?"

Chessy's motor roared into high gear, signifying complete satisfaction.

"I'll have one of those little porthole things installed so you can go out onto the terrace and come back in whenever you want to, even when I'm not home. And I'll be able to grow some flowers for us to look at, and we can lie in the sun whenever we feel like it."

Chessy rolled over in ecstasy at the mere thought.

"You see, it's not that I don't like this apartment, not at all. I love this apartment," she emphasized, just in case the walls needed a little more convincing. "But the building is going co-op, and I heard about the penthouse becoming available, and I figured it was now or never. I'm sure it'll prove to be the right decision."

Hearing no objection from either the cat or the walls, Nina continued.

"Of course, there *are* a few little problems—like having a whole new kitchen and bathrooms put in, and having the floors scraped and sanded and refinished, and rearranging a few walls. And of course there'll be the carpets and drapes to select—but when it's finished it's going to look very much like this place, only better! Are you pleased? Of course you are! And you're the first one to know, pussycat. The very first. I haven't told a soul . . . not even *him*."

Nina took a long sip of her drink and searched around in her mind for the answers to a two-part question she'd been avoiding ever since the idea of the larger apartment first presented itself: What would Dino's reaction be, and why was she so apprehensive about discussing it with him?

"I'm home!" At the sound of his voice she stubbed out her cigarette, put the casserole into the microwave oven, and checked her watch. Exactly on time, as always.

"Hi, darling, kissy-kissy?" She gave him his standard greeting.

"How is your day going, buttercup?"

"The usual, lover. Mmm-mmm. You taste so good!" Actually, his mouth tasted like stale broccoli, but it was what he wanted to hear.

"Not as good as you, poochy." Thanks to the tobacco industry, her mouth tasted like a dirty ashtray.

"Is everything set up, poochy?"

"Of course, sugar lump. You know I'm always ready on time."

He loosened his tie and went into the bathroom as she turned on the oven to high at three minutes. Over the years, ever since he'd arranged to be home for lunch every day at two P.M. the ritual had been repeated so often it was finetuned to split-second precision. He finished washing his hands and face and stepped into the kitchen at the exact moment the timer on the microwave oven went "ping!" signaling that lunch was ready and *The Turning Seasons* was about to start.

She put the kettle on its lowest setting and set the casserole on the table as he flicked on the portable television set and adjusted the volume control.

"Oh good, they're picking up the Melanie-Norman story right off!"

"*Ssh.*"

They viewed the episode and demolished the casserole in silence, as always, comparing only cursory notes between scenes when the twisting story lines were interrupted for commercial messages.

At the end of the program, she sighed in deep satisfaction and began to clear the table while he stared out the window, lost in concentration.

"It seems to me they aren't handling this the right way," she said, spooning instant coffee into the twin mugs.

"What do you mean?"

"Melanie isn't being very smart about Norman."

"How so?"

"Oh come on, look at the way she believes every lie he tells her. She's too smart for that."

"You've got to be joking. How is she supposed to know he's lying to her? This needs more sugar."

"All that business about wanting to collaborate on the Driver campaign. Who wouldn't see through that nonsense? That is *very bad* for your waistline."

"Look, she doesn't know beans about the Driver business, but she's not stupid. She knows when she needs a helping hand."

"Well, she couldn't have forgotten that Victoria warned her to stay away from that man!"

"You make me laugh. Victoria is nothing but a nosy old bag."

"I'm telling you, Victoria is eaten up with envy because Norman pays so much attention to Melanie!"

"Are you crazy? Victoria is old enough to be Norman's mother!"

"If you want to know what I think, I think she *is* his mother!"

"That's the stupidest thing I ever heard! She couldn't have children, we've known that for years!"

"If you believe *that*, you probably still think Charlotte adopted Walter and Gigi!"

"God damn it, you haven't got the brains of a cow! There was medical evidence that those kids could not have been Charlotte's own children! They don't look anything like her!"

"No? They look an awful lot like Matthew Granville, though, don't they?"

"Don't get so smug with me! Matthew was *sterile*! Can't you remember *anything*?"

"I remember *everything*, and that's exactly what you can't stand, isn't it?"

"Look, just drop it, okay?"

"*Isn't it?*"

He smashed his fist onto the table. "I said to drop it!"

"Well, certainly. Goodness, what a fuss." She looked at her watch. "Oops, you're going to be late. Better get a wiggle on."

"Good grief, you're right." He stood up and gulped down the rest of his coffee. That Melanie Prescott was one good-looking dame. He dreamed about her all the time, even when he was awake. If he could just meet her someday, he'd make her forget all about that jerk Norman Chandler. . . .

"Bye-bye, love bucket."

"See you later, sweetie pie."

"Jeannie! Did you hear about the Gorgeous Hunk?"

"No, like what is it?"

"I could die, I could just *die*!"

"So like what happened? Did you see him washing his car in short pants again?"

"No!"

"Did you trap him in the supply closet and tear his shirt off, like in your dream?"

"No!"

"Did he finally notice you and grab your buns on the staircase, like in *my* dream?"

"No, this is real! This actually *happened*!"

"So tell me!"

"He got married!"

"Oh, *shit*! Like when?"

"Over the weekend. My mother heard about it in church yesterday. I could have *killed* her. She comes like waltzing in later, yakking on and on about this and that, and then she just like *happens* to mention that she heard he got married on Saturday morning."

"Oh, no! Who'd he marry?"

"You'll barf. He married that jerky mouse whose father runs the hardware store on North Street!"

"That *Melinda*?"

"That one."

"Oh my God, and *she's* the one who like got the G.H. in the sack? That gorgeous hunk. Those eyes. Those shoulders. That hair."

"Those *hands* . . ."

When the news circulated through Rutland High School that Michael R. West, teacher of English literature, had married Melinda S. Hale, daughter of a hardware merchant, grief was general among the female student population. The G.H. had been had, and life was barely endurable.

Months later, even though the end of the school year was approaching and there were dozens of term papers to be marked, the G.H. himself was still observing a routine that the young ladies of Rutland High would have found as unbelievable as his unexpected marriage. For Mike West continued to do something he'd been doing for years—married or not, he still found a way to steal the time every afternoon to give himself a treat.

It wasn't something a mature young husband should need, and he certainly wasn't proud of it, but he enjoyed it so much he was willing to take a few risks to get it.

At first, right after he married Melinda, Mike imagined he'd broken the habit. But then he realized it wasn't so—he still needed it just as much as before. Maybe even more.

Before his marriage, it was relatively simple. The high school where he taught was close to his apartment, so he'd just go home for a short time every afternoon, "for lunch."

But with Melinda in the apartment every afternoon, he'd had to become more inventive. Damn, if only she'd chosen to work in the afternoons instead of the mornings! Well, that was his own fault. She'd wanted to find a full-time job, but he'd insisted that part-time was all she should take on, at least at first. Actually, he was hoping she'd get pregnant almost immediately and not want to work at all, but he knew what her opinion of that old-fashioned attitude would be, so he kept it to himself.

Then, when the daily schedule was shifted and he had to take his lunch at noon instead of one-thirty or two, he was forced to resort to a drastic and expensive measure: Mike West bought a rebuilt VCR and a used television set and hid them in a storage room in the basement of his building. Each day at two P.M., while the G.H. was teaching English literature at Rutland High School, the wonderful little machine obeyed its programmed instructions and taped *The Turning Seasons* for him.

That was the easy part. The hard part was finding the opportunity to watch the show. At first he used to let the week's five programs pile up on the cassette and then find an excuse to "do errands" on a Saturday or Sunday and sneak down to the storage room for two and a half hours of bliss. But then he grew dissatisfied with the six-day wait between sessions and resorted to leaving school promptly some days and stealing into the basement for half an hour before going upstairs to Melinda. To vary the routine, on other days he'd disappear for a while after dinner "to put out the trash" and then get "trapped" by some gabby neighbor—or he'd "have to meet briefly with a working parent" to discuss a student's progress, or simply take a stroll, or go for a pack of cigarettes. . . .

One way or another, Mike West got what he wanted, which was a chance to spend half an hour every day watching *The Turning Seasons*, or, more accurately, watching that incredibly exciting redhead, Nina McFall.

Mike's deepest wish was that some day he could see

Nina McFall in person, an event he never for a moment believed might actually happen. But had he been aware of a plan that was hatching in Meyer Studios, his Gorgeous Heart might have skipped a beat at the realization that maybe, just maybe, he might actually get his wish, and not too far in the future. . . .

Dino called Nina early Friday morning to talk about their weekend plans. The forecast was for an extremely nice day Saturday and a just so-so Sunday, so they decided to do something outdoors.

"Let's go upstate for a picnic," Nina suggested. "I'll bake some chicken, and we'll have hard-boiled eggs and potato salad and chips and chocolate cookies, and anything else you and Peter want. We'll do the classic American picnic, how does that sound?"

"Sounds great to me, and I'll bring some chilled wine. But I don't know about Peter."

"Don't tell me he doesn't like baked chicken."

"No, he loves it. But I think he has plans. He said something about going to a movie."

Nina heard more than "going to a movie" in Dino's voice, and she didn't like it. Dino's relationship with his son was a roller-coaster affair. After Peter's mother died, the boy had been withdrawn and quiet for a long time. Growing up without a mother had to be hard on any child, but the best Dino could do was to hire a live-in housekeeper, Mrs. Bartolucci. She soon grew to adore Peter almost as much as Dino did, but at most she was a surrogate grandmother, not a mother. Nina was happy to realize that since she herself had entered Dino's life Peter had begun to come out of his shell. She knew Peter liked her, but she had to be careful not to seem to be taking Dino away from the boy. As though anyone could.

"Oh, it's going to be too nice to spend the day in a movie house. Is he there? Let me talk to him."

Dino put Peter on the phone.

"Hi, Nina. How you doing?" He always sounded older than his going-on-thirteen years.

"Hello, Peter. Doing great. Listen, your dad and I were just talking about taking a picnic somewhere tomorrow and getting out of the city for the day. Baked chicken and all the trimmings. How does that sound?" She didn't wait for an answer, but pressed on to sweeten the pot. "We could drive upstate a ways, maybe to Bear Mountain. Bring your bat and softball. I'm sure there'll be some playing fields there."

"Guess I could use the practice. I don't know, some of the guys were talking about seeing a movie . . ."

"Oh come on, you can save that for a rainy day. And after lunch we could visit West Point."

"Yeah? Hey, that sounds okay."

"Terrific. Now put your dad back on."

As Dino got back on the phone Nina could hear Peter's voice retreating into the distance as he rushed to tell Mrs. Bartolucci he was going to see the cadets at West Point.

"How did you do that? I could never get him to give up going to the movies 'with the guys.'"

"Just a little simple bribery. I offered him food and West Point."

"Good idea. But frankly, I think what attracted him wasn't West Point or the menu. I think he likes to be with you."

"Does he? I'm glad." She dropped her voice to its sultriest level. "I hear it runs in the family."

"Careful, or you might see a grown man try to crawl through a telephone wire."

"If anyone can do it, you can."

He laughed. "I just might. God, I can't wait to see you. Listen, after we get back to the city, we'll drop Peter off here and then finish up the evening at your place, okay?"

"Well, I don't know, let me consult my calendar. . . . Hmm. There seems to be a slight problem. Apparently I already have a date to meet a particular attractive and steamy police detective. He's been nosing around here for months now, I just don't know if I can get rid of him."

"Yeah, policemen like to nose around."

"He's very insistent."

"I know the feeling."

"But I'll try to squeeze you in."

"Hey, easy. There's a law against phone calls like this."

"Why, you overgrown masher, there's a law against entrapment, too. You entrapped me. Hey, officer, would you lend a girl a hand?"

"I'd like to entrap you."

"Mmm. The feeling is nuptial."

"What?"

"The feeling is mutual."

"Yeah. So I'll pick you up about ten?"

"Don't you mean '*we'll* pick you up'?"

"Okay, don't get technical."

"Make it nine-thirty. Let's get a good start on the day."

"Right. See you then, sweetheart."

"Good. And Dino, don't forget Peterrrr . . .'s baseball things." She'd nearly said, "Don't forget Peter," but caught herself in time.

At the studio that day, Nina vowed to concentrate on her work and steer clear of Helen, the producers, the publicists, and anyone else not connected directly with her scenes. It wasn't hard to do—Helen was apparently spending the day at Leatherwing, her estate in Westchester, Horst and Ken were scarcely in evidence, and the publicists were behind closed doors. Where publicists should be kept at all times, Nina told herself. She didn't know what they were doing, and she didn't care. Had she overheard their discussion, she would have cared a great deal.

"But Ferde," Doris said, "you know how Helen feels about Nina McFall. She'd never spring for such an idea."

"Helen Meyer might not be too fond of Nina," Ferde said confidently, "but the only thing she really cares about is this show. *The Turning Seasons* is her baby, and she'll agree to anything that will improve the ratings. You heard what she said yesterday. She wasn't kidding. She hired us to boost the ratings, and we better perform or else."

"You don't like her much, do you?"

"She's okay. A little crazy sometimes, but maybe you have to be a little crazy to work in this business."

"I think she has her eye on you."

He let out a hoot of laughter. "Forget it! I don't go for older sister types, no matter how loaded they are. Besides, you're wrong. Haven't you seen the way she follows Rex Reynolds around, with her jaw hanging open?"

"So? That's true of most of the women on the show. Anyway, Sexy Rexy seems to be sniffing around Robin Tally."

"I'm surprised he's not after Nina herself. They seem like such a believable team. Especially in the love scenes."

"I don't think he turns Nina on. When they're doing a scene you'd swear she's really got the hots for him. But when the little red light goes out, thud. She turns it off like a water faucet."

"That's called acting. Happens all the time around here."

"Besides, I hear she's very tight with some policeman."

"A cop?"

"A detective. Plainclothes type. I don't think our Rex would want to tangle with him."

"Or anybody else. Have you noticed that nobody is exactly buddy-buddy with him? Most of them probably view him as a threat, and I guess that's understandable. If his mail continues to build, he's going to be onscreen more and more, and they're going to be off."

"Speaking of fan mail, we better get down to cases. Run that idea by me again."

Ferde paced back and forth as he described the plan that he felt would put the twinkle back in the TTS weekly ratings, take the razor edge off Helen Meyer's teeth, and keep both him and Doris off the unemployment line.

The notion had struck him the day before, while Helen and Nina were having that idiotic go-round about Nina's avalanche of fan mail. If Nina McFall was so damned popular, why not capitalize on it? It didn't matter to him or anybody else *why* people watched TTS as long as they watched it. If the reason for turning it on was to see the latest plot development, fine. If the fans wanted to see Rex Reynolds or Rafe Fallone take a shower, terrific. If they wanted to see Nina McFall scheme and plot to take over the world, so be it.

And what, he'd asked himself, would excite Nina's fans more than anything else? A chance to come to New York, meet the lady herself, take a look behind the scenery to see how it all gets put together. Yes, but there wasn't anything so extra juicy there. That sort of thing had been done before. It needed the extra jolt that would make people pant and grab for it. It just rolled out of Doris's mouth like music. They fairly jumped up and down in glee. They loved it! Nina would love it! The fans would go berserk!

They couldn't wait to tell Helen.

Chapter Four

On that Saturday morning in the middle of May, New York awoke to weather worthy of the middle of August. From the moment the sun rose, the day showed all the signs of being a scorcher, and Nina had a sudden brainstorm as she slid the pan of baked chicken into the oven to warm. She reached for the phone and tapped out Dino's number.

"Hello?"

"Peter, hi, it's Nina. Hope I didn't wake anyone."

"No, we're nearly ready to leave. What's up? Is it off?"

"Would I do that to you? Not a chance. I just had a nutty idea and I wanted to bounce it off you."

"Shoot."

"Have you noticed anything odd about today?"

"Yeah. It's *hot*."

"Right. And where's the best place to go when it's hot?"

"The *beach*?"

"You got it. If you want it."

"Great! I'll ask Dad."

"No, don't do that. Don't ask him, *tell* him. Tell him we have decided we're going to the beach, and if he wants to come along, that's fine with us."

"I don't think I ought to do that."

"Oh, come on. I dare you. Majority rules."

". . . I better ask him."

"Peter Rossi, you are a wimp."

"Hey, cut it out! Okay, I'll tell him. You can wire my jaw together later."

"Don't be silly—he probably won't do more than break your arms. And look, since we're heading east, it's dumb for you guys to come all the way into Manhattan to get me. I'll leave here in about fifteen minutes and be in front of your place in about forty-five."

Nina was delighted. Not only had she come up with an idea that Peter was really enthused about, she had also given herself an excuse to drive her car. She burrowed to the back of her bedroom closet and dragged out her beach bag. The aroma of suntan lotion and salty sand crept into her nostrils and she suddenly felt like a child again.

First beach trip of the season! Hot dog!

Maneuvering the shiny new green Nissan 300 ZX up the exit ramp that led from the Primrose Towers garage to West 74th Street, Nina was on top of the world. No doubt about it, this was the day to tell Dino about the new apartment.

The beach traffic was very light; people had apparently been caught unawares by the unseasonal weather and weren't taking it seriously. Parking at the beach was a breeze, and the threesome was soon trudging across the sand, lugging the standard paraphernalia of a family out for a day at the seashore—food chest, beach umbrella, blanket, towels, and the inevitably unopened magazines and books. Who could read at the beach, when there was all that nature to gaze at?

They walked far enough to be sure of solitude from even the few groups of beach nuts who could be found romping in the sand or huddling behind a dune on just about any day, including Christmas Eve.

Peter and Nina spread out the blanket while Dino

wrestled with the umbrella that only Nina would lie under. If she turned up for rehearsal Monday morning with a sunburn, the makeup girl would moan and Helen would have a fit.

Nina slowly unbuttoned her white cotton thigh-length pleated beach shirt, wondering suddenly if she'd made a mistake about her swimsuit. It was a green and white striped spandex monokini, cut low at the top and high at the bottom, with the nearly separate pieces joined by gold metal rings at the hips. She knew it would make Dino's eyes pop in appreciation, but she hoped he wouldn't get all stuffy and object because she was showing so much skin in front of Peter.

Oh, don't be silly, she told herself, the boy has surely seen girls in much skimpier outfits on the beach. She tossed the beach shirt onto the blanket and turned to face Dino. His gaze swept her body from head to toe and back up again, and then he looked out to the open sea, his lips silently forming the words, "God help me."

"I want to go up that way, okay?" Peter asked, gesturing vaguely to the east, and pointedly ignoring Nina's near striptease.

"Sure. Just don't try to go in the water."

"Dad!"

"There aren't any lifeguards yet, and I want to keep an eye on you when you're in the water. No argument."

"Okay, I'm just going to explore for a while. Anyway," he paused nonchalantly, "you two probably want to be alone for a little close combat."

Nina suppressed a giggle and Dino shot back, "Watch your mouth, kid!" But he was grinning broadly.

Nina watched Peter running along the edge of the water, thinking he looked like a puppy let out to frisk after a long day cooped up in the house. She loved it when Dino and his son were relaxed enough with each other to exchange a little verbal sparring.

"He's such a good kid," she observed, settling onto the beach blanket. Dino was still standing, watching Peter's receding figure. "Takes after his father," she added, looking with open admiration at Dino's body.

They'd never been to the beach together before, and she marveled at how his body could look so different in the open daylight than in a romantically lit bedroom. Some men—probably most men—surely looked better in dim, artifical light. But Dino's wonderfully strong arms and beautifully muscled shoulders took the sunlight magnificently, and the sight of his hard, rippled stomach, slim waist, and powerful chest made her breath suddenly come short. A slight breeze rearranged the mass of curly black hair that lay across his forehead and ruffled the thick mat that covered the upper part of his chest. She suddenly wanted very much to put her hands on that chest and caress it.

He looked down at her and laughed.

"What's the matter? Didn't you ever see a man in a bathing suit before?"

"Certainly," she purred. "Thousands of them. But I've never seen anything like you."

"You could give a guy a swelled head," he said, sinking to his knees on the blanket and then lying down next to her, much closer than the size of the blanket required.

"In my humble opinion, you already have a swelled head."

"I didn't think it showed."

"Dino! This is a public beach!"

"I'm not sure we're talking about the same thing," he said, his gorgeously flat stomach rippling with suppressed laughter.

"I don't know what we're talking about, and please change the subject. Isn't this better than Bear Mountain?"

"Yeah. Listen, I have to say something before Peter gets back." Not liking the shift in the tone of his voice, she waited in silence. "Don't misunderstand, coming to the beach was a great idea, but after you called this morning we almost got into a fight."

"I think I know what you're talking about. That was all my doing, I put him up to it."

"Well, I didn't like it."

"Dino, you have to recognize when he's just kidding around with you and when he's serious. He's a smart kid, and he adores you. He's not going to step over the line. But you have to let up on him and give him the room to grow."

"Okay, I didn't say we had a fight, I said we *almost* had a fight."

"Well, I'm sorry you almost did and I'm glad you didn't."

"Yeah."

"And I'm glad we came."

"Yeah."

"And I'm glad I'm in love with you."

She saw the slow grin start to spread across his face. "Yeah?"

"Yeah. And I can't wait to get you alone later."

"Yeah? Why's that?"

She turned on her side to face him directly, and spoke very slowly, with a tiny space after each word. "Because . . . I . . . want . . . to . . . get . . . my . . . haaaaands . . . onnnnn . . . yourrrrr . . . *Ideas!*"

"How would you like me to throw you in the drink?"

"Seriously. I have something to discuss with you. I'm not kidding."

He sat up, recognizing the change in her mood. "Well, whatever it is, you better get it out in the open now. You can't keep me in suspense the whole day. What's up?"

"Okay. I am. I'm up. Five stories up, to be exact." He waited. "Remember I told you the building is going co-op? Well, I know it makes sense to buy an apartment, and I was going to buy mine."

"You *were* going to?"

"Right. Until I heard that the penthouse was becoming available, and I got to thinking, and I went to see it. Oh Dino, it's a wonderful space! It needs some renovating, but the result would be a knockout!"

"Your place is a knockout already," he said with the beginnings of impatience in his voice. She remembered the awe he'd registered the first time he entered her apartment. "What's the difference? You just want to be five floors higher?"

"No, it's not the height. Dino, it has the most marvelous terrace! We could have a garden, and a place to eat outside whenever we wanted to, or sit in the moonlight and enjoy the stars! It'd be like living in a little house in the sky, with the living room and dining room and kitchen and terrace downstairs, and the bedrooms upstairs, and . . ."

"The bedrooms?" He'd caught it immediately. "How many bedrooms?"

"Well, only two. Apartments like this often have three, so this is really unusual. What do you think?"

Dino began to pick grains of sand off the blanket methodically. He suddenly seemed quite far away. "If you think it's a good investment, what's the problem?"

But that was the question she wanted to ask him. This wasn't going well. It was clear he felt the unspoken pressure and didn't know how to handle it.

"There really isn't a problem. It's an opportunity that I wanted to get your opinion on."

"You said you had something serious to talk about. Was that it?"

"Yes, that was it. It's a sizable investment, and I wanted to know what you thought."

"I'm sure you can afford it."

Damn! The money thing again! Always the money thing! So she earned a staggering salary, far greater than his would probably ever be. So what?

"It's not a question of affording it. I'm shaky about the renovation part. I don't feel equipped to deal with contractors and electricians and plumbers and so forth. They'd run circles around me. I thought maybe I could ask you to . . . help me out."

He scanned the horizon of the ocean for a long time before answering.

"Got any plans for the second bedroom?"

"Well, it's always nice to have a guest room. I've been trying to talk my mother and father into coming to New York for years now, and sooner or later they're going to do it. It'd be nice not to have to put them up at a hotel or on a sofabed."

"Any other plans?"

"No plans I'd make without you," she said quietly.

"Can't argue with that."

"Good. I hate arguing." She leaned over and kissed him lightly on the shoulder. His skin was warm from the sun, and she brushed her lips across it several times. "Would you do my back?" She handed him a tube of suntan lotion with a very high protection level and turned over on her stomach.

Dino stroked the lotion across her back, reaching his fingers tantalizingly under the straps of her bathing suit top and lingering along the edges of the bottom piece.

Peter came bounding back to the blanket in a spray of sand and high spirits. Good kid or not, Nina could have drowned him.

"Let's eat!" Peter cried.

"You want to have lunch at ten-forty-five in the morning?" Dino asked.

"Why not?"

"Because you'll be starved by one o'clock and the food will be all gone."

"Aw, c'mon, Dad."

"Peter, it's really too early for chicken."

Nina felt it was time to side with the voice of authority. "Why not have a piece of fruit to tide you over? Besides, if we eat now we won't be able to go into the water for at least an hour."

"You're going *in*?" Peter asked incredulously.

"Certainly. What do you think I am, a sissy?" And she was up and running toward the crashing waves before they could get to their feet. She knew if she paused to test the temperature of the surf she'd be lost, and made good her boast by plunging directly in.

Moments later she was back on the blanket, shrieking and shivering as Dino and Peter rubbed her quivering skin vigorously with towels.

"You're a nut!" Dino said between shouts of laughter.

"You're a goofball!" Peter said.

Teeth chattering, Nina forced out the only two words that made any sense to her at the moment.

"Let's eat!"

They spent the rest of the day in a series of cliché activities. Dino and Peter raced up and down on the hard sand along the waterline, and then played with Peter's softball. Peter had brought his camera along and took a lot of pictures of Nina and Dino, some posed, some candid. While Nina started to build a sand castle, Dino and Peter drifted over to watch and then to join her.

Nina was amused at the sight of a New York police detective on his haunches in swimtrunks, engrossed in dribbling wet sand into a fantastic series of spires. She was even more amused when Peter quietly took out his camera and snapped several shots of the muscled hulk patting and shaping sand turrets before he looked up and realized what his son was doing. Peter was convulsed.

"Hey, cut that out!" Dino yelled.

"Sure, pop. I have enough now, anyway. Any time you get out of line, I bet the guys at the precinct house would just *love* to see a picture of Lieutenant Rossi making a sand castle!"

"How about a shot of Lieutenant Rossi giving his son a fat lip?"

"Police brutality!" Peter yelled, dodging Dino's playful punch.

The unseasonal weather gave way to a chilly breeze late in the afternoon, and they gathered up their things and trudged back to the car. The salt air had a predictable effect on Peter, and he slept all the way back to the city, where Nina and Dino delivered him to Mrs. Bartolucci before heading for Primrose Towers.

"I feel so gritty!" Nina said, entering the apartment. "First thing I want to do is take a shower. How about you?"

"Is that an invitation to scrub your back?" Dino said, kicking away his loafers and peeling off his shirt.

"You can scrub anything you like," she answered, wrapping her arms around his bare torso. "Mmm. I've been wanting to get my hands on you all day long. Do you know how good you look in a bathing suit?"

"I'd rather concentrate on how good you look *out* of one."

The shower was a prolonged event from which they both emerged squeaky clean.

"This has been one of the all-time great Saturdays in the middle of May," Dino said as Nina toweled his back dry. "Did you see how Peter wolfed down that chicken? You know your way around the kitchen, don't you?"

"Certainly. It's one of the rooms I'm most at home in. Wait until you see what I'm going to make for dinner."

"Why don't you just relax and let me start on the hors d'oeuvres right now?" he said, turning around to face her and nibbling on her ear. "I could make a meal of you here and now."

They sank down onto Nina's bed, exploring each other's bodies eagerly with their hands and mouths. Nina and Dino knew each other's secret signals and subtle responses so well that each could prolong the other's moments of deepest pleasure and wildest passion almost indefinitely.

When finally they crashed over the edge and whirled out of control, they were in perfect synchronization, even to the point of gasping in unison. As their deep heaving subsided and their breathing slowly returned to normal, they lay together, still united.

"Nina, I adore you," Dino whispered, his lips against her ear, his hand gently caressing her still tingling breast.

"And I adore you, my darling," she answered, moving a hand slowly across the smooth skin of his back. His body was still glowing from the sun, and she thrilled at the realization that this magnificent man made her happier than anyone she'd ever known or ever would know.

She giggled as his tongue began to explore the inside of her ear, but suddenly the giggle stopped as she felt a flame spread through her entire body. Dino felt it, too. He began to move inside her, growing and throbbing uncontrollably. Within moments they were writhing again in a fresh esctasy that made their earlier delirium seem tame in comparison.

"Dino," Nina gasped as she drifted back to reality. "Don't move any more. Don't do a thing."

"What's the matter?"

"If you start again, I might not live through it!"

When she knew she had control of herself again, she kissed him gently and slid out from under his body.

"Time for another shower, love."

"Me, too. Definitely."

"Oh no you don't. This time you'll wait until I'm finished."

"Too bad we don't have two showers."

She smiled to herself as she adjusted the water temperature again. Before very long, they *would* have two showers, she thought. But she hoped they wouldn't be labeled His and Hers.

Wrapping herself in a terry robe, Nina went back to the bedroom and stopped abruptly in the doorway, rendered speechless by the sight of Dino lying naked and asleep in her bed. For all his wildly insatiable lovemaking, he was uneasy about his own nudity, and she didn't often get the chance to admire him openly and at length. Nina wondered if the discomfort he felt when she looked at him was a throwback to his old-world upbringing, or if his wife, Carla, had somehow caused it. Had she mocked him? Did her infidelity rob him of some self-confidence? It wasn't a subject she could ever discuss with him, but she was determined to cure him of it.

She sat lightly next to him on the bed and leaned down to deliver a light kiss on his stomach, just above the hairline.

"My God, what a way to wake a man," he muttered.

"I have several other ways you might like even better," she whispered, moving her mouth to his side and sprinkling a trail of light kisses up and down his hip.

"Hey, hey, hold it right there," he said, laughing and pulling her face up to his. "How many showers do you want to take in one day?'

"Who's counting?"

"No one, but I'm starving. Aren't you hungry?"

Suddenly she realized she was famished, and she shoved him into the bathroom while she began to dress for dinner.

Ten minutes later he emerged, a towel wrapped around his waist, and began to take fresh underwear and a knitted shirt from the small wardrobe he kept at her apartment. She was very pleased that he did that; not only did it facilitate their comings and goings, it seemed to her an encouraging sign of permanence.

"Dino, I don't really feel like cooking tonight," she said, going into her walk-in closet to select an outfit. "Would you mind if we went out?"

"Whatever you say," he answered. But something in his tone told her that he wasn't too pleased at the suggestion. She looked out from the closet and saw him removing the knitted shirt he'd just put on and shoving it back into the drawer.

"We don't have to go out if you don't want to," she said. "I'd be delighted to cook for us."

"Haven't you cooked enough for one day?" he answered, taking out a fresh white shirt and a striped tie.

"Oh, the knit shirt was fine," she said quickly. "Don't get all dressed up with a tie and everything. I just feel like a fancy burger. I'm going to wear slacks and a top. You don't even need a jacket."

"Nina, will you make up your mind? You want to stay in, you want to go out; you want a dinner, you want a burger; you're getting dressed, you're wearing slacks. It's hard to keep up."

She was shocked at the abrupt change of mood. What had happened to the warmly romantic man she'd spent the last two hours in bed with?

48

"Darling, I'm sorry. I didn't mean to seem so . . . changeable. We're having such a nice day. Let's not spoil it. Please?"

She went to him and folded her arms around his neck, pulling his head down to hers. They looked deeply at each other for a moment, and then he seemed contrite.

"Sorry, babe. I didn't mean to snap at you. I just get so . . ."

"You just get so what?" She felt it was important to find out what bothered him at moments like that.

"I don't know, so . . . irritated."

"At me?"

"No, not at you. At me, I guess. Why wouldn't I want to go out with you? Or stay home with you? Or do anything at all, just to be with you?"

"Oh, sweetheart, I love you so much."

"Same here. You know that."

"Yes, I do know it." They embraced in silence for a long moment, and then backed away from each other to continue their dressing. Nina had an inspiration.

"And I know something else!" she said, selecting a pair of beige linen slacks and a white pullover top. "We need a vacation!"

"Hey, that sounds good. You got any time coming up?"

"Sort of. I'm not scheduled for a long break until August, but I know the script is very flexible regarding Melanie Prescott for the next few months, and I think I can approach Helen on the subject. How about you?"

"No problem. I've got all kinds of time coming to me."

"Terrific! Where would you like to go?"

They finished dressing and went out for dinner in a volley of enthusiastic suggestions: tours of New England, trips to the Caribbean, an idyll on the Hawaiian Islands, a pilgrimage to the capitals of Europe, an African safari . . .

Before they finally fell asleep that night, they found it necessary to take yet another shower.

Chapter Five

At the studio on Monday, Nina took advantage of her first break in rehearsal to visit Helen Meyer's office and bring up the subject of vacations. Her timing proved unfortunate.

"A vacation!" Helen said lightly, vastly amused at the suggestion. "Don't bother me with such nonsense now. We've scheduled a full cast and staff meeting for eleven o'clock. This is no time for personal requests, so just run along."

"A meeting? What's going on?"

"We are going to positively electrify our viewers," Helen said in the low tone she reserved for Important Statements. *"The Turning Seasons* is about to pull off a first!"

Nina knew when to back away; good-bye vacation plans. "Sounds exciting, Helen," she said with as much enthusiasm as she could muster. "What's it all about?"

"You'll hear all about it at eleven o'clock." Helen suddenly threw Nina an accusing look. "Shouldn't you be in rehearsal, or studying your lines? Does Bellamy know where you are? This is very unprofessional of you, Nina, and I for one am shocked. When I think of some of the problems you've caused . . ."

Nina groaned to herself. Helen was on a roll, and

there was no use pursuing anything with her. "It's all right, I'm on a break. See you at the meeting."

Nina decided to ignore the thrust about not knowing her lines and returned to the rehearsal hall. Even though the accusation was totally unfounded, the last way to get anything out of Helen Meyer was to quarrel with her.

"Have you heard anything about a meeting at eleven?" Nina asked Noel Winston, taking her place across the battered table that was used at rehearsals to represent the gleaming mahogany antique that graced Melanie Prescott's executive office.

"Horst just announced it," the silver-haired actor told her. "It'll be here at eleven. All hands wanted for a command performance."

"What's going on?"

"That's all he said. The scuttlebutt is that it's got something to do with some new controversial storyline."

"I don't think so. I just came from Helen's office. She was dropping hints about some kind of a first. Sounded like more than a storyline twist."

"Why don't we wait and see?" Noel suggested. He'd been around long enough to know better than to waste much time and energy on rumors. But despite Noel's good advice the minutes dragged by like hours until eleven o'clock, when Bellamy called a halt and the executive staff members joined the expectant group in the rehearsal hall.

"All right, settle down, folks," Horst Krueger said. "To get right to the point, as you all know, we've been concerned lately about the ratings, and Mrs. Meyer has challenged us to come up with something that will get those numbers back up where we like to see them." He chuckled and grinned, but his delivery lacked conviction.

"So our publicists put their heads together."

"And discovered they had about half a brain between them," Robin muttered at Nina, who poked her in the ribs with an elbow. This was no time to start giggling.

"And came up with an idea that I think is a lollapalooza!" Horst continued, and then ran out of steam. "So why don't we have Ferde and Doris tell you about it themselves?"

"Before they do," Helen Meyer interrupted, "I just want to say that in all my years in the business, I've *never* been as thrilled and inspired by a publicity program as I am by this one! All right, Ferde and Doris, go ahead. Share the excitement!"

"In other words, 'you *will* like it,'" Robin murmured. "I may puke."

"At least wait until you hear the idea," Nina uttered with motionless lips. "You may be in good company."

Ferde Ungar looked over his audience with anticipation, then rolled out his revolutionary plan to boost *The Turning Seasons* ratings. Before long, even the skeptics in the group had to admit that the idea was new and different, and that it just might work. One thing was certain—it would create frenzy among the viewers.

"Here's the idea we've come up with," Ferde said, generously including Doris in the credit. "It's a contest," he began, "but not your usual fur-coat-and-a-week-in-Hawaii giveaway. The prizes we're going to offer will be the stuff they fantasize about."

Again Helen interrupted. "Ferde, dear, save that part for the end. First tell them about the contest itself."

He glanced at her, smiling but annoyed. What did she think he was going to do, give away the punchline too soon? "Right. Okay, here's how it works. Starting as soon as possible, we're going to shorten the program by about two minutes each day . . ." He paused for effect. That got them all right. Now there wasn't a sound in the room.

". . . and we're going to use the time to ask questions, questions that viewers will have to answer on a contest form that will run in *TV Guide* each week for an entire month. Each week's answers will have to be postmarked by the Monday of the following week. At the start of the fifth week, we'll use the two minutes a day to start to give the answers, so the viewers can keep track of how they did."

"You mean the answers to the first week's questions will be given in week five, and the second week's questions will be answered in week six, and so on?" Angela asked.

"Right. That way, they'll know how they did as we go along."

"Won't the losers lose interest in the show?" Noel asked.

"No, because at first there'll be hardly any losers. The questions will be pretty easy until the last week, when they'll have to be more difficult. And at the same time the scripts are really going to sizzle; Dave and Sally have some twists coming up you're not going to believe."

"What kinds of questions will there be?" Robin asked. Despite her cynicism, she was getting curious.

"Doris, that's your baby; you take over."

Doris Kinling stood up and faced the group. "We want to make the questions thematic and promote interest in the contest beyond the what's-in-it-for-me prize level," she explained. "So we're going to base the questions on TTS *history!*"

They looked baffled. "For example?" someone called out.

"For example, 'Where did Melanie Prescott first meet Norman Chandler?'"

"That's easy," ingenue Sirri Ballinger said. "At Victoria Allender's birthday party."

"Right," Doris said. "But try this one: 'Why didn't Mark Stonington marry Hedy Durango?'"

Dead silence.

Finally Sylvia Kastle spoke up. "Who the hell are they?"

A buzzing arose as they compared notes about the mysterious couple Doris had named.

"I think I remember," Mary Kennerly said. As the resident grandmother on TTS, Mary had been on the show almost from the start. "Wasn't Mark Stonington the character who used to live in Peter Kingston's house about six years ago?"

"Right! Very good!" Doris was fairly jumping up and down with excitement. "Now, who was Hedy Durango?"

Mary was stumped. "Never heard of her."

"I know! I know!" Angela cried out. "While Mark Stonington was fooling around with his secretary, he was *really* in love with the waitress at the Firelight Cafe. And she was Hedy Durango! Am I right?"

"You're right!" Sally Burman answered. "Very good, Angela!"

"But the question was, 'Why didn't he marry her?'" Doris reminded Angela, who looked crestfallen.

"I can't remember," she admitted.

"Because she was already married!" Noel burst out, after racking his memory. "To Alan Jeffries!"

"You got it!" Sally said, and there was a good round of applause in recognition of Noel's feat of memory.

"Hey, this is fun!" Robin said, voicing the reaction of the whole group. "Ask us another one."

"No, you've got the idea. That's as far as we're going on the questions right now," Helen Meyer said, standing and taking command of the meeting. The burble of conversation died down as she waited, a sly expression on her face. "You see how exciting this idea is? And you don't even know about the prizes yet," she said teasingly, provoking a chorus of demands for more information.

"All right. Here's the real kicker. The people at home are going to eat this up and keep very careful track of the right answers, because there are going to be only three winners, and they're each going to get to come to New York with their husbands."

"Or wives? Or boyfriends, or girl friends?" Robin threw in.

"Yes, of course," Helen continued, refusing to be thrown off stride by this gadfly, "and stay at the Plaza for a week!" The group waited expectantly; no matter how swanky Donald Trump made it, a week at the Plaza couldn't be the big "kicker" Helen had referred to.

"But, in addition to a fun-filled week of glamorous activities," Helen continued, "it'll be a week of work! *Because* . . . the winners are all going to appear on the show!"

She waited to let it sink in, trading smug smiles with Ferde and Doris and ignoring the long-suffering expressions on the faces of Horst Krueger and his co-producer, Ken Frost, who would have to handle the logistics of this enterprise.

"Can you imagine the impact this is going to have on soap-opera viewers? A chance to actually appear on *The Turning Seasons*! It'll be a dream come true! As soon as this is announced, nobody will dare miss a single episode. We'll be back on top! And we'll stay there!"

The planned ten-minute meeting went on for nearly half an hour as more details of the contest were revealed.

No, the questions and answers were not worked out yet; the Mark Stonington/Hedy Durango question was just an example. The actual quiz would be put together by Myrna Rowan and Mark Viner, who usually assisted Dave and Sally as dialogue writer. They'd research the material by reading the mountains of old scripts in the Meyer Studio's vault.

Myrna would be in charge of security, keeping the questions and the answers in a passworded document in her word processor. Only Myrna and the writers would know how to access the secret document.

The questions would be given to the public at the rate of three per episode: one at the start of the show, one somewhat near the middle, and one at the end.

The answer forms would be printed in *TV Guide* each week; some questions would be multiple choice and some would be write-in.

The answers were expected to be voluminous; they'd be tabulated by an outside service that Horst and Ken would hire for the occasion.

No, the cast would not be given the questions in advance, and certainly not the answers.

Yes, the winners would actually be on the show for

three consecutive episodes, and they'd be paid the going rate. A special arrangement would be made so they wouldn't have to join the actors' union.

No, the winners wouldn't have lines; they'd play what was known as "silent bits," although each would receive at least one "big fat close-up." And the first-place winner would be allowed to bring along members of her local TTS fan club who would not appear on the show.

No, Hedy Durango was definitely *not* the minister's cousin from Iowa, that was Helga D'Amore. . . .

It was a wildly exuberant group that burst into Corrigan's Pub for lunch that day. The neighborhood establishment, just around the corner from Meyer Studios, was used to groups of actors in all kinds of moods from gloomy to elated, but today's crowd was something else. Even the most blasé denizens of Corrigan's turned to stare at them.

Helen had concluded the meeting with a stern admonition to the group not to reveal the contest plan to any "outsider," and the loyal TTS crew, well aware of the murderously competitive nature of soap-opera practitioners, had no intention of disobeying. Yet they were tickled by the possibilities of the quiz and were indulging themselves in lampooning the legitimate questions.

"When did Florence McGinly begin her affair with Sergeant Cassidy?"

"What color was Florence McGinly's blouse the day she began her affair with Sergeant Cassidy?"

"What color was Florence McGinly's *hair* the day she began her affair with Sergeant Cassidy?"

"What color was Sergeant Cassidy?"

"What was the name of Doug Shultz's fourth wife and how long did it take her to get him to go on a second honeymoon after their third child was the first seven-pound boy in five generations of six-pound girls?"

"Seriously, how many people do you think will enter this thing?" Mary Kennerly asked.

"Thousands," Sylvia Kastle said. "Tens of thousands."

"Sylvia's right," Nina said. "If the letters they send are any indication, getting on the soaps has replaced becoming a movie star as the world's favorite daydream."

"I hope Helen knows what she's doing," Angela said.

"That never stopped her before," Robin said darkly, remembering how some of Helen's previous ideas had backfired.

"That's true," Nina said, "but the idea of putting fans on the show is really unique. I think it's going to be a great success. I really think people are going to be very excited."

"Are you saying nothing can go wrong?" Robin challenged.

"Well, it's just a *contest*. What could possibly go wrong?"

The man in the remarkably clean work clothes carried his bag of groceries up to the second floor, let himself into his apartment, and hurried over to turn on the television set. His wife wasn't home—probably over at her friend Patti's house, watching the show. Ought to be just in time, he told himself.

And he was. The opening set of commercials for *The Turning Seasons* was just finishing, and a moment later the Allender living room came into view.

He lowered himself carefully into his favorite armchair and immediately became absorbed in the unfolding events. When the previous episode ended, Victoria was just beginning to suspect that Melanie Prescott wasn't telling the truth about her dealings with Peter Kingston. Of course, as a viewer he knew Melanie was lying through her teeth, but the suspense was in waiting to see how long it would take Victoria to figure it out. If she ever figured it out . . .

When the day's episode was over, he got up, and while he put the groceries away, he tried to decide if Victoria had ever had any reason to know the truth about Peter and Melanie. He reviewed everything he knew about the relationship among those three, and decided that Melanie was safe so far. . . .

Unless he'd missed something important when his television privileges were taken away that time. His mouth drew into a tight line at the thought of how unfair that punishment was; he was just a bystander in that fight. The warden had no right to punish everyone just because he didn't know whose fault it was.

Eddie had pretended not to care at the time, pretended to be as tough and hard as his fellow inmates. But he wasn't, not really. He was serving a few years for armed robbery, and before his term was even half over he knew he was going to have to smarten up and not make the same mistakes over and over. So he was trying real hard to keep his nose clean until he got out. But some guys just weren't happy unless they were getting other guys into trouble. Like that Marty, the one who started the fights all the time and then let somebody else take the fall.

Eddie had figured out how to avoid that s.o.b., but that day he was all wrapped up watching his favorite program, minding his own business when Marty started in. Came up and started fooling with the knobs on the TV, making the lines spoil the picture, changing the channel. Anything to get Eddie's goat, especially when he was watching his favorite program.

He knew Eddie would resist, and from there it was only a short hop to a slugfest with the bastard. When the guards separated them the TV screen was busted and nobody was talking. That was what Marty counted on, that nobody told on anybody else. You did that inside, or you were really dead meat. Lucky the warden liked him, or Eddie would have got lots worse than a month without TV. Damn it, he really missed that show!

When the month was over, he kind of asked a few questions from some of the other guys to find out what he missed, and they started to laugh at him. So he just shut up and watched, gradually picking up the threads and trying to figure out what had happened meanwhile.

So he liked to watch *The Turning Seasons*. So what? A

lot of guys inside got the habit of watching soaps. Christ, what else was there to do most days? Some of them, like Eddie, really got hooked on the stories and really looked forward to seeing what would happen next. Besides, some of those women were so beautiful—like that knockout redhead, Nina McFall. Too bad the show was only a half hour. Eddie could have watched her lots more. She was the most beautiful woman he'd ever seen. Well, now that he was out, he could watch all he liked because Louella was as devoted to *The Turning Seasons* as he was. She was even a charter member of the local TTS fan club. But Louella didn't know how crazy Eddie was about that Nina McFall. Nobody knew—it was his very own secret.

Now Eddie sat down at the little desk in the living room and pulled out a pad of Louella's stationery. It had flowers on it, and ordinarily he wouldn't have been caught dead writing on anything so sissy looking, but this letter was different. Like the others he'd written every time Louella was out of the house, this was a very special letter to a very special lady. The flowers kind of inspired him, in a way—made him able to write more romantically.

Eddie gripped the pen tightly, stared off into space for a while, then began:

"Dear Lovely Lady . . ."

Monday was the longest day in anybody's work week, and that was particularly true for Nina McFall that day. After the giddy lunch at Corrigan's, the mad rush to get through the final rehearsals and into the taping of the day's episode hadn't gone too smoothly.

"What's going on here?" Bellamy Carter had asked after the third take of a perfectly simple scene was interrupted due to maniacal laughter from a cast member. "This sounds like a Girl Scout camp-out! What do you say, people, are we going to straighten out or what?"

The next to last scene called for Rex Reynolds, as the

devious Norman Chandler, to put a few heavy moves on Robin Tally as the trusting Buffy Kingston, ending in a heavy embrace that the girl was supposed to resist halfheartedly as Melanie Prescott walked in on them. But they couldn't get through it without one or the other cracking up.

Nina, waiting for her cue, was at first amused by the shenanigans but then grew weary of the goings-on and wished they'd get through it so she could tape her final scene, go home, put her feet up, and plan her new apartment.

It took a temper tantrum from Bellamy to get Rex and Robin through the scene, and Nina went smoothly through her paces on cue. She came upon the pair unexpectedly, watched them unnoticed for a moment, gave them a long calculated look, then turned and started toward her office. But when Melanie turned away from the embracing couple, she came face to face with another unseen observer, Turner Caldwell, played by Rafe Fallone.

Rafe, as Turner, the tough guy who was madly in love with Buffy despite her engagement to Gregg Thomas, was registering extreme hatred for Norman Chandler, and Melanie persuaded him to restrain himself and go with her to her office. There, in the final scene of the day, Turner confessed his love for Buffy and uttered vicious threats against Norman for bothering her.

Rafe was known as a solid, dependable actor, but even so, Nina was unprepared for the burning rage in his face as he watched Rex fold Robin in his arms for the long embrace. And when they took their positions on the Melanie office set for the final scene, she was impressed to note that he kept the rage level constant.

The scene was a firecracker, with Rafe raging almost out of control as he spat out Turner's violent hatred for Norman. It ended with Turner's blood-chilling promise to tear Norman's head off if he didn't leave Buffy alone.

"And cut!" Bellamy called. "Really fine work, everyone. Rafe, that was particularly great. A truly compelling moment . . ."

But Rafe wasn't listening to his director. Neither was he shaking off Turner's rage. Instead, he tore across the set and grabbed Rex Reynolds by the shoulders, whipping him around so fast his face was a blur.

"You lousy crud, you better leave her alone!" Rafe told the startled Rex. "If you go near her again, you're going to be sorry, count on it! You got that?"

Rex stared at Rafe as though he'd gone mad. "Go easy, friend," he said with his most engaging smile. "The scene's over, you know."

"The scene's over?" Rafe sneered. "The scene won't be all that's over if I catch you bothering her again! Don't forget it!"

Nina watched in fascination. She'd never seen Rafe, usually the mildest of men, in such a fury. Her eyes moved to Robin, who'd been watching the sudden outburst, and Nina tried to read her friend's expression, but wasn't sure of what she saw. Catching Robin's glance, she motioned with her head toward her dressing room and Robin nodded in agreement.

A few minutes later, with the door closed and locked, Nina let out a long, low whistle. "What was that all about?" she asked Robin.

The dark-haired beauty suddenly looked somewhat smug as her attitude changed from mystification to satisfaction. "Just what it sounded like."

"What it sounded like was a very jealous boyfriend."

"No! Really?"

"Robin Tally, have you been setting something up?"

"Oh, Nina, he deserved it. Rafe's been taking me for granted again. You know that drives me wild."

Nina certainly did know. Every few months Robin would come to her weeping and wailing because Rafe was spending too much time watching football on television, palling around too often with his buddies, making too many decisions without consulting her. In short, spending too little time paying attention to Robin. And Nina would counsel patience and understanding, pointing out gently that men were different from women, etc. etc. etc., that it didn't mean he'd stopped loving her, etc. etc. etc. . . .

But this time Robin had obviously taken the ball in her own hands. "I realized that Rex was kind of hanging around me more than our scenes required, and he was definitely putting something extra into the romantic scenes, so I didn't exactly discourage him. I wanted to find out if Rafe would notice."

"I don't know how smart that was, honey."

"Well, I found out. He certainly noticed!"

"Oh yes, he noticed, all right. Now you've got a suspicious boyfriend and probably a very nervous leading man."

"But I don't have the problem of being taken for granted!"

"True. Only tell me—what are you going to do if Rex decides the prize is worth the chase and goes right on hanging around and putting that 'something extra' into your warmer scenes?"

"Oh, I don't think that will happen."

"I hope not, for everyone's sake. Rex Reynolds strikes me as the type who doesn't give up easily, even when he should. And though Rafe may be a pussycat most of the time, he's not one to make idle threats, is he?"

Robin looked conscience stricken. "I didn't think of that."

"Think of it, baby, think of it!"

Chapter Six

For the next several weeks, Myrna Rowan thought she'd be in a hellish sort of heaven. Her assignment to scrounge through hundreds of old TTS scripts to find suitable contest stumpers was the hellish part, because she had to relinquish all her regular responsibilities to an untrustworthy-looking young lady who seemed far more interested in the young studs of the Meyer stable than she was in learning the routines.

The heavenly part of Myrna's temporary assignment had a lot to do with the fact that she'd be virtually closeted with Mark Viner, Dave and Sally's assistant. Myrna prided herself on her reputation for being totally impervious to the stunningly handsome men she dealt with every day at Meyer Studios, but ever since Mark Viner joined the staff, she'd had to work very hard to avoid outright gawking.

It wasn't that Mark was particularly good-looking. In fact, he was rather ordinary, particularly in comparison to Rafe Fallone, Rick Busacca, Bob Valentine, Rex Reynolds, and the rest. Those were the stuff torrid dreams were made of, and next to them Mark Viner wouldn't have rated a second glance. But there was just something about him that gave Myrna an instantaneous gut reaction. After his first day at the studio it took her stomach a week to relax and she lost four pounds. And ever after, she went to extremes to avoid speaking to him, and she never looked at him for longer than a few seconds. When he passed close to her desk, she stopped inhaling for a few moments. She was convinced his personal scent would destroy her self-control. The only thing she couldn't do anything about was his voice—she couldn't very well clap her hands over her ears when he spoke or command her eardrums to stop functioning, so when he spoke she had to endure waves of pleasure so intense they bordered on nausea.

But Myrna was so successful in hiding her reactions to this perfectly ordinary young man that no one had the slightest idea how she felt about him. So when Helen assigned them both to the contest project, she actually took Myrna aside and laid it on the line.

"Listen, Myrna, I know you go out of your way to avoid talking to Mark, so I have a pretty good notion how you feel about him. But business is business, the show must go on, and all that rot. I don't want to hear any complaints. It'll just be for a few weeks."

Just a few weeks! If Helen only knew! This was Myrna's big chance. By the end of the first week she was planning to be three months pregnant! Her only worry was what to talk about.

"My God, where do we start?" Mark asked her the first morning as he stared at the rows of filing cabinets and stacks of cartons, all crammed to overflowing with TTS scripts.

Myrna's first thought was to start by tearing off his clothes and pulling him down on top of her, but she took a firmer grip on herself than ever before and adopted a thoroughly businesslike tone.

Beats the shit out of me, she thought, and then intoned idiotically, "Wellllll, you know what they say—it's always best to start at the beginning."

For that piece of timeless wisdom she was rewarded with a slowly spreading smile and a growing twinkle of delight from his big brown eyes. "What's that from?" he said. "That's from some movie, isn't it?"

"Is it?"

"Sure it is. 'It's always best to start at the beginning . . .' 'It's always best to . . .' Follow the yellow brick road! *The Wizard of Oz*, that's it, where the Witch of the North comes down in the big pink bubble after Dorothy's house lands on her sister, the Witch of the East. You know, in Munchkinland, which in my opinion was one of the greatest sets Hollywood turned out. That and the valley of Shangri-La in the original *Lost Horizons*. Wow, I had no idea you were a movie freak."

"Oh, sure. I go all the time."

"But there's something about the storyline that always intrigued me. If the fairy godmother figure was the Witch of the North, and the house landed on the Witch of the East, and the really bad one who went after Dorothy and her friends was the Wicked Witch of the West, then what about the Witch of the South? I don't remember any Witch of the South, do you? Maybe there's going to be a sequel some day. Wouldn't that be terrific?"

Myrna stared at him for a very long moment as the familiar weak-kneed feeling rapidly became only a memory. "You know, Mark, you were absolutely made for this job."

"So let's take your advice. Mrs. Meyer said all the scripts were carefully filed, so we'll just start with the oldest ones, go through them in chronological order, and make a note of anything that might be useful. Okay? Myrna, did you hear what I said?"

"I'm hanging on your every word."

Myrna watched in fascination as Mark hauled the oldest set of scripts out of a filing cabinet marked "No. 1" and began to read. Every time he came to a specific factual item he stopped, consulted Myrna, and either made a note of it or rejected it. He reached the end of the script for the very first TTS episode an hour later and immediately flipped open script number two.

Myrna stopped listening to the ancient dialogue and consulted her pocket calculator for a few minutes.

"Mark, hold up on that. This is impossible!"

"What's the matter?"

"*The Turning Seasons* has been on the air for more than twenty years. At the rate we're going, if we work ten hours every day—which I for one have no intention of doing—it'll take us *two years* to get through this entire roomful of scripts. Of course, by then there'll be two more years of scripts piled up, and that'll take us another five weeks to get through. And by then there'll be another etcetera, etcetera, etcetera; get it?"

"You mean we better figure out another way to do this?"

"Yes. Now you are definitely using the old noodle. Got any ideas?"

"Well . . ."

"Okay, now listen. There are about fifty-two hundred scripts here. If we each go through two scripts an hour for seven hours a day, we can get through a hundred forty scripts a week, right? Okay, let's say we want to finish this thing off and get back to the outer world in about three weeks. That means we have time to go through about four hundred twenty scripts, give or take a few dozen. That's about eight percent of the total output. So we've got to select about twenty scripts from each year's two hundred sixty—are you with me?—and pick the questions and answers out of those twenty and the hell with the rest, now let's get moving."

"Is that—"

"One other thing, Mark. *No talking.*"

By the middle of the first afternoon, Myrna had zoomed through her quota of seven scripts and Mark was on his fourth. Resisting the urge to bully him along faster, she began to stroke the resulting questions and answers into the portable word processing workstation that Helen had had installed in the storage room for that express purpose.

Mark looked up when Myrna turned the machine on, but she gave him no encouragement, riveting her attention on the task as her fingers flew over the keyboard and the resulting data appeared instantaneously in green on the black screen in front of her.

When they were finished, she commanded the electronic slave to respond only to a code that she invented on the spot, programmed the machine to print out the first day's work in the computer corner of her office above, and raced up the stairs in time to whip the pages out of the printer and slap them in a closed envelope on Helen Meyer's desk.

Helen looked up in surprise.

"Well, Myrna, how's it going?"

"Fine, just great. You'll be able to start your contest on schedule, don't worry about it."

"Wonderful! That means we can go ahead and air the first set of questions on June fifteenth. I can't wait to see what musty old facts you've dredged up," Helen said, opening the envelope. "Oh, what fun it must be to delve into those glorious old storylines and relive the great moments in TTS history!" She was actually smiling.

"Let me put it this way," Myrna said. She was *not* smiling. "If this 'temporary' assignment lasts longer than you said it would, you're gong to have to give me a fifty dollar bonus every day. And as soon as it's over, I'm going on vacation. Three weeks, with pay."

"You certainly have a strange attitude. Don't you realize this assignment is an honor? You should be proud we've entrusted it to you. Now what's the problem? Does it have anything to do with Mark? Myrna, where are you going?"

"Over the rainbow. Emerald City. Shangri-La," Myrna's voice trailed off as she disappeared down the hallway toward the exit.

True to her word and with assistance from a sullen but silent Mark Viner, Myrna kept the stream of TTS questions and answers flowing, and the stack of pages in the contest file that Helen now kept under lock and key grew accordingly.

Horst Krueger and Ken Frost hired a firm to handle the blizzard of contest entries that was expected; the writers were ordered to shorten the scripts for *The*

Turning Seasons by the required number of minutes to accommodate the daily quiz installments that were scheduled to begin on June 15; and the contest entry forms to be printed in *TV Guide* were designed.

An optimist would have said that nothing was going wrong; a pessimist would have said the smooth sailing was too good to be true.

"Oh my *God*! Did you see this?"

"See what, Patti?" George Martinus was too familiar with his wife's enthusiasms to get excited no matter how high her voice rose. The last time she'd screamed at something in the paper and brought him running up from his basement workshop it proved to be a story about the cancellation of a giveaway quiz show she'd become addicted to.

"*This!* This item in Bev Gilmore's column. It's unbelievable! Listen to this, Georgie." The newspaper quivered in Patti's hands as she read the item to her glowering husband in a voice that started at fever pitch and climbed straight upward.

SHINE WITH THE STARS

Get set, girls. During the last week of August, a small number of you lucky fans will get to live out your fantasies for a week when you join the cast of America's favorite long-running television soap, *The Turning Seasons*. Seems Meyer Studios has come up with the bright idea of running a trivia contest based on the daily drama's past storylines, and the winners will get a week-long luxury trip to The Big Apple where they'll spend their days in close contact with Nina McFall, Angela Dolan, Sylvia Kastle, Noel Winston, and all the other stars as they join the cast in "cameo roles" (that means walk-ons, in case you don't know the code). The contest is set to run for four weeks, with entry forms appearing in *TV Guide*. Okay, you TTS devotees, sharpen your pencils and your memories; we hear some of the questions are really going to be pips!

Patti tossed the newspaper over her head and let out a shriek that was heard by a workman using a pneumatic drill to cut through a sidewalk three blocks away.

"Patti, will you turn down the volume? Jesus, you want me to go deaf?"

But Patti was beyond such petty considerations as the state of her husband's eardrums. *"The Turning Seasons! The Turning Seasons!* I'm going to be on *The Turning Seasons!* I'm going to be on TV! I'm going to meet *Nina McFall!* I'm going to be on TV!" She reached wildly for the phone. "I've got to call Louella! And Pauline! I've got to call them all! Thelma and Connie and . . . Hello, Louella! Did you read—you *did*, you read it, too! It's real, isn't it, tell me it's real, tell me somebody's not playing a joke on me! . . . You bet I am! Why not? Who's been watching it as long as I have? Who started the club? Who . . ."

George scowled and trudged down to the basement. Woodworking was very soothing at such moments. Whenever Patti drove him over the edge with her insatiable appetite for the excesses of daytime television, George went to his workbench and started to work on a new lampbase or a footstool or a chair. The Martinuses were the only family in town with a set of twenty matching dining-room chairs. But even though George was very good at his hobby, sixteen of the chairs had to be kept in the attic due to space limitations in the combination living/dining area of the Martinus bungalow.

It was ironic that the only time all twenty chairs were required was for Patti's monthly meeting of the local Nina McFall Fan Club. As founder, president, secretary, and treasurer, Patti felt it only right that she host every meeting. And this contest thing probably meant she'd call a special meeting, since the regular date was still three weeks in the future. It also probably meant more club members.

George selected a piece of planking sturdy enough for a chair seat and turned on his bench saw. He wasn't ready to cut any wood yet, but it helped drown out Patti's excited chatter overhead.

Goddamn television. Goddamn soap operas. Goddamn Nina McFall! It was bad enough Patti had all those batty broads come to the house every month for those stupid meetings, but she spent so much goddamn time on it in between. Talking about that goddamn program. Talking about that goddamn Nina McFall. All the time! It was Nina this and Nina that and where she lives and where she came from and what she does and where she goes and who the hell gave a rat's turd?

Worst of all, Patti had started to *look* like goddamn Nina McFall. First she dyed her hair red, then she had the beauty parlor do it exactly the same stupid way goddamn Nina wore it, then she learned how to sew and started to make copies of the goddamn clothes goddamn Nina wore. Then, son of a bitch if she didn't start *talking* like her, using the same goddamn voice that came out of the TV every afternoon.

George tried to ignore all this, but every once in a while it got to be too much for him and they'd have a big blowup over it. Like the time Patti read somewhere that goddamn Nina McFall was dating some jerky detective, and she tried to get him to quit his job and join the police.

"Forget it, Patti, just forget it!"

"It's a smart idea, George. As a policeman you'd get a better pension than the bank is going to give you."

"I said forget it! In the first place I'm not interested in being a cop, I'm a bank guard. In the second place, I got too many years with the bank already to give up the seniority. And in the third place, even if I was interested in being a cop, I'm too old!"

"You're only forty-four!"

"I'm too old!"

"*That* is a rotten deal."

"You're doing it again, Patti. Cut it out."

"Doing what?"

"You know what. You're trying to sound like *her*. It's bad enough you try to look like her and dress like her. Christ sake, why don't you find out what kind of perfume she uses and smell like her too? Don't you understand? I don't *want* to be married to goddamn Nina McFall! I want to be married to Patti Martinus! Jesus!"

After George left for work the next day, Patti sat down and began to write a letter.

"Dear Ms. McFall," she wrote. "My name is Patti Martinus (Mrs.), and I'm the president of our Nina McFall Fan Club. And we got together and decided we'd like to send you a little something to show you how much we think of you, as you are our all-time favorite. So after much talking it over, we took a vote and decided to send you your favorite perfume. The problem is, we don't know what scent you wear. If you could drop a line and let us know, we'd be real pleased and the shopping committee could go right to work. Much respect from your devoted admirer, Patti Martinus (Mrs.)."

The letter composed by Patti Martinus (Mrs.) was very clearly stated and quite sincere, but it wasn't the most interesting letter being addressed to Nina McFall that day. Not by a long shot.

"My sweetest darling Nina. I have been waiting for a long time now to hear from you, but your letter has not arrived. Is it possible that you haven't written to me? I can't believe that, not when I've told you so many times how I feel about you, what you mean to me, and how wonderful our future together is going to be. I won't allow anyone to come between us!

"Perhaps you don't realize I'm serious. But you'll know that I am, just as soon as I hold you in my arms and you look into my loving eyes. Soon, even before we meet, you'll have proof that your own Secret Lover has dedicated his life to his Melanie.

"Oh, sweet angel of love, how ecstatic I am just to think about you, to picture your lovely face, to whisper your name, and to know that one day soon you will whisper mine. I am yours forever. Until we meet . . ."

He read it over slowly, mouthing the words silently, wondering if he'd said enough this time to convince her of his intentions. Maybe so, but just in case the letter didn't impress her, she'd change her mind when she opened the box!

Idiot! How will she know who sent it? He tore the gold-foiled gift wrap open, realizing that he'd forgotten to include a note, even a clue, as to the donor. After long thought he penned a brief note and slipped it into the box.

Two hours later he parked his car and walked into a post office in another town, a place where no one knew him. The city he lived in was big enough so that a postmark would be a useless clue, and the letters could safely be dropped into any mailbox. But the package was a different matter—it had to be weighed for postage and he didn't want to leave a trail that could be used to identify him, in case there were questions later.

"Parcel post?"

"No, first class."

"That's two forty-five. Want to register it or insure it?"

"Uh . . . No, that's not necessary." He was certain those forms required return addresses.

"You left off the return address."

"Oh, did I? Thanks for noticing. Just let me have the stamps and I'll fix it up."

The postal clerk put the stamps on top of the little box and shoved it back at him across the counter. He took it to another counter at the rear, stuck on the stamps, pretended to inscribe a return address, and dropped it into a mailbox near the door.

Soon Nina McFall would know what she meant to him. Soon . . .

The news of the TTS contest produced interesting and varied effects across the country.

In Little Rock, Arkansas, Miss Dora Gilbert, aged

eighty-three, became so excited at the prospect of winning a trip to New York City and a part on *The Turning Seasons* that she went to her dentist and had herself fitted for a completely new set of false teeth. Then she went to her opthalmologist and insisted he write out a prescription for contact lenses, tinted bright blue. And finally she made a ruinously expensive visit to La Boutique Chique. Miss Dora didn't care what anyone said; she was going to look her best for the cameras.

In Camden, Maine, Alice Murchison waited until her pulse stopped racing and hesitantly considered seeking her husband's opinion about the wisdom of entering the contest. The only time she had ever missed an episode of *The Turning Seasons* was when the hurricane of 1979 left the town without power for three days. And even then, after the lines were repaired she telephoned her sister Margaret on Cape Ann and squandered eight dollars and eighty-nine cents on the toll charge while Margaret described exactly what had happened during those three episodes, right down to the clothes Nina McFall and Angela Dolan wore. There was nothing Alice Murchison didn't know about *The Turning Seasons*, so she was sure to win. But she wasn't sure that Wilbur would want her to win and go to New York. Actually, she was sure he'd forbid it. Maybe she could just enter under an assumed name, and then when she won she wouldn't have to go to New York. Was that too silly?

In Las Cruces, New Mexico, Hilda Hotchley exchanged a knowing smile with her husband. "This is it, Harold. This one has our name written all over it. Start packing."

In Warhole, Wyoming, Della Graves turned off the television, happily let out a string of oaths having to do with her fornicating herd of fornicating cows, and picked up the telephone to call the real-estate man and put her fornicating farm up for sale. She was going to New York and she was never coming back. No fornicating way!

In Coral Gables, Florida, four women who met every Friday for lunch, a few rubbers of bridge, and a few pitchers of martinis before watching *The Turning Seasons* weekly cliff-hanging episode, planned to pool their considerable knowledge about the program and enter the contest as "Saramae Globar." But the plan, the bridge games, and the friendships came to an immediate and final end when they tried to decide who would go to New York and have a part in the show when they won. Sara thought she should go because she was the oldest. Mae thought she should go because she was the youngest. Gloria thought she should go because she'd never been married. And Barbara thought she should go because she'd never finished college. In the end, they each decided to enter the contest separately and never spoke to each other again.

In Rutland, Vermont, Mike West made an amazing discovery one day when he came home from school unexpectedly: his wife Melinda watched soap operas! Not only that, but the one she was engrossed in when he let himself into the apartment was *The Turning Seasons*! He was privately amused when she said she thought she'd enter the contest, just in case. After all, she said, she'd been tuning in to the program "off and on" for several months, and she was pretty familiar with the plot, and *somebody* had to win. At the end of the first week of the contest, when the final question was asked, Mike was further amused to see Melinda think deeply for a long moment and then come up with the wrong answer. And these were probably the easy questions; as the contest went on they were sure to get harder. He didn't like to spoil her fun, but he knew she didn't have a ghost of a chance—unless she had help. And no one knew even half as much about *The Turning Seasons* as he did. . . .

In Hicksville, New York, Dottie Wooten started another diet.

In Chicago, Illinois, Eddie Croydon surreptitiously checked Louella's answers on the entry blank. She knew her stuff, all right. Wouldn't it be great if somehow she could win?

Chapter Seven

The atmosphere inside Meyer Studios on the Monday of the second week of the *The Turning Seasons* contest was only slightly more jubilant than the beach in Fort Lauderdale on the first day of Spring Break.

To get the show on tape by three every afternoon demanded rigid adherence to the daily production schedule: first call for line rehearsal at eight A.M.; blocking the actors' movements, timing, and script adjustments from nine-thirty to eleven-fifteen; lunch from eleven-fifteen to twelve-thirty; the first runthrough of the entire show from twelve-thirty to one; makeup and costumes from one to one forty-five; dress rehearsal from one forty-five to two-fifteen; fifteen minutes for last-minute fix-ups; and the final taping from two-thirty to three.

But today was obviously going to be different. It was nearly eight-twenty A.M. and the first word of the script had yet to be uttered. Ordinarily, had Helen Meyer walked into the rehearsal hall and found such flagrant disregard for the timetable, she'd have blown her stack at everyone in sight. But today the lady herself was leading the parade of procrastinators. At the moment, she was blissfully reading excerpts aloud from one of a large fistful of newspaper clippings.

"... one of the most wildly successful publicity ploys ever devised ... Will take its place in the Ballyhoo Hall of Fame ... *The Turning Seasons* days of sagging ratings are over, at least for the foreseeable future ... *TV Guide* reaped an unexpected windfall from the daily soap *The Turning Seasons* last week when hordes of fans descended on newstands to buy copies of the weekly telemag just to get their hands on a contest entry form ... Publicity flacks for other soap operas are hanging their heads this week ... It looks as though getting on a soap opera has replaced owning a home as The Great American Dream ..."

The group that had gathered around Helen to hear these glowing opinions cheered and whistled at each fresh statement. And when Ferde and Doris arrived, the heroes of the day received an earsplitting ovation. It was as though *The Turning Seasons* and everyone connected with it had won all the Emmys and a few Oscars and Tonys for good measure.

When finally Horst Krueger interrupted the proceedings to point out that there was still a show to get on the road, gang, he was greeted with a chorus of good-natured catcalls, boos, and hisses. It wasn't until Spence Sprague sided with Horst that things in the hall began to return to normal.

"Horst is right," Spence called from the sidelines, where he'd been observing the circus. "If you don't all buckle down and get this rehearsal underway, we're going to run way over schedule today. And you know that running over schedule means running over budget, don't you? Of course, if the management doesn't care ..."

Ordinarily Helen's hackles would have risen at even this mild rebuke, but today she was in too good a mood. "Spence, what can I say? You're right. When you're right, you're right. I'll have some of these posted on the board so you can all read them later. Now let's get with it, people!"

The excitement that permeated the morning rehearsal sessions was still going strong when final taping got underway—exactly on schedule. It was as though the flood of good publicity had inspired a parallel burst of cooperation and professionalism on everyone's part.

"If I didn't know better, I'd swear this group was on uppers," Robin whispered to Nina as they took their places and waited for their entrance cues.

"I could use some more of this boundless energy myself," Nina said, suppressing the urge to yawn.

"Pooped?"

"Thoroughly. This business with the renovation has me going in circles. I can't *believe* what that contractor—uh-oh, here's our cue. I'll tell you later."

But "later" was deferred indefinitely. As soon as the taping ended, Robin joined the crowd at the bulletin board, where Helen had posted the best of the articles sent by Meyer Studios' clipping service from newspapers all over the country.

In her dressing room, Nina noticed that the stack of newly arrived fan mail was much larger than ever before. She also saw there was a small package along with the letters; it caught her attention because the amount of postage on it was unusual for such a small package.

It would have to wait until tomorrow; at the moment, she had to hurry home and fight with the contractor.

If Monday morning's atmosphere had been euphoric, Tuesday's could only be described as ominous. The early warning was sounded as soon as Nina arrived at the studio.

"Hi, Sylvia," she said cheerily, and was rewarded with a strangely restrained "Morning" from the usually warm and outgoing woman.

"How's it going, Mary?" she called to the senior member of the acting team, who looked at Nina for a moment too long before issuing the terse rejoinder, "Going fine."

Puzzled but not concerned, Nina figured it was a letdown after the previous day's jollity, and proceeded down the corridor to her dressing room. En route she crossed paths with Angela Dolan.

"What's happening, Angela?" she asked in her friendliest tone. "Are they keeping you busy?" she added, to fill the unexpected silence that met her first greeting.

Angela's frigid gaze would have left icicles on the sun.

"Angela? What's the matter?"

The trim blonde seemed to grow another two inches as she prepared to speak. "*Busy*? Are they keeping me *busy*?" she repeated sarcastically. "What an interesting question, particurary considering the source. Well, yes, they *are* keeping me busy, since you ask. But not as busy as they're going to be keeping *you*, it seems."

Whatever had frosted Angela's tips this time, it was a lulu.

"Angela, I recognize all the signs of a hard freeze coming from your direction, but honestly, I don't know what you're talking about."

"Of course you don't, you busy little beaver. So why don't you just drop in on one of our prize-winning publicists and find out? I'm sure they'd just love to tell you all about Nina McFall Day."

"Nina McFall Day? What's that? Oh, Angela, I'm so tired today. For heaven's sake, just tell me what you're talking about."

"You'll have to excuse me now. I have a scene to prepare," Angela said with a deadly cold smile. She moved with deliberate grace into her dressing room, punctuating her exit with a hard slam of the door.

Here we go again, Nina thought. It seemed that she and Angela couldn't go longer than a week without some kind of hard feelings erupting. Well, it was understandable, Nina supposed, at least some of it. Before Nina joined the cast of TTS, Angela Dolan had definitely been the best known of the principal actors. But as Nina's popularity began to grow, Angela's shrank, a condition attested to by the running tally of fan mail that Myrna Rowan kept at Helen Meyer's bidding.

Well, it wasn't Nina's fault! She hadn't done anything deliberate to harm Angela, and she certainly wasn't going to hold her own career back just to protect someone else's overdeveloped sensitivities. This is a tough business, she thought, and if Angela can't take the bumps then she doesn't deserve the smooths.

But still Nina paused at the door to her dressing room, then consulted her watch. She had just enough time. Oh, hell. Angela's not a bad person, she just overreacts sometimes. Better go see what this is all about.

"That's terrible! How could you *do* such a thing?" Nina demanded of Ferde Ungar when he explained the meaning of "Nina McFall Day."

"You have to understand, we were ordered to find a way to goose the ratings. So what was more natural than to build on our strengths? And what's our biggest strength? You are."

"Never mind the grease job," Nina said. "When Helen outlined all this contest business, she didn't say a thing about 'Nina McFall Day.' No one did."

"We weren't sure about that part of it. Now we are."

"What does it involve?"

"Oh, it isn't all that much, really. On the last day of the week the winners are here, they'll get to do a scene with you." He rushed on quicky at the reaction on Nina's face. "Which only means that you'll be the mainstay in the scene that they'll appear in. In the background," he finished lamely.

"What else? I know that's not all."

"And you'll be their hostess. Later."

"Here it comes. What does 'later' mean? How much later?"

"Well, at a cocktail party."

"A cocktail party. Isn't that cozy? Where's it going to be?"

Ferde looked particularly uncomfortable at this point. "Helen thought it would be best to have it at your place."

"Forget it!"

"But . . ."

"Forget the whole thing! Don't you understand how embarrassing this is? First it sounds like we're having a contest to boost the show's ratings, and everyone is treated equally and everyone is going to benefit. Now suddenly it's all changed and it looks like *I'm* being dangled as the main attraction, boosted at everyone else's expense. Ferde, I have to *work* with these people. They're my friends and they're going to resent it. Ferde, *I* resent it!"

"You resent what, Nina dear?" Helen asked, walking into Ferde's office.

Nina went through her tirade again for Helen's benefit, and then waited for a response.

"Nina, you're too much of a professional to question the value of publicity," Helen said sweetly.

"I'm not questioning the value of publicity, I'm questioning the wisdom of poor relationships among the cast. Already this morning I felt chilly breezes from Sylvia and Mary, and Angela is ready to kill me. Now I find out why. Suddenly you're promoting a prize on this TTS contest as 'Nina McFall Day' and you want me to go along with it. *And* have a crowd of people in my apartment when I'm trying to get ready to move. Impossible!"

"Yes, I heard about your penthouse," Helen said, smiling. "Sounds wonderful. Sounds like the perfect place to entertain. Think how thrilled your fans will be to see the photographs later on. Pages and pages and pages of pictures of Nina McFall's fabulous new penthouse as she welcomes her adoring public into it!"

"It won't be ready on time! The old tenant hasn't even moved out yet! It needs a total renovation!"

"Just the terrace and the living room, dear. And the kitchen, of course. It's always good to include the domestic side, isn't it, Ferde?"

"Helen, I am *not* going to . . ."

"And think how much you'll enjoy that week-long vacation afterward."

Nina's eyes narrowed. "You're trying to bribe me."

"Is that what I'm doing?"

"Yes, that's *exactly* what you're doing. Because nowhere in my contract does it say that I have to open my home and allow my privacy to be invaded for publicity purposes!"

Helen looked only slightly miffed by the truth in Nina's statement.

"Well, Nina, if you don't wish to cooperate, I'm sure we can make some other arrangement. Meanwhile, I'll tell Dave and Sally not to write you out of the script for that week."

Nina gave up. "*Two* weeks."

"Of course—two weeks. Isn't that what I said?"

"I'll talk to my contractor tonight. Maybe he can change his work schedule."

Helen laughed lightly. "Of course he can, if you tell him to. After all, you're the boss, aren't you? I mean, it *is* your home, isn't it?"

"I'm beginning to wonder!"

The unpleasant turn events had taken was lightened considerably when Nina went home to her apartment late that afternoon, for she received the information she'd been waiting for—the penthouse had finally been vacated, which meant that the renovation could begin. It also meant she could at last show the place to Dino.

"Oh, Chessy," she told the purring ball of fur in her lap, "this is something I've been looking forward to. And dreading."

Dino was coming to meet her as soon as he was off duty, and she planned to relax with him for a while over a drink, get him in a receptive mood, then casually suggest that he might like to see the new place before the renovating began.

It was a perfectly fine scenario, so why did she have

the nagging feeling it wouldn't play? She gave up trying to figure it out and concentrated instead on the knottier issue of deciding which flavor cat food would make Chessy happier at the moment—Deli Delight or Chunky Chicken.

Then she stretched out on the sofa and put in a solid hour studying the next day's script. Oh, Lord, another heavy breathing scene with Rex Reynolds! The scene itself was fine, but Nina was having problems finding inner justifications for Melanie Prescott's failure to see through Norman Chandler and realize what a slimy character he really was. Surely the viewers had him pegged from the start; it was very difficult to fool an audience, and a dangerous thing to do.

Nina recalled the time about three years earlier when one of the TTS plotlines involved a robbery. The writers had insisted it would be good to mislead the viewers into believing that the guilty character was Stewart, a suspicious type who'd been introduced into the story only a few days earlier. Actually, the thief turned out to be Brent, a character of long standing. In truth, Brent was played by an actor who didn't want to renew his contract. Since Helen was loath to recast the role on the grounds that it destroyed believability until the audience got used to the new actor, the writers devised a flexible solution: Brent was given a long jail term. Later, if the actor wished to return to TTS, it would be a simple matter to have Brent released from jail and return, chastened and wiser by the experience. On the other hand, if the actor decided not to return to the show, Brent could simply be reported as having moved to another town to start life with a clean slate.

It sounded like a clever solution, but the audience hated it; letters poured in, reviling TTS for making Brent into a thief, and ratings were on the soft side for several weeks thereafter.

It provided a lesson for an actor that Nina never forgot: Always be careful about what your character is called on to do, and if it seems the fans are going to disapprove, then fight with all the clout you can muster.

Of course, the less experienced actors didn't have any clout, and sometimes had to find ways to justify some pretty outrageous behavior. But if you hung on long enough, you built up the clout and could eventually use it for self-protection. As Helen had said time and time again, it was a tough business.

Helen. Angela. Nina McFall Day. Oh, why did things have to get so complicated?

By the time Dino arrived, Nina had the next day's script under control, particularly the motivations, and had changed into a sophisticated blue and green silk crepe de chine dinner dress with padded shoulders, a V neckline, and a two-tiered flounce just above the knees that seemed to have a life of its own.

She had rearranged her hair from the Melanie Prescott knot into a mass of shimmering waves that fell softly over her shoulders, slipped a few gold bangles on one wrist, and surveyed the effect in her mirror. No, off with the bangles; they looked cheap somehow. Instead she put on a massive silver cuff bracelet. Bingo. Instant class.

Satisfied with her outfit, she applied a few squirts from her perfume atomizer, smiling at the memory of that sweet letter she'd received from the head of a fan club somewhere out west, wanting to know what perfume she used because they wanted to send her some. She'd answered immediately, naming Joie de Vivre, the less costly of the two scents she used, secretly delighted to know that it was the scent Dino strongly preferred over the other, vastly more expensive, Ecstasie.

Funny, she couldn't recall ever receiving the perfume. Well, no matter; it was the thought that counted, she told herself as she hurried to open the door.

"Hello, darling."

"Babe, you look terrific," Dino said, taking her in his arms for a kiss that would have burned up the home screens if Melanie Prescott and Norman Chandler could have reproduced it.

"Come in—let's relax for a while."

"Bad day?"

"How can you tell? Tattletale lines around the eyes? Grim jawline?" she asked, mixing him a martini and wondering if it would be worth the effort to try to get him to become a champagne drinker. No, definitely not.

"Something in the voice."

"That's right, you can tell over the phone, too. Clever man. For that, you get another kiss."

"Hey, if this is a contest, I'll really show off and claim the big prize right now."

Nina groaned at the word. "Don't mention contests!" She related the latest details of the situation, including the conversations with Angela and Helen, but omitting the part about hosting a cocktail party for the winners at the end of August in her new penthouse in exchange for a two-week vacation. She wanted him to see the new apartment first.

Dino listened without comment until she was finished, then heaved a philosophical sigh.

"Honey, I have to tell you that I can see both sides here."

"That's all right, I can, too. You don't have to hold back. Tell me what you really think."

"Well, this might surprise you, but even I have become aware of what a big deal this damn contest thing is."

Nina raised her eyebrows. She knew Dino didn't watch soap operas—not even *The Turning Seasons*—and she was certain that his colleagues at the stationhouse didn't watch, either, at least not in public. Had he been reading the entertainment columns?

"Mrs. Bartolucci," Dino explained. "She's become a dedicated fan of yours, and she was chewing my ear off the other day, telling me how she loves the show, and how she loves you on the show, and how her friends love you on the show, and maybe she could get me to get you to give a few little hints about some of the tougher questions. Then the next day I was driving to investigate a robbery with Bruno Reichert, and damned if he doesn't pull the same line. His mother-in-law in Detroit watches and she knows he works for me and she knows you and I have been seeing each other."

"A woman in *Detroit* knows about us?" Nina asked incredulously.

"Yeah. She remembered from when the papers carried all that news about the Minton murder, and then the Triano thing last winter. So of course she figures your show is all Bruno and I ever talk about, and maybe he can ask me a few little things, because that's probably all you and I ever talk about, too. And you know what? Maybe she's right. Two minutes after I walk in, we *are* talking about the goddamn contest!"

She suddenly felt very uncomfortable. "Well, it's only a game, really. It'll be over soon."

Dino rose from the sofa and wandered over to the window, where he gazed down into the street. "I'm sick of it already. So much goddamn publicity. You know, I have to tell you that it used to tickle me when we were out somewhere and somebody would recognize you and maybe throw you a hello or ask for an autograph. Hey, I used to think, this lady is really a celeb! Now every time we step out somewhere and somebody interrupts us, I feel . . ."

"What, darling? What do you feel?" Nina asked anxiously.

"I feel *mad*, that's the only word for it. It makes me mad when strangers poke their noses in and interrupt us. How can you relax when you know that can happen any time? Damn it, I like my privacy and I feel like it's gone whenever one of your fans butts in."

He fell silent. Nina put her wineglass on the coffee table, rose, and walked over to join him at the window. Uncertain of the right words, she wrapped her arms around his muscular torso from behind and gave him a long, gentle hug.

He turned to face her, and she read genuine concern and worry in his eyes.

"I'm sorry, babe. I dumped all over you for something you can't help. All that is part of your job, and it goes with the territory. I know that. What I'm doing is taking it out on you because I'm stewing over Peter."

"Peter? Is something wrong?"

"I don't know. I suppose it's called becoming a teenager. Yesterday we were talking about his schoolwork, which isn't all that great, and the subject of summer vacation came up. I told him I didn't think he should just loaf around all summer, hoping I could get him to think about catching up a little by spending some time in summer school."

"Uh-oh. I can image what his reaction was."

"Yeah, not wildly enthusiastic. At first I thought I was on the right track, because he brightened up when I said he should do something with his time. But it turned out that what he wants to do is get a job. The kid's not even thirteen yet!"

Go easy here, Nina told herself. This is quicksand country. "Summer school would be a wonderful thing, absolutely wonderful . . ."

"Go on. I hear the 'but' coming."

"You're such a smartie, aren't you? But—if he's not really failing and he's dead set against it, maybe a job, just a part-time job, wouldn't be the worst idea in the world. Much better than just hanging out with his pals."

"Maybe so, maybe so." But Dino didn't sound convinced.

"Isn't that the way kids get into trouble? Not that Peter isn't trustworthy, but even good kids can be led astray if they spend too much time with troublemakers."

"You might be right . . ."

Nina suddenly had one of her brainstorms, but first she wanted to lay the groundwork properly. "Let's kick that around over dinner, shall we? But first, I have a little surprise for you. Are you ready?"

"I don't know. I'm not too crazy about surprises."

"Well, I think you'll be interested in this one. At least, I hope so. The tenant finally moved out of the penthouse, and renovations are going to start tomorrow. But first I want you to see it. Okay? Let's bring our drinks."

She dangled a key in front of him and prayed he'd express at least a little bit of interest.

"Sure, babe, why not?"

Well, that certainly was a *little* bit of interest—certainly better than nothing.

"Come on, Chessy," she said, picking up the purring tom. "You want to see your new home, don't you?" At least she'd have one ally.

On the way up in the elevator she warned him that the place was a mess, but she wanted him to see the "before" so he'd be able to evaluate the "after." When they reached the top floor, the elevator doors parted to reveal a small and somewhat dingy elevator lobby.

"Kind of gloomy," Dino observed.

"Yes, but not for long. The lobby will have a new paint job and new lighting, and I thought I'd put a little table there, with maybe a flower vase or a table clock and a mirror above it."

"Who lives in the other apartment?" Dino asked, nodding at the only other door in the lobby.

"Oh, that's not another apartment—that's the service door to the penthouse."

"Well, pardon me! Talk about privacy!"

Yes, he loved privacy—score one point for the good guys.

When Nina pushed the door open they were instantly bathed in the light of the setting sun that was spilling across the good-sized foyer through a pair of French doors, one of several such pairs that led onto the terrace. The light flooded the rooms with a warm golden glow that temporarily concealed a myriad marks and flaws on the walls and ceilings, and Nina felt like a princess entering a forbidden castle. If only the prince wasn't too much of a grouch . . .

"This is the foyer," she whispered, as though apprehensive about being caught trespassing. "Look, a walk-in closet for outerwear and a separate closet for guests' coats. See, the lights go on when you open the door, just like a refrigerator. All the closets are going to be like that."

"That's important," Dino said in somber tones. "If I had to flip a light switch every time I wanted to go into a closet, I'm not sure I could deal with it."

She gave him a playful punch on the shoulder. "Go ahead, make fun of me. But you'll see; this place is special."

Nina led the way through an archway into a long, wide hall, setting the squirming Chessy on the floor so he could do his own exploring. "This is the gallery," she said.

"The gallery? Where I come from, we used to call them hallways."

"That may be, but this is too wide for a hallway. In this neck of the woods it's a gallery."

"As in picture gallery?"

"You got it."

"Okay, it's a gallery. What's next?"

"The living room."

"Don't you mean the grand salon?"

"No, you galoot, it's the living room. And just look at it."

He whistled in genuine admiration at the huge room with its generous moldings, high ceilings, inlaid parquet flooring, and double set of French doors.

"Is that the terrace out there?"

"Yes. Come see. The view is heavenly."

It was. The magnificent vista of the Hudson River stretched both north and south, providing a panoramic sweep that Dino couldn't even pretend not to admire. As they stood there sipping their drinks and gazing at the Jersey cliffs across the river, Chessy mewed his way onto the terrace, attracted by the scent of fresh air and the gentle breeze.

It was an idyllic moment, and a domestic stillness settled over them. Nina wondered if Dino was aware of it. Certainly Chessy was; he weaved between Nina's feet and found a choice spot to curl up near the living room wall, where the sun had baked the bricks to a delicious warmth.

"I guess Chessy approves," Nina said.

"What's not to approve?" Dino muttered, then took another sip of his drink and said, "So come on, show me the rest." That sounded encouraging. Definitely.

They went back into the living room and then entered the dining room, which was almost as large as "the grand salon." Dino stared at the vast space.

"Wow! Now that's a dining room even my father would have called big enough." He smiled at the memory. "He loved to entertain, any time at all. He didn't need an occasion, and the more people the better. When I got older I used to wonder how my mother did it, all that cooking and cleaning up afterward. She never even had a dishwasher," he reflected.

"I'll bet she was a wonderful cook," Nina said.

"She sure was. Wasn't everyone's mother a wonderful cook? Kitchen through here?" he said, barging through a swinging door. There was an even greater note of interest in his voice, Nina thought. She wished she'd warned him about the kitchen. . . .

"What the hell? . . ." Dino stood in the doorway, staring at the room before him. It wasn't a kitchen by any stretch of the imagination, but a conglomeration of wooden tables and overhead racks, all stained and exuding a strong chemical smell. Pipes led from an old porcelain kitchen sink to several other battered and stained industrial-sized metal sinks that had been rigged up jerry-style at various places around the room. "Who lived here? A mad scientist?"

"A photographer. Apparently he turned the kitchen into a photo lab, and when the management found out they had him evicted. Commerical enterprises are a violation of the lease. That's why the place became available. You don't find spaces like this in New York every day of the year."

"All the negatives you can eat, huh?'

"Something like that. But just ignore what's in it now and think what it could be."

"Peter should see this. He's got the photography bug—wants to take a course in it next term."

Nina knew an opportunity when she heard one, and quickly seized on this one. "Dino, what a wonderful idea! There's so much space here, we could easily chop off a piece of it and turn it into a little darkroom. Wouldn't he love that?"

Damn! Why had she said "we"? He had that same look she'd noticed on the beach when she first mentioned the second bedroom.

"I'm sure he would. At least until the novelty wore off. You know how kids can be."

"Anyway, it'd be an excellent investment. Add to the value of the place when I sell it."

Dino burst out laughing. "When you sell it! You haven't even moved in and already you're talking about selling it?"

"It's always advisable to keep an eye on the future," she said primly, refusing to feel foolish. "I don't necessarily intend to spend the rest of my life here. Who knows? In a few years I might be ready to leave New York and go live in the country somewhere. . . ."

"Sure. And raise chickens and get up at four A.M. to slop the hogs. You are the nuttiest fruitcake in the window." He put his glass on one of the makeshift tables and took her in his arms. "Maybe that's one of the reasons I'm so gone on you. Listen, I've heard everything you've said, and you're right. This is going to be a fantastic apartment; it's terrific just the way it is. And if you're serious about a darkroom, Peter would flip for it. I'm starting to flip a little myself."

After a lingering kiss they stood quietly hugging in the rapidly darkening kitchen. And then Nina had her second inspiration of the day.

"Dino, I just had an idea. Why don't we let Peter design the darkroom himself?"

"Hey, he'd really like that! You're full of good ideas, aren't you? Maybe that's why you taste so good."

"Wait, there's more. This could be the answer to the problem of how he spends the summer. Kids love to work with tools and carpentry and all that stuff. I could get my contractor to hire him as a part-time apprentice, say a few hours a day three days a week. That way, Peter would learn something useful, earn a few dollars, and keep out of trouble! And the contractor would have a little extra help at minimal expense. Do you love it? What do you think?"

"I don't know . . ."

Don't rush it, give him time! "Well, look, it's getting dark and you haven't seen the rest of the place. Let's finish the tour and then talk about this over some food. I, for one, am starving."

Without waiting for a response, Nina took Dino by the hand and quickly led him through the rest of the apartment. The kitchen had three other doors; one led to the pantry, one to the service entrance, and one back into the foyer. From there they went upstairs to the bedrooms.

They walked through in silence, Nina opening doors for Dino to glance in closets and bathrooms. As they passed through the master bedroom, she wondered when they'd christen this particular chamber in their own private way. When they got to the second bedroom, Dino uttered his single comment on the entire upper level. "Convenient, very convenient." Then he turned and went back down to the foyer.

"Some layout, I have to admit," he said in an even tone of voice. "Sure we didn't miss anything?"

"No, we covered ev— Oh. There's one more thing. This." Nina went to a door that Dino had supposed was another closet and opened it to reveal a paneled study lined with built-in oak bookcases. Another door at the far end opened into a half bath.

Dino walked in and ran his hand over the smoothly shining oak shelves. Nina knew that would get him; men are always pushovers for bookcases. But she wondered whose books he imagined on those spacious shelves—hers, his, or theirs.

"Okay, enough. I don't care if there are four more rooms, a garage, and a heliport for the private chopper. I'm hungry."

* * *

Two hours later, after a pair of perfectly grilled steaks, an excellent bottle of Chateauneuf du Pape, and a perfectly managed psychological campaign by Nina, Dino agreed: If the contractor was willing, Peter would have a job for the summer as part-time carpenter's apprentice on the penthouse renovation project. And he could design the darkroom.

Nina had one more reason to feel just a trifle smug about getting Dino to agree to the idea—she hoped it would give Peter a proprietary feeling about the penthouse. But this wasn't anything she could discuss with Dino, of course. Not yet.

Nina arrived for rehearsal the next morning in a happy frame of mind. She'd had a wonderful evening with Dino; he seemed to accept the fact that she was upgrading her luxurious apartment for a superluxurious penthouse, he was agreeable to the idea of Peter working part-time—and he was crazier about her than ever. The scene in her bedroom before he finally left at one certainly proved that.

So she felt there wasn't anything she couldn't handle that day—except possibly the growing load of fan mail. She wondered, in view of the sheer quantity, how much longer she'd be able to continue her practice of signing each letter personally, even the standard form responses that went out. As for the totally individual responses, she'd have to be much more selective about those, limiting herself to the really special ones, either letters to people who wrote her regularly, those few whom she carried on a continual correspondence, or the occasional letter that touched her deeply—like the one from the woman who told her how happy it made her dying mother to forget her pains and problems every day for the half hour she spent in the company of Ms. McFall and the rest of *The Turning Seasons* cast.

But in no case was she going to respond, even via

form letters, to writers of *strange* letters, letters that included unsavory suggestions or threats to punish Nina for Melanie Prescott's unscrupulous deeds. As for the unhinged admirers . . .

Nina's eye fell on the little package she had set aside two days earlier, the one with so much postage. She picked it up and wondered what could be so small yet weigh so much. She was used to receiving gifts from fans—all sorts of things, from hand-knitted scarves and caps to embroided handkerchiefs, costume jewelry, and books. She was amused to note that the package was addressed to "Melanie McFall."

She tore off the packing tape and removed the brown paper outer wrapping. Inside was a layer of gift wrap, a beautiful heavy gold-foil paper. And inside that was the box itself. She shook it but learned nothing from the clunking sound that resulted. Well, time to see what weighs so much.

Inside the box, wrapped in protective cotton batting, she found the gift itself: a massive pendant suspended from a gold chain. The pendant was an unusual design—two cobras twined together in the classic lovers' knot, with green-colored stones for eyes. Nina thought it was odd, intensely interesting, even beautiful in a way, but somehow threatening, as though it had been designed by an evil genius intent on attracting admirers and then mesmerizing them.

Under the piece of jewelry was a neatly folded note. She had an impulse to throw it all in the wastebasket, including the unread note, but she was too curious to resist.

"Dearest Angel. You are what other women want to be, even try to be. But no woman could ever be what you are. Here is proof of my love. Wear it, Melanie, as a sign to me that you accept your Secret Lover, who will soon be at your side. Anyone who tries to come between us is doomed. Faithfully and forever . . ."

Nina slowly refolded the note and put the pendant back into its box, rewrapping it with the gold-foil paper. She shuddered to think that this man might really mean what he said. This was no ordinary fan, idly yearning for a glimpse of a celebrity; this was a truly disturbed person. The letters proved that, along with the choice of gift.

The strong impression of the sinuous and insinuatingly designed pendant lingered in Nina's memory. She'd never seen such a unique design in a piece of costume jewelry.

And a nagging thought crept into her mind, but she dismissed it. Of course it was costume jewelry. Anything else would have cost a small fortune, and only a true madman would go so far as to . . .

Chapter Eight

It was the middle of July, and the heat of the New York City summer was rivaled only by the heat of *The Turning Seasons* Trivia Contest. The entries had avalanched beyond anyone's expectations, and the temporary staff hired to handle the tabulations had been doubled and then some.

Finally, after four weeks of questions that built steadily in difficulty, it was time for the second phase of the competition—publicizing the answers. For maximum security, the heavily safeguarded answers were given to the announcer only a few minutes before he was to go before the cameras and put them on tape. Then the special segment would be aired that same day, at the end of the shortened TTS episode.

The announcer who had been hired for the job, Gary Johnson, was an actor who'd been trying for years to land a role on *The Turning Seasons*. He'd been so persistent about it that he'd become his own worst enemy and was suffering from a sort of backlash effect, although he didn't know it. Spence Sprague and the assistant directors had secretly agreed never to use him on the show because he had made such a fuss when Rex Reynolds was hired to play Norman Chandler. But Johnson was so aggressive in his efforts that they realized he wasn't going to go away until he was hired. He wasn't the first actor to get a job that way, and he certainly wouldn't be the last—but this wasn't the job he wanted.

Although Johnson was electrified at finally receiving the long-awaited call, he was crushed to learn that he was wanted only as an announcer, not as a member of the cast. He was so distressed, in fact, that he promptly turned the job down, which irritated Spence Sprague so much that he personally phoned Johnson.

"Gary," Spence growled into the phone, "I've had my eye on you for years, looking for just the right spot in the cast, but there hasn't been anything exactly right for your particular qualities. It's time you realized that this is really all that's probably ever going to come your way in regard to *The Turning Seasons*."

"But it's not acting," Johnson whined. "I want to be a part of the real show!"

"For God's sake, grow up! You know all about the competition, so you understand that the spot will last for a full month. You'll be seen daily, and thanks to the craze this thing has become, your exposure will be tremendous. You know how this business works—you're going to be seen a lot, and afterward you'll have a much better shot at getting on one of the other shows. *Any* of the other shows! You'll be *known*!" And you'll be off our necks, Sprague added silently to himself.

After far more persuading than Johnson deserved, he finally agreed to take the announcer's spot, on condition that one of the TTS cast appear with him each day to announce the answers.

That was when Spence lost it. "*Condition!*" he exploded. "Who the hell do you think you are? My actors are too busy doing the show to add contest announcements to their schedules! Besides, it'd be lousy for their images to appear on the show out of character. If that's your attitude, forget the whole thing!"

Sprague later reflected that it was interesting to note how quickly Johnson backed down. All right. He'd do the announcments. But, Johnson told himself after the talk with Sprague, one day, somehow, he was going to get on that show and play opposite lovely, luscious Nina McFall.

In Hicksville, New York, Dottie Wooten sat breathless in front of her television set, clutching a pencil and her duplicate copy of the answers she'd sent in to *The Turning Seasons* competition. After four weeks of anxiety, finally she'd start to learn how she did. As she watched she automatically chewed mouthfuls of lettuce and cottage cheese without dressing and sipped from a glass of water. Dottie had lost six pounds already, and if she could lose another nineteen by the time the final answers were revealed, she'd be ready for the big time! Thank God she'd never thrown out all those dresses she couldn't get into anymore. Some of them were even back in style!

The Monday episode churned on, ending several minutes earlier than usual. After a commercial break that seemed to go on forever, there was a drumroll leading into a blazing fanfare of brass instruments, and an unfamiliar face came onto the screen.

"Hello, all you fans of *The Turning Seasons*!" he said as the music quieted down to a steadily pulsing rhythm. "My name is Gary Johnson, and I'm privileged to be the fellow you've been waiting to hear from! . . ."

George Martinus slammed out the back door as the shrill squealing in his living room swelled to an unbearable pitch, threatening to drown out the announcer's words.

"Girls, now shush! Shush up!" Patti commanded. "We don't want to miss a word of this!"

"For a month now you've been sending in your answers to our questions in hopes of winning the prize of a lifetime—a chance to actually appear on *The Turning Seasons*! And today's the day you start to find out if *you* are among the lucky ones whose dreams are going to come true! Are you ready?"

"Are we ever!" Louella Croydon cried.

"Then here we go! Now, do you remember . . ."

"Let's go!" shrieked another.

"Jill and Louella, if you don't quiet down, both of you, I'll put you out, I swear I will," Patti warned the boisterous pair. "Now *ssh!*"

". . . it was only four short weeks ago when you heard the very first question in the competition? This was the question we asked you to answer: Exactly how long did Roger Drusdale stay in prison for the attempt he made on the life of Victoria Allender?"

The background music quickened in tempo as increased urgency crept into Gary Johnson's voice.

"Do you remember your answer?"

"For Pete's sake, 'course I remember it," Hilda Hotchley fumed. "Think I'm an idiot? Get on with it!"

"Well, fans, we thought that was an easy one! After all, it wasn't that long ago when Roger Drusdale was thwarted in his cowardly attempt to put an end to Mrs. Allender's life . . ."

"Oh, my Great Aunt Fanny, they're going to stretch this out till Christmas Eve! Harold, don't trip over the ironing board!"

". . . but you'd be amazed at the variety of answers we got. For example, the longest prison term anyone sent in was 'Life plus one hundred years.' Sorry, but that is not the correct answer! And on the other end of the scale . . ."

"What was your answer, honey?" Mike West asked his wife.

"I think I said eighteen months," Melinda answered. "Or maybe sixteen."

". . . several of you said that it was a trick question, that the attempt on Victoria Allender's life wasn't made by Roger Drusdale at all but by someone else. Now, shame on you! Do you think we'd start right off with trick questions? No, sir! *Those* came later!"

"Didn't you make a copy of your answers, honey?"

"I meant to, but—*ssh*, let's listen."

"All right, here it is—the correct answer to the first question: For trying to kill Victoria Allender, Roger Drusdale was sentenced to two years in prison! *But*—with time off for good behavior, he served exactly *eighteen months!*"

Hilda Hotchley nodded in satisfaction and turned Harold's blue plaid shirt over to iron the other sleeve.

Patti Martinus's fan club went wild with jubilation; they were off and running.

Dottie Wooten screamed in disappointment as she pulled herself to her feet and headed across the room to her cache of Hershey bars. On the way she flung the remains of her cottage cheese salad into the garbage.

Eddie Croydon smiled knowingly. Maybe he should have entered this thing himself instead of leaving it to Louella and that nutty fan club.

Alice Murchison put a check mark in the first space on her homemade score sheet and began to worry again about how to handle Wilbur when it came time to go to New York.

Della Graves stared at the television screen and grimly told Gary Johnson exactly what to do with his fornicating competition and precisely how to go about it.

And all across the country at that moment, the groaning from those who had answered the first question incorrectly was drowned out by the crowing from those who got it right. Had the latter group known how simple that question would prove to be in comparison to some of the grim stumpers they had subsequently fouled up, the cheering would have been very subdued.

But at Meyer Studios at the end of the first day of the fifth week of the competition, no one was terribly excited. A scoresheet for the unofficial contest pool that Robin Tally and Sirri Ballinger had cooked up was posted on the bulletin board. All cast members were listed down the side, with the question numbers running along the top. At the end of the competition, whoever received the highest score would have his or her dressing room repainted and redecorated at the expense of the others.

Well, Angela Dolan thought, as one of the cast members with the longest seniority, this is going to be duck soup. She believed a nice flattering shade of peach would be appropriate. Mary Kennerly had chosen green. And Noel Winston was planning on sky blue.

As soon as he was alone again, he took the manila envelope from its hiding place in the bottom bureau drawer under some old sweaters he never wore and emptied the contents onto the bed. Dozens of sheets of paper covered with his handwriting fluttered across the bedspread. It felt good just to look at them. He liked to write to her—it was almost like talking to her in person. And when he read them, he could imagine how she felt whenever she opened one and read it for herself.

He picked up one of the sheets of paper and began to read it silently, slowly mouthing the words, losing himself in the intensity of feeling he put into every line:

"Dearest Love," it began, "You kept me awake last night, you really tortured me with the things I know you're going to be saying when I hold your naked body against mine and teach you what my love is really all about. Believe me, you are going to scream your pleasure into my ears when you know what I am capable of doing to you. There's no way you are going to settle for any other man after you've spent an hour, no, even a minute, with your Secret Lover. . . ."

No, not yet. It was too soon for that one. He picked up another.

"My sweetheart. Sometimes when I get a sudden vision of how your beautiful swelling breasts are going to feel in my hands, it makes me . . ."

No. Not yet for that one, either.

"Dear Angel. Today I concentrated on only two things—your lips and your voice. I know your voice very completely, of course, because I get to hear it almost every day. But your lips are the things that get me very excited, since so far I have only looked at them but not yet felt them against my lips, or anywhere else that you are going to want to put them, on my face and my ears and my neck and my shoulders and my chest and . . ."

No, still too soon.

"Dear Melanie. Today you made me very goddamn mad by keeping Nina away from me. I watched as always, but this was one of those days you stayed away from me. That makes me furious! Don't do that too often or I'm going to get so angry I'll do something that I don't want to do! I mean this!"

No, that was wrong. He felt that way whenever she stayed off the show, but he realized later it probably wasn't her fault, at least not every time. Sometimes she couldn't help it. But sometimes he was sure she was punishing him for not coming to her and being with her.

But she couldn't feel that way many more times. Soon she'd know what she'd been missing.

Very soon.

He heard the front door open and quickly slid the papers back into the manila envelope and hid it again beneath the sweaters.

In just a few more weeks . . .

Chapter Nine

Nina crumpled the letter angrily and threw it into the wastebasket. That was it, that was the end! From now on, she'd be on the outlook for that all-too-familiar handwriting and tear the letters up without even opening them. Whoever he was, he was becoming too weird for Nina; the insistent tone of the letters was starting to upset her.

Besides, she had quite enough to worry about without a "Secret Lover" emerging from the woodwork just at the moment.

It was only a month now until the penthouse reception she'd been blackmailed into promising Helen in exchange for her two-week vacation, and the renovations weren't anywhere near completion.

She stared at her image in the dressing room mirror and reflected on the crash course she'd unintentionally been given in the realities of apartment renovation in New York City. She'd learned a lot in only six short weeks.

Oh, the demolition had been accomplished immediately, as soon as she paid the first third of the contracted price for the entire job. Within a few days walls had been ripped open, old plumbing torn out, ancient appliances removed. Frayed wires dangled from holes in the ceilings, and a horrible mess of crumbled plaster and scraps of lumber covered the floors. She'd been awed and thrilled; the wrecking crew had attacked the penthouse with the zeal of crusaders. But then it was as though someone had blown a whistle and everything had ground to a halt.

Every day when Nina finished taping and got back to Primrose Towers, the first thing she did was go up to the penthouse to see what progress had been made. It had become an exercise in frustration. On the first day after the demolition was complete, she'd opened the door to the penthouse with a breathless air of expectation. She knew she shouldn't expect miracles—after all, how much could be accomplished in one day?

As it turned out, not much at all. Nina ventured into the apartment still looking for signs of progress, but it didn't take her long to get the message. Nothing had been done. Nada. Zero. Zip. In fact it appeared that no one had even been there!

Forcing herself to remain calm and persuading herself that there had to be an excellent reason for the disappointing situation, Nina went down to her old apartment and headed straight for the phone, not even stopping to greet Chessy. She dialed the contractor's number.

"You have reached the office of Al Gastanos," the machine told her. "No one can come to the phone now. At the sound of the beep, leave a brief message and your call will be returned as soon as possible. Have a nice day. And remember to wait for the beep."

Nina remembered and waited. "Hello, Mr. Gastanos? This is Nina McFall. Please call me as soon as you can, any time up to ten o'clock this evening. Thank you. And *you* have a nice day, too."

Then she picked up her purring pet and settled down with him on the sofa for a good long snuggle. It was the least he deserved after guarding the castle by himself all day. "Oh, Chessy, Chessy," she whispered into one of his twitching ears, "why do I have the feeling that this is only the beginning?"

It was then shortly after five P.M. By eight o'clock she had fed both Chessy and herself, changed into a sea-green lounding robe with matching slippers, studied her script for the next day, studied it again, and discovered that instead of getting the relaxation she needed, she was pacing around nervously, glancing alternately at her watch and the phone.

At eight-thirty she could stand it no longer and dialed Gastano's number again.

"You have reached—"

She hung up abruptly, then regretted it. Suppose he was there monitoring his calls? He would have picked up once she identified herself, wouldn't he? Of course!

Nina dialed the number again, and waited through the unnecessarily long message, gritting her teeth at the inevitable and inane "Have a nice day." Then came the beep. Nina's second message was shorter than her first.

"Mr. Gastanos, Nina McFall. It's eight-thirty-five. I'm still waiting to hear from you. Please call me."

At ten o'clock, after a brief but pleasant conversation with Dino, she climbed into bed. She was determined not to bother him with her renovation problems; it was quite enough that she'd gotten him to agree to let Peter work for the carpenter on the job.

At ten-thirty she took a mild sedative.

At eleven-thirty she finally dozed off.

It went on that way for three days before she finally spoke to Gastanos himself.

"Mr. Gastanos? Nina McFall. I've been trying to reach you for days and days, but you've never—"

"Calm yourself, lovely lady, calm yourself."

"But I left so many messages!"

"Ah, these terrible machines. Not reliable. Would you believe, I only got one message, just now. Anyway, here we are. Now what can I do for you?"

"Mr. Gastanos, I—"

"Please, it's Al. Call me Al. My friends all call me Al. And all my customers are my friends. That's the way I like to work things. Okay?"

"Fine—Al. But why isn't anyone working on my

105

apartment? I stop in every day, but nothing's been done. Time's flying by! You know my schedule. And my young friend is waiting to start work, too. We're both waiting. Al, is there a problem?"

"Ah, it's that cursed strike that's holding us up."

"What strike?"

"You haven't heard? The corrugation-material deliverers are on strike . . ."

But when the corrugation material people were all squared away, then came the curled-wire shortage, followed by the ceramic-tile crisis, and compounded by the lintel finishers' walkout.

After a week, Nina began to think of "call me Al" Gastanos by the more fitting nickname of "Alibi Al." With the planned reception staring her in the face and an eager Peter waiting to start work, she was getting desperate for a way to apply some pressure. Help came, as it often does, from an unexpected source.

"Nina, you've been looking worried lately. Something bothering you?"

It was Rex Reynolds who asked the question during a rehearsal break.

"I was hoping it didn't show. You see, I'm renovating this apartment . . ."

She poured out her troubles and was astounded when Rex laughed and said, "Contractors, they're all the same. You have to know how to talk to them."

"Apparently I don't."

"Ah, but *I* do."

"You do? How?"

"Both my father and my brother are contractors. I speak the language. It may not be language a lady should listen to, but I speak it nonetheless. Would you like me to have a word with your Mr. Gastanos?"

Would she!

Within forty-eight hours after Rex had his "word" with Alibi Al, two men were busily at work installing new sheetrock walls, a plumber and two assistants were installing new radiators and uncrating the new bathroom fixtures, and a team of electricians was making sense of the dismaying snarl of wires. And the master carpenter, who was there to oversee the preparation and installation of new woodwork and kitchen cabinets, had taken Peter Rossi under his capable and protective wing and was initiating the enthusiastic youngster into the mysteries of grades of lumber, types of molding, sizes of nails, and how not to mar either the wood or one's thumb when countersinking a finishing nail into a smooth piece of wood.

"Nina, I don't know when I last saw Peter so happy," Dino told her over dinner a few nights later. "It may not last, but for now he loves what he's doing. All he talks about is carpentry and woodwork."

"Don't be pessimistic. Why shouldn't it last?"

"You know how kids are. Today's fad is tomorrow's bore."

"Well, let's just wait and see. Maybe he isn't exactly ready to enter a profession, but he's learning something that will always come in handy."

"You're a smart cookie, Ms. McFall. Nutty, but smart. How did you ever get that contractor off his duff?"

Nina told Dino about the unexpected help from Rex Reynolds, and detected more than a hint of annoyance.

"Why didn't you ask me to do something?"

"Oh—I thought of it, but I know how busy you are. And anyway, Rex's family is in the business, so it was nothing for him to lean on Alibi Al a little."

"You think I don't know how to lean on people?"

She gave him her sultriest through-the-lashes gaze. "You, Lieutenant Rossi, are one of the best leaners in the business. When you lean on a girl, she knows she's been leaned on."

"Is that so? I don't know, maybe I could use a little more practice."

"Practice makes perfect, right?"

"Something like that. Will you stop with the eyes? People will think I've drugged you."

She bent her head close to his and whispered softly, "Help! Help! This man is trying to have his way with me."

"I have an idea. Let's skip dessert and you can show me what's been happening in the penthouse so I'll have an idea of what Peter's talking about."

"And then?"

"And then we'll go down to your old apartment and discuss the fine art of leaning on a girl."

"I'll race you to the roof!"

For the next week, progress on the penthouse had gone so smoothly and fast that Nina couldn't believe it. Every day, instead of dreading what she'd find, she went home eagerly to review the work. But then she began to notice things she didn't understand and didn't really know how to evaluate—items not done as she'd expected, things left partly complete or changed entirely. She wasn't sure what needed to be done, but she knew better than to try to "lean" on Alibi Al herself. It was time for a little more input from Rex Reynolds, but this time she thought she just might forget to mention it to Dino.

The only problem was, how to approach Rex? She didn't want to give him any reason to think she had an ulterior motive; finally she decided on the direct approach.

"Rex, may I ask you another favor?"

"Certainly, Nina. More problems with the renovation?"

"Maybe. I'm just not sure. The things I see might be perfectly okay, but I don't really know. And I don't want to complain without a reason, and I certainly don't want to ask a lot of dumb questions that'll remind my friend Alibi Al I don't really know what I'm talking about . . ."

"So you'd like me to come up and take a look, right?"

"Would you?"

"Sure, no problem. After we finish today?"

"That would be wonderful. Meet you at the exit. Four o'clock?"

"Fine. Or better yet, as soon as I've changed I'll just come by your dressing room and knock you up."

"You'll *what?*"

He laughed at her startled expression. "That's a British term. They use it to describe the act of knocking on someone's door to wake them or call them. Colorful, isn't it?"

"I'll say! See you later."

She was used to the sly technique some men had of using off-color references to test the waters, see what kind of reaction they provoked. Was Rex one of those? If she'd laughed heartily and come back with a salty retort of her own, would he have taken it as encouragement that her interest in his abilities went beyond renovation? She wasn't sure. Rex was so damned handsome he could surely have his pick of any female in sight; he didn't need to go to the trouble of gamesmanship. Yet some men liked exactly that, the game itself even more than the prize. She couldn't help remembering Rob Bryant, the sexy assistant director who'd had every female on the TTS set drooling.

She was glad Dino wasn't one of those. Dino didn't like games at all, but he adored the prize.

She was also glad Dino didn't know that she'd asked Rex Reynolds to look at her new apartment.

Nina was ready before Rex arrived at her dressing room, giving him neither the chance nor the opportunity to do any "knocking up."

When they opened the exit door to the street, a small group of devoted fans were waiting. Such groups often formed outside Meyer Studios, as many of the faithful made it their business to become familiar with the comings and goings of many of the TTS cast. The current favorites were Nina, Angela, Robin, Rafe, and Bob Valentine. Rex hadn't been on the show long enough to attract his own following.

Nina always made it a point to stop and greet her fans; the only time she ever had to cut them short was when she was rushing to an important appointment or to catch a plane. And even then she'd call out to them a quick greeting and an explanation: "Hello! How nice to see you! Sorry I have to run or I'll miss my plane! Goodbye!" It wasn't much, she realized, but who knew how long some of those people had been standing there waiting to see her? At such times it was the least she could do. But usually she paused to chat for a few minutes, to thank them for watching the show, to ask how they liked the way it was going, to sign as many autographs as she could. Nina was mystified by cynical actors who had such overinflated egos that they considered fans as nuisances and brushed by them impatiently. Those fools didn't deserve such adulation and probably soon lost it anyway.

So she didn't begrudge the five minutes it took to greet this group and sign their autograph books. Several of them had comments to make about the current storyline, and a few seemed particularly delighted at the unexpected bonus of seeing Melanie and Norman together. "Is Melanie going to wind up with Norman?" "Do you think he's the right one for you?" "Isn't he the most *gorgeous* thing!" Most of the excited references to Norman came from the women in the group: the few men just gazed at Nina as though they were tongue-tied, throwing occasional glances of envy at Rex.

Nina's eye was caught by one man in particular, a slightly built man in his late thirties who seemed to be staring only at Rex with a rather sullen expression.

"Why is Melanie so mean to Victoria Allender?"

"Peter Kingston is the one to watch out for."

"Are you still seeing that detective?"

"I don't think Melanie should *ever* get married."

Nina saw that Rex had succeeded in hailing a cab and eased her way toward the curb, keeping up a stream of easy chatter even as she stepped into the taxi.

"Thank you for coming!" she called as the cab pulled away.

"You handled that very nicely," Nina said to Rex as

the taxi carried them away from Meyer Studios and toward Primrose Towers.

"Let's not kid ourselves, it was you they were there to see," he said. It was a gracious statement and the only one possible under the circumstances, but Nina detected an air of resentment underneath it. Oh well, she thought, a little envy won't hurt him—and with the kind of good looks he has, his day will come soon enough.

As if to bear out her suspicion that he envied her popularity, Rex immediately turned the conversation to the subject of the renovation and the problems Nina suspected were cropping up. But Rex's "inspection" didn't go at all as she'd hoped, for when they arrived at the penthouse and opened the door, Nina came face to face with Alibi Al before she even stepped into the foyer.

"Oh! Al! . . . I didn't know you'd be here."

"You know me, little lady. Always on the job."

"Yes . . ."

Before Nina could collect her thoughts and decide how to handle the situation, she was aware that the beefy contractor was staring admiringly at her body. She wished she was wearing something less revealing than the formfitting pearl-gray slacks and clinging white blouse in which she'd left for the studio that morning.

"I gotta tell you, Red, this job of yours is turning out to be something else. Let's us go talk about it over a couple of drinks someplace quiet, what do you say?"

The nerve of this so-and-so!

"The lady is already engaged for this evening," Nina heard the deep voice say from behind her. And when Alibi Al looked over her sholder and saw Rex standing there, his repulsively confident expression vanished and was replaced by an immediate look of instant suspicion.

The situation didn't get any better when Nina had to introduce the two men.

"This is Mr. Reynolds. Rex, Mr. Gastanos is my contractor."

"Pleased to meet you," Alibi Al said slowly, shaking hands with Rex. But Nina could feel the immediate chill in the air as the contractor's icy blue eyes narrowed to slits. Oh, Lord, would Alibi Al realize that Rex was the one he'd already spoken to on the phone, the one who'd "leaned" on him?

"I've been hearing quite a lot about Ms. McFall's new apartment," Rex said, but there was something different about his voice, and Nina realized he was deliberately disguising it.

"Yeah? There's a lot to hear about."

"Indeed. I'm considering a similar project and she kindly offered to show me the work in progress so that I'd have a better idea of what I might be getting into. There's nothing worse than a babe in the woods, is there?"

"Yeah, that's right. Do I know you?"

Nina laughed and quickly jumped in. "I wouldn't be surprised. Mr. Reynolds has been on so many television shows lately it seems half of New York recognizes him."

"Yeah? Like what?" The air of suspicion was only slightly diminished.

"Oh, you name it, Rex has been on it. You know how the acting business goes—when you're hot, you're hot."

"*L.A. Law*, a couple months ago?"

"Guilty," Rex said at his most charming.

"*Cagney and Lacey*, the one where Mary Beth gets locked in the stable with the wild horses?"

"That one, too."

"And *Beauty and the Beast*, when Vincent nearly got buried in the foundation for the new office building, right?"

"Not that time. Sorry to say, I've never been on *Beauty and the Beast*."

"Oh, but it's only a question of time," Nina said archly, wondering how to end this idiotic conversation. But again Rex came to the rescue.

"Nina, we don't have much time. Let's take a quick look around, shall we?"

"Yeah, come on, I'll show you what's what," Alibi Al said, leading the way.

Throughout the tour of inspection Nina had the feeling that every time she turned her back on Alibi Al he was running his eyes up and down her body, mentally peeling off her clothing. When they finished and were about to leave, Rex offered his hand to the contractor and thanked him for the information.

"This has been very enlightening. If I decide to go ahead with renovating my place, perhaps I could ask you to give me an estimate on the job?"

"Sure, sure thing." Alibi Al took a soiled business card out of his shirt pocket and presented it. "But I don't know . . . ," he said to Nina while still looking at Rex, "there's still something tells me I've met this guy someplace."

"Well, anything is possible. Thanks again, Al."

When the elevator door closed behind them, Nina let out a long repressed giggle. "Your powers of improvisation are remarkable," she said. "That bit about getting an estimate from him was an inspiration."

"He is one sleazy character," Rex said. "I'm sure he meant what he said—sooner or later he's going to realize that I'm the guy who spoke to him on the phone. I think I'll stay away from this building for a while."

"Well, no matter. I want to hear what you think about the job he's doing. Do you have time for a drink?"

They spent an easy half hour in the living room of Nina's old apartment talking about the renovation project, and Rex persuaded Nina that even though nothing serious was going wrong, Alibi Al was cutting as many corners as he thought he could get away with.

"Is there anything I can do about it?"

"Sure. You could spend all your time up there policing the job, driving yourself crazy and annoying them so much that they'd cut corners even more just to get it over with. No, unless something serious goes wrong, it's just a fact of life you have to put up with. Of course, if you were really anxious about the whole thing, you wouldn't have any trouble convincing your friendly neighborhood contractor that there's a good reason to give you a really bang-up job . . ."

Nina stiffened slightly. There it was again—that

sudden touch of crass. Why did he do that? Or was she just imagining it?

"Well, I don't know how to thank you for what you've done," she began as a way of steering him toward the door.

"I know how."

I don't want to hear this, she thought, but only raised her eyebrows in cool curiosity.

"You can tell me something in return."

"What's that?"

"How serious is it with Robin and Rafe?"

Good grief, is he still sniffing around after Robin? Nina wondered.

"Oh, Rex, you'd better forget that. It's very serious. I wouldn't get involved if I were you. Take it from me, Robin is a close friend and I know where her fluffy little head is. And where her heart is." I also know where Rafe's fists are, she added to herself.

Rex shrugged. "That's about what I thought. Can't blame a guy for trying, can you?"

After he left, Nina washed the wineglasses and polished the glass top of the coffee table until the rings disappeared, all the while deep in thought. Coming to a decision, she went to the phone and called Dino's number. It was still too early for him to be home from the station, but this time she wanted to talk to Peter only.

"Hello, Peter. It's Nina."

"Hi!"

"How's the boy carpenter doing?"

"Oh, it's great. The main guy, Tommy, he's terrific. He's teaching me everything! I'm gonna ask Dad if I can have some tools and set up a shop in the basement."

The enthusiasm in the boy's voice was a welcome sound.

"Peter, I was up to the penthouse just a little while ago, and I saw a few things that make me wonder if Mr. Gastanos is following instructions."

"I don't like that guy. He's got some mouth on him."

"Well, to be honest with you, I'm not crazy about him

either. But I just want to get this job done. You know I've promised the studio they can use the penthouse for a big party at the end of August, and I'm worried it's not going to be finished on time. So I have a favor to ask of you."

"Sure. What is it?"

"I'm going to instruct Mr. Gastanos to concentrate exclusively on the downstairs rooms, not to touch the upstairs until the downstairs is completely finished, to be sure we're ready for that party." And to be sure I get my two weeks' vacation, she added mentally.

"Okay, what do you want me to do?"

"Actually, I don't want you to *do* anything; I just want you to keep your eyes open. And if you see any work being done upstairs, call me that evening and let me know."

"Gosh, I could go down to the lobby and use the pay phone there and—"

"No, Peter, don't do that. Just call me when you get home and if I'm not here leave a message on the machine. Okay?"

"Sure."

"And, Peter, this might sound a little strange, but I think it'd be better if you didn't—well . . ."

His laugh interrupted her. "I know. Don't tell Dad. Don't worry, I won't let on."

"Good. It's just for a little while, until I'm sure we're going to be ready for that party."

After she hung up, Nina was struck by the amusing parallel between the favor she'd just asked of Peter and the arrangement she'd entered into with his father: Peter was to be her eyes and ears at the penthouse, whereas she was Dino's eyes and ears at the studio. Some day they'll all have a good laugh over it, she was sure.

All that had happened just when the contest was getting underway. In the ensuing weeks, Peter had called Nina only twice, to report that although he hadn't actually *seen* anything, he'd heard noises coming from the upper level. And both times, when Nina had braced herself and gone up to the penthouse as soon as she returned from the studio, Alibi Al convinced her that the work being done upstairs was necessary to the completion of the mechanical work downstairs. She was very brusque and businesslike with him, and only once had he referred to "that Reynolds guy that I'm still trying to remember where I met."

Now, at the end of July, things actually seemed to be shaping up. The penthouse was coming along with incredible smoothness and was actually almost on schedule. The contest was a howling success, with TTS ratings the envy of the entire soap world. Peter was still bubbling with enthusiasm about his part-time job as an apprentice carpenter. And best of all, Dino seemed to have lost his resentment about Nina's soaring popularity and high public profile as well as her ability to afford the penthouse and the staggeringly expensive renovation.

With the contest about to enter its final week of answers, Nina's mail soared. She was tickled by some of the letters—

"Dear Nina. So far I've gotten every one of the questions right, and am I looking forward to coming to New York and meeting you and best of all being on the show with you! (Just don't tell my wife.) Yours, Dick Olcott."

—and a little saddened by others—

"Dear Miss Nina McFall: I am very sorry that whoever put together this stupid contest made it so hard. Now I'll never get to meet you. But I still watch the show anyway. I'm just not going to write anymore. So good-bye. Dorothy Wooten."

—but unaware of the most important letter of all, the one she threw away unopened as soon as she recognized the handwriting:

"Dearest Angel Blossom. Although you have not yet given me the sign by wearing my gift, I have reached a decision. Even if my answers to your contest don't bring me to New York, I'm going to come there and be with you anyway. There's no way I can stay away from you any longer. My body aches for yours. I have sworn to be with you, to become part of you forever and ever. Without you, there can be no life for me. This is what you have done to me, and I adore you for it. And without me, you will not want to live. No one else will have you, either, I promise you that, my angel. There is no way for you to escape our destiny. Your Secret Lover is on his way."

Chapter Ten

It was the final day of the second phase of the contest. It was the day the winners were to be announced. It was the day a lot of people had been waiting for, not least of whom were the cast members of *The Turning Seasons*.

Only hours before air time an entire scene was trimmed from the taped episode of TTS that was to air that day, to make enough room for the big announcement. Angela Dolan was in a rage because the trimmed scene was one of the best she'd had in a long time, and she knew she had played it to perfection.

"But, Angela," Sylvia Kastle said soothingly, "why get yourself so upset? It won't go to waste; it's too important to the storyline. It'll just be moved into next week."

"Next week! What good is that?" Angela ranted. "Next week nobody will be watching! This week *everybody* is watching! It's all *her* fault again!" she said accusingly, and nobody needed to ask who the culprit was, in Angela's opinion.

Nina was going to say something to Angela but wisely decided against it and buried her nose in her script, trying to ignore the tension in the studio. None of the cast had been told the answers to the final set of questions or the identities of the winners. The day's schedule had been revamped so that when the shortened episode ended and the taped contest announcement came on, there would be a pause in the proceedings and everyone could gather around the monitors and watch the grand finale.

Gary Johnson's script, complete with final answers and winners' names, had been prepared early that morning behind locked doors by a team consisting of Helen Meyer, Horst Krueger, Sally Burman, and Myrna Rowan. When it was ready, Gary Johnson was brought into the room, given a copy to study, and then escorted to a secured soundproof set for immediate taping.

Afterward, following the terms of his contract, Gary was escorted from the set to yet another locked room— one without a telephone—where he was to wait for his release until the segment had aired later in the day.

"My God, Helen," Spence Sprague muttered when he learned of the security precautions, "the CIA could use you!"

"Perhaps I'll make myself available," Helen responded, refusing to be kidded on the subject and glowing with smug contentment over the continued record-breaking ratings TTS was garnering.

Despite various pretensions to jaded sophistication, no one in the Meyer Studios that day was immune to contest fever. Even Angela was keeping an eye on the clock; she was confident she'd win the redecorated dressing room as the TTS insider with the most detailed knowledge of the show.

Bellamy Carter was hard put to it to keep his actors' minds on the business at hand. A scene between Turner Caldwell and Norman Chandler was in rehearsal, but all eyes were on Gary Johnson as he was called into the secured office to receive the script for his final announcement. Even the normally dependable Rafe and Rex, as Turner and Norman, were distracted.

"Turner, will you *please* give this total concentration?" Bellamy said to Rafe, reverting to the standard theatrical practice of addressing the actors by the names of their characters. "Norman has just made a particularly obvious pass at Buffy, and you're on the verge of decking the bastard. Buffy, you're over here by the sofa," he said, placing Robin in position. "And Norman is at the door, anxious to make a getaway. Ready, Norman?" Rex nodded. "All right then, action!"

"Chandler, I want a word with you," Rafe said menacingly.

"What's on your tiny mind, Caldwell?" Rex responded.

"I don't like what you just said to my Buffy."

"*Your* Buffy? Don't make me laugh."

"I'm warning you . . ."

"Don't bother me," Rex said lightly, turning to go.

But he didn't get very far. Rafe reached out, spun him around by the shoulder, and threw a powerful punch to his jaw.

"What the hell are you doing!" Bellamy screamed as Rex expertly ducked and Rafe's fist smashed into the doorframe. Robin threw down her script in disgust as Rafe stifled a moan of pain. Several people crowded around the two men, realizing that far more than the script was in motion at the moment. Bellamy advanced on Rafe with a crazed look of frustration, spitting out words about stupidity, idiocy, and lack of professionalism.

Nina rushed over to Robin, who was pointedly examining her nails and ignoring Rafe. "Honey, what's going on here? That's not in the script."

"I know it isn't. The green-eyed monster is back."

"Good grief, are you still baiting Rafe with Rex?"

"No, I'm not. That happened exactly once, weeks ago, and not since. But jerko can't seem to understand it. God, if only he could give that overactive imagination of his a rest!"

"Do you want me to talk to him?"

Robin cast a glance at Rafe, who was standing to one side now, nursing his throbbing hand while Bellamy worked him over with a few thousand well-chosen words. "No, I think he feels stupid enough. I know how his mind works. Later we'll play the big reconciliation scene and he'll apologize sweetly and shamefully and promise never to let it happen again. And it won't—until the next time he imagines someone is looking at me cross-eyed."

"Will he apologize to Rex, too?"

"No way. He really hates that guy's guts, for some reason."

"Oh, I think it's understandable. Rex gives off some very contradictory vibes sometimes," Nina said, recalling the smarmy innuendoes of several weeks earlier. "He pretends to be a nice guy, but then all of a sudden, ping! And you know you're strolling in quicksand. I think it's better just to stay away from him."

Robin gave Nina a look of surprise. "Well, I do. It's Rafe who can't seem to keep his nose clean."

"People! People!" Bellamy shouted. "Can we get back to the scene? *As written*? Isn't it bad enough the day's schedule is screwed up with this contest interruption? Do we have to make things worse? Now let's try it again. Buffy, over here. *Gentlemen*, places please?" His tone of frigid sarcasm was instantly received and acknowledged by an embarrassed Rafe, who went through the scene perfectly. As written.

But Rafe didn't apologize to Rex.

Myrna Rowan let herself out of the secured office and heaved a great sigh of relief. As far as she was concerned, the blankety-blank contest was over, and it had been nothing but a gigantic pain in the aspidistra. Now Johnson had the final script, the security of the contest answers had been carried out successfully, and she could relax. Next week, when the winners arrived, she'd have absolutely no part of any of it. Little Myrna was going to her everyday duties and life could return to normal.

"Myrna? Hey, Myrna, how did it go in there?"

"Great, Mark, just great."

"So what's happening?"

"Exactly what's supposed to happen, Mark."

"For instance?"

She ground her teeth. Would this boob never let her alone? "For instance, Johnson has the final script, he's locked up until the taping, then he gets locked up until after the airing, then he goes home. Then we tape the daily episode. Then I lock my desk. Then I stand up. Then I say 'Good night, boss' to Mr. Krueger. Then I go home."

"Ah, come on, quit kidding me. You know what I mean—the contest."

"It's over, Mark. The winners' names will be on the air in about an hour. Everyone will be watching."

"You want to watch it with me?"

"Why would I watch it? I know what's going to be said!"

"Oh. Hey, maybe Mrs. Meyer will run another contest sometime, and maybe we can do the research again, you and me. That was fun, wasn't it?"

"Sure, it was great fun," Myrna sighed.

"Like in *Magic Town*!"

"Never saw it. Listen, I have to—"

"You never saw *Magic Town*? That's a great movie. Contests always remind me of *Magic Town*. That's the one where Jimmy Stewart runs a poll to find out which town is the most average town in the whole country, and he meets Jane Wyman, and they . . . Myrna, don't you want to hear the rest? Myrna?"

"You watching that damn fool program of yours again, Alice? Don't let me catch you on the long-distance phone later talking to your sister about it."

"I did *not* miss the last question, *you* missed the last question! If we lose, it's your fault!"

"Girls, quiet down! George, are you coming back for din— Oh, who cares? I can't stand the excitement, I'm gonna scream! Somebody turn up the volume! Louella, you ready with the recorder? What? I can't hear you! Girls, shut up! This is it!"

"Oh my Lord, it's time! It's time! Donnie, get off me! You can finish that yourself—right now I got to hear if I got the last question right!"

"I don't know why you want to watch the rest of this, Mike. I know I didn't get all those questions right. 'Specially the really hard ones. I just haven't been following it long enough to know those things. It was just silly to guess at so many of them. You should have let me just drop out . . ."

"Harold, put the ironing board away for me. This is one time I'm not going to miss a word! *Ssh*! Now here we go."

"Time out! It's starting!"

The cast gathered around one of the monitors in the studio, watching almost as raptly as the viewers at home. Gary Johnson's face swam into focus and he began to speak the words everyone wanted to hear as the brass fanfare died away and the familiar TTS competition theme began to throb in the background.

"Hello, all you wild and crazy fans of *The Turning Seasons*! Today's the big day, isn't it, the day you've all been waiting for—the day we give you the answers to the final questions in the *Turning Seasons* Trivia Contest! *And* . . . the day we reveal who has won the dream prize of a lifetime: the chance to *actually appear* on *The Turning Seasons* with all your favorite characters!

"All right, we don't want to keep you in suspense any longer. First, the answers to the last questions: To repeat the first stumper from the final set: Who was Melanie Prescott's godmother? . . . And the answer is—did you get this one right?—Melanie Prescott's godmother was her Great Aunt Marion! *Marion Stingle!"*

The music surged, the lighting effects behind Gary Johnson's wildly smiling face sparkled, and thousands of TTS fans screamed in anguish. Marion Stingle! Wasn't it Lorelei Mason? Wasn't it Jennifer Frobusher? I could have sworn it was Dulcie Dwinnell! Who'd know a thing like that?

"All right, now settle down, two more answers to reveal before we get to the big winners. Our next to last question was this doubleheader: When Simon Wentworth attended Jensonville College for the *first* time, what was his major subject and what was his minor subject? Now we did put a tiny hint in there, for those of you who were listening carefully. Remember that Simon dropped out of college for a while and then went back after his divorce from Shirley Vivaldi. You probably remember that the second time around, when he earned his degree, he majored in ethnic musicology and minored in botany. *But* the answer we were looking for was this: During his very first term at Jensonville College, Simon Wentworth studied political science for his major and home economics for his minor! And you might also remember that the home ec lab was where Simon fell in love with the gorgeous Professor Vivaldi— but that, as they say, is history!"

Again the music and lighting effects were put through their electronic paces as the tension built. In the studio, the cast was keeping track of the answers and rapidly calculating the scores to see who would soon enjoy a redecorated dressing room. Two of the contenders were head and shoulders above the others, but they were at a dead tie. "It's between Angela and Mary!" scorekeeper Sirri Ballinger whispered. Angela and Mary nodded to each other grandly, in the manner of warring royalty, polite to the last.

"All right! All right! Now for the last question, the *very last one*—and are you still in the running? This is it. I will repeat the last question before giving you the official answer. It was this: Who did Peter Kingston suspect was the *real* mother of his daughter Buffy after he found out

Buffy's mother was not the wife of his business partner Cory Sloane? Did you get it? Did you say Martha Renfrew? We hope you didn't, because that was *wrong*! She was his third suspect. The *second* suspect, and the correct and final answer was . . . *Alberta Prendergast!*"

"*What?*" Angela squawked.

"Mary won! Mary won the dressing room!" Sirri squeaked.

"That's ridiculous!" Angela fumed. "It *couldn't* have been!"

"And now, hold on to your seats, because you are about to find out who among you will be right here in New York in only one short week, appearing on *The Turning Seasons*! But first, a word from our sponsor . . ."

Miss Dora Gilbert didn't care. She looked great in her new wardrobe, and the blue-tinted contact lenses hardly gave her a headache at all anymore.

Alice Murchison breathed a sigh of relief. Now she wouldn't have to worry about telling Wilbur she was going to New York City.

Judy Olcott snapped off the television set, walked over to her husband Dick, and smacked him in the face.

Mike West sat back in his chair and pretended to doze as he watched Melinda out of the corner of his eye. She was sure she hadn't won, she wasn't even excited.

Hilda Hotchley got up to fetch her mending basket while the fool commercials were on. No use to waste the time.

Patti Martinus had fainted dead away and Louella Croydon was slapping her wrists to revive her.

As the last commerical ended, the music swelled to a mighty crescendo and the lights danced around Gary Johnson's beaming face. "I won't prolong the agony a moment longer. Here's what you've been waiting for—the names of the winners of the trip to New York and the cameo roles on *The Turning Seasons*! Our tabulations were completed several days ago, and we had them audited not once but *twice* to assure total accuracy. *And* we are pleased to welcome to *The Turning Seasons* cast our three top scorers. Let's hear it for our third place winner, who is . . . *Mrs. Hilda Hotchley of Las Cruces, New Mexico*! Hello out there, Hilda, and welcome to *The Turning Seasons!*"

"Harold, go next door and ask Mrs. Gorman if she'll take in the mail while we're away. I don't want that nosy mailman to know we're gone."

"And in second place we have a fan from Rutland, Vermont! Welcome to *The Turning Seasons*, Melinda West! Start packing, Melinda!"

Mike's smile opened into a broad grin and gave way to a whoop of delight when Melinda screamed and dropped the dish she was drying. "It must be a mistake! Mike, I told you I was guessing at half those questions! What are we going to do? We can't accept! I don't even want to go to New York! Mike, stop laughing!"

"And in first place . . . the person who knows more about *The Turning Seasons* than anyone in America— Mrs. Patti *Martinus*, who is president and founder of the Middle West Nina McFall Fan Club! Welcome and congratulations to you, Patti!!! Our representative will contact you within twenty-four hours to make travel arrangements for you and your group!"

The noise that erupted from the Martinus house was off the Richter scale. Hours later, when George came back for his supper, the celebration was still going on. The husbands of several of the fan club members, including Eddie Croydon, had arrived to take their wives home but had stayed to join the party when they saw that Patti had thrown open the doors to George's liquor cabinet.

All right, you dizzy broad, George Martinus thought as he walked away from his house again, this time in search of a diner where he could enjoy some food in peace and quiet. Sounds like you fixed it so we're going to New York. Too bad you don't know who isn't coming back!

Chapter Eleven

Nina stared at Helen Meyer. She couldn't have heard right. It must have been the heat, or the Monday-morning blahs.

"They're bringing *how* many people?"

"Sixteen. There are the Martinuses and all fourteen members of the fan club, along with five of their husbands. Actually, that makes it twenty-one."

Nina groaned. "And the other two winners, I suppose they're bringing their husbands, too. That makes twenty-five all together! How could you *do* this to me?"

Helen treated Nina to one of her thinnest, frostiest smiles. "Come now, we've all heard so much advance publicity about your enormous new penthouse—surely you can handle a crowd of twenty-five. Or was the publicity not accurate?"

"But it *isn't* just twenty-five! There's our whole crowd—the cast, their dates, the staff, *their* dates, the caterers . . ."

"Caterers? What caterers?"

"The caterers who are going to provide and serve the food and drink for your little bash. I agreed to let it be held in my new apartment; I didn't agree to do all the work that goes along with it."

"Now listen here, Nina, don't try to wriggle out of an agreement that you—"

"Stop where you are, Helen! I'm not wriggling out of anything. I've been wrestling with the slimiest contractor east or west of the Rockies just to get the downstairs ready in time, and I've had to think about furnishing the place and decorating it so it looks as though someone is actually already *living* there. Now you want me to plan a *menu?* I suppose you also expect me to do the marketing, scrub the vegetables, polish the silver, and wait on tables!"

"All I said was—"

"I know what you said. And I know what you meant. I am supplying the hall for this little shindig, which in itself is no small feat. And in exchange I am going on *a two-week vacation* immediately afterward. But the hall is *all* I'm supplying. If you don't want to provide the food and drink and the furniture I'm going to have to rent for the occasion, they can just sit on the bare floor and eat peanut butter out of a jar! *With their fingers!*"

"Rented furniture? Why rented?"

"Because after this party I'm going to have to let the work crew back in to finish the renovation. And I'm not going to move my own furniture up five flights on Saturday and back down on Sunday!"

There was a long pause during which both women went through a peculiar neck-stretching and clothing rearrangement exercise that somehow filled the gap while the emotional temperature in the room cooled down.

"You do have a point," Helen conceded at last mildly.

"Thank you. I didn't mean to get so excited," Nina responded in equally civilized tones. "I will make all the arrangements, including renting the furniture, hiring the caterer, selecting the musicians, and ordering the flowers. But *you'll* get all the bills. After all, it was your idea."

"Yes, it was," Helen said, making a rough estimate of the cost of the party and adding it to the already staggering expenses for the entire contest promotion.

But then she thought about the ratings and felt ever so much better. It's an investment, she reminded herself, and already it's paid off. Think of how much bigger the payoff will be when coverage of the winners' visit reaches the public.

And despite everything, it was all going so smoothly. . . .

"Al, this isn't good enough."

"What's on your mind, Ms. M?" the paunchy contractor said, expressing an even raunchier attitude than usual.

"You're falling behind schedule again."

"Well, we had a problem with the—"

"I don't want to hear about it! Whatever the problem is, it's your problem, not mine. So you find a solution. All I'm concerned about is getting these downstairs rooms in shape by the end of the day one week from this Thursday. On the following Monday morning you can come back in and finish it off. Any questions?"

"No, no questions, Ms. M."

"Good!" Nina was learning how to speak the language. Then she let him have the crusher, calculated to make him treat her with more respect. "And while you're at it, you'll have to tear out all the sheetrock you just put in the downstairs powder room."

"What do you mean, Ms. M?"

"Which word didn't you understand, Al? You know what I mean; that sheetrock is not waterproof and the New York City building code requires waterproof sheetrock in all areas with plumbing. Do you want to dispute that?"

"I guess not, Ms. M."

"Good. So rip that junk out and don't charge me for it. Then get a load of greenboard in here, and start cutting."

"Oh, *now* I understand. You been talking to your boyfriend again, that tall, dark, and snotty Rex Reynolds guy, the one who likes to call up contractors and lean on them."

"Don't be ridic—"

"I *knew* that guy's voice was familiar. You know, he ain't as smart as he lets on. Why don't you do him a favor, Ms. M? Why don't you tell him to stick to his soapsuds and leave the tough jobs to the men?"

She stared him down, repressing the urge to spit in his eye. Maybe she'd overplayed her hand after all. "Why don't you tell him that yourself, Al?"

"Yeah, maybe I should."

From then on, relations between Nina and Alibi Al were cool at best. But the substandard sheetrock was replaced the next day, and Nina never saw a charge for it because the cost was divided into ten equal parts, each of them buried in the charges for other items.

Keeping Alibi Al on schedule proved to be child's play compared with the complexities of arranging to have the walls and ceilings painted on Thursday evening, the floors scraped and finished on Friday morning, the draperies hung on Friday afternoon, the furniture brought in on Saturday morning, and the food and drink delivered by five P.M. Saturday evening.

Nina spent her off-hours that week in a frenzy of phone calls and rushed visits to select paint colors, furniture, and draperies. She accomplished the ordering of music, food, and drink over the telephone while stretched out on the sofa with Chessy, who exhibited a sublime indifference to his mistress's tension.

"If there's such a thing as reincarnation, I'm coming back as a cat," she told the purring puss after a lengthy phone conversation involving hot hors d' oeuvres versus cold canapes. "Then somebody can scratch behind my ears while I just loll all over the place. *Oh, my God!* I forgot to order any rugs!"

The rug crisis was solved by deciding to keep the dining room floor bare for dancing and by the impulsive purchase of a huge oriental rug for the living room, an item Nina had been coveting for some time but had been resisting for the simple reason that she had no place to put it. At least that's one item Helen won't complain about, Nina told herself as she wrote out a check that would have gone a long way toward reducing the national debt.

"I'm exhausted! I'm worn out, and the hard part is still ahead of me!" Nina complained to Dino at the end of the week over dinner at the English Pub. It was an off-night, with very few patrons, and they were almost whispering to avoid being overheard in the quiet dining room.

"Well, you don't look it, if it's any comfort," he said, groaning inwardly at the prospect of more talk about the renovation. "You look terrific."

She looked better than terrific. Nina was wearing a simple yet sophisticated off-white linen coatdress, subtly shaped, with peaked lapels and flap pockets. Her jewelry was a matching necklace and bracelet of pink coral, so light she could barely feel it. With white pumps and a small white purse completing the ensemble, she looked like the embodiment of a totally calm and poised woman.

But looks were deceiving.

"I'm telling you, I'm ready for the loony bin," she muttered through barely parted lips.

"I don't know why you don't let me go up there and talk to that guy. Why do you have to be so damned stubborn?" he demanded.

"I'm not so damned stubborn, I'm so damned independent! And I'm so damned *hungry*. Can we just drop the subject of the renovation and order?"

"You're the one who keeps bringing it up."

Anyone observing them would have thought they were exchanging sweet nothings.

The following day, Nina shuddered involuntarily at the sight of the familiar handwriting, and once again she overcame her natural curiosity and resisted the urge to open the envelope. Curious or not, she had the instinctive feeling she was better off not knowing what was inside that envelope. She stared at it for a long time before dropping it unopened into a drawer.

Now what? Nina thought as she came through the studio door on Friday morning and saw a knot of people clustered around the bulletin board. The sheet of paper that drew their attention was posted in the center of the board; all other material except for notices required by law had been removed.

SCHEDULE OF EVENTS FOR OUR GUESTS

"Dear People," said the brief paragraph at the top of the sheet. "Listed below is an outline of what we've lined up for our visitors this week. Logistical details for each event are available through Myrna Rowan. If you are scheduled on this sheet to host a particular event, *it is your responsibility* to pick up the appropriate sheet from Myrna. No substitutions will be allowed without my express consent. Thank you, my angels. I love you all. Helen Meyer."

"'No substitutions'? Sounds like a Chinese restaurant," Robin grumbled. "Oh, look at that, I'm on for Sunday!"

Nina ran her eye quickly down the notice, looking for her own name.

Day	Time	What	Where	Who
Sun	3:45 P.M.	Meet arrivals	LaGuardia Airport	Tally, Fallone, Valentine, Ballinger
	5:00	Hotel check-in	Plaza Hotel	Ungar, Kinling
	7:00	Dinner	Oak Room, Plaza	Dolan, Winston
Mon	9:30 A.M.	Tour studio	Here	Viner, Rowan
		Meet cast	"	All; stay loose
	11:15	Lunch	Corrigan's Pub	Levy, Bell
	12:30 P.M.	Observe	Rehearsal hall	Viner, Rowan
	4:00	Return to hotel		Viner
	7:00	Dinner	Le Perigord	McFall, Reynolds
Tues	9:30 A.M.	Observe	Rehearsal hall	Frost
	11:15	Lunch	Host's choice	Kastle, Kennerly

	12:30 P.M.	Costume fitting*	Wardrobe	Galano
		Hair & makeup*	Makeup	"
	1:45	Observe	Rehearsal hall	"
	3:30	Return to hotel		Viner
	6:00	Depart hotel	(via limo)	Viner
	7:00	Dinner	Leatherwing	Meyer, Krueger, Frost, Gelber, Burman
Wed	8:00 A.M.	Observe	Rehearsal hall	Carter
	11:15	Lunch	Host's choice	Tally, Fallone
	12:30 P.M.	Observe	Rehearsal hall	Carter
	1:00	Costumes etc.*	Wardrobe & Makeup	"
	1:45	Normal production routine through to final tape		"
	3:30	Return to hotel		Viner
	7:00	Dinner	21	Ungar, Kinling
Thurs	8:00 A.M.	Same as Wed.	Same as Wed.	Sprague
	11:15	"	"	Busacca, Haney
	12:30 P.M.	"	"	Sprague
	1:00	" *	"	"
	1:45	"	"	"
	3:30	"	"	"
	7:00	Gals: Dinner Windows on the World		Dolan, Kennerly
		Guys: Night out Various low places		Fallone, Valentine
Fri	8:00 A.M.	Same as Wed.	Same as Wed.	Krueger
	11:15	"	"	Meyer
	12:30 P.M.	"	"	Krueger
	1:00	" *	"	"
	1:45	"	"	"
	3:30	"	"	"
	8:00	*Phantom of the Opera*		Kastle, Winston
	11:00	Supper	Sardi's	" "
Sat	All day free for shopping etc.			—
	6:00 P.M.	Buffet dinner	Primrose Towers	McFall and FULL CAST, Krueger, Frost, Gelber, Burman, Viner, Rowan
Sun	12:00 P.M.	Depart hotel for LaGuardia		Viner
		Farewell Committee		TBA

*These entries apply only to Mrs. Martinus, Mrs. West, and Mrs. Hotchley. All others are *observers*.

"Please note that at all times there will be at least two photographers in attendance, and they have orders to 'shoot on sight.' So don't be caught doing anything you wouldn't want to see printed in a fan magazine. Best behavior, darlings! Isn't this *fun*? *HM*"

The moaning and groaning that issued from the group at the bulletin board came chiefly from those with late-hour or repeated assignments. Nina didn't feel she'd made out too badly, noting that Helen had taken on a fair share of the chores herself and hadn't even grabbed off the *Phantom of the Opera* tickets for herself. Of course, she had already seen it twice. . . .

As for that ominous "TBA"—to be announced—on the departure date, Nina knew that was Helen's cute way of holding a club over all their heads; whoever misbehaved during the week's festivities would become part of the Farewell Committee. Well, Helen wouldn't be Helen if she didn't engage in such shenanigans, Nina told herself, planning to be the best little Nina ever and definitely stay far away from the Farewell Committee. She had no intention of spending the first day of her long-anticipated vacation waving bye-byes at a gritty airport.

The plane carrying Melinda and Mike West left the small airfield outside Rutland at ten in the morning, headed for Burlington and a connecting flight that would get them into New York's LaGuardia Airport just shortly before the plane from Chicago that carried Patti Martinus and the entire riotous group of fan clubbers and spouses.

Oddly enough, the couple who had the longest distance to travel, Hilda and Harold Hotchley, weren't on the plane from Las Cruces, New Mexico that should have taken them to El Paso, Texas, for the flight to New York. In fact, the Hotchleys weren't on any plane at all, although they were definitely in motion.

Chapter Twelve

An airport in the middle of a Sunday afternoon is an interesting place. Anyone who cares to do so may observe endless and varied scenes of human emotion—tearstained farewells, joyous reunions, uneasy arrivals, awkward introductions, and a whole panoply of relieved departures—all played out by a generous spectrum of people ranging from doddering grandparents with aching feet to obstreperous toddlers with mighty lungs who clamor for incredible quantities of airport food, which they rapidly consume and periodically disgorge onto the thronged floor, instantly creating a clear area where moments before no such thing seemed possible.

An airport is a wonderful place for an actor in training to look and learn the physical behavior that unconsciously accompanies the expression of specific emotions. But the quartet of actors from the cast of *The Turning Seasons* that arrived at LaGuardia Airport just before three-thirty on the afternoon of Sunday, August 21, was in no mood to learn anything—with the definite exception of how to strangle Helen Meyer and get away with it.

Sirri Ballinger was resentful that she was missing out on a day at the beach.

Bob Valentine was resentful that he was missing out on a day at his favorite fishing hole.

As for Rafe Fallone and Robin Tally, they were resentful that they were missing out on an afternoon in bed together. Deeply resentful.

"How are we supposed to recognize these people?" Sirri asked.

"I think we can assume they're going to recognize *us*," Robin muttered.

"Why, ladies, didn't you pick up your logistical sheets from Myrna Rowan?" Bob asked in his best Eagle Scout manner. Robin and Sirri had to admit they hadn't, and Rafe sheepishly unfolded from his jacket pocket a rather garish sign proclaiming Turning Seasons Contest Winners.

"The idea," Rafe said in disgust, "is to hold this damn thing up until they spot it. Then we greet them, they greet us, the photographers immortalize the touching scene, we show them to the baggage-claim area, and then we usher them into the limousines."

"All the time carrying on a sprightly line of chatter, of course," Bob added.

"What did we do to deserve this?" Sirri asked the heavens. "This isn't in my contract."

"Are you sure?" Robin queried. "The way Helen Meyer draws up a contract, I wouldn't be surprised if we were obligated to wash dishes at Leatherwing on New Year's Eve."

At that moment a very pleasant-looking young man tapped Rafe on the shoulder and said, "Excuse me, but I think we're looking for each other."

"Well, that's a novel approach," Robin whispered to a giggling Sirri.

"My name is Mike West, and this is my wife Melinda. She's the winner of *The Turning Seasons* contest. Anyway, she's one of the winners."

Strobes flashed as photographers began immortalizing, and Sirri was instantly transformed from a grumbling young lady into an enchantress. She practically broke into a southern accent, so coy and flirtatious did she become. Robin gaped open-mouthed at Sirri's performance, thinking that this guy was cute all right, but not *that* cute.

Rafe assumed the chores of emcee and introductions were performed all around, followed by explanations that the larger group was due in from Chicago in fifteen minutes, followed immediately by an awkward silence. Young Mr. West seemed at ease, but his pretty young wife was apparently petrified.

"First time in New York?" Bob finally ventured.

"That's right," Mike said, looking at his wife for confirmation.

"Well! . . . Well . . . how do you like it so far?"

"Sure is noisy," Mike said, and Melinda nodded in agreement.

"Where are you folks from?" Rafe said.

"Vermont. We're from Rutland, Vermont."

"Well, I hear great things about Vermont," Rafe said heartily, hoping to hell he wouldn't be asked to quote any.

"Yeah, it's nice there."

"Congratulations on winning the contest," Robin said directly to Melinda, who was clearly expected to respond. But she only smiled wanly.

"You must have been watching our show for a long time," Robin pursued. Melinda nodded weakly.

This is all backward, Robin thought to herself. *They're supposed to be the ones who ask the questions, not us!*

This sparkling flow of easy conversation was interrupted by a sudden eruption of noise coming from the direction of the arrival gate of the Chicago plane. The babble grew to a crescendo, and Robin told Rafe to put away the sign. The fan-club contingent had unmistakably arrived.

The initial contact with the Chicago group more than made up for the dreariness of the Rutland contingent.

As the photographers did their thing, "*Rafe Fallone!* It's Rafe Fallone! Look! Trudy! Edna! Louella! Girls! It's Rafe Fallone, I'm gonna lay me doon and dee!" Patti Martinus had made the most of the refreshment cart during the brief flight from Chicago, and nearly all of the "girls" had followed suit.

Introductions proved both impossible and unnecessary. As soon as Patti realized that her favorite soap-opera personality was not among the landing party, she led the ladies in a rousing chorus of "We Want to See Nina" to the tune of "K-K-K-Katy."

"Come on girls, let 'em know how we feel! We want to see Nina! We want to see Nina! She's the only s-s-s-star that we adore! When the sh-show ends, on the b-boob tube, we'll be calling out for m-m-m-m-more!"

"My dying wish is that Angela Dolan could hear this," Robin giggled to Sirri.

"Cheer up," Sirri said. "Angela's one of the dinner hosts tonight, and Nina's not going to be there, either. Maybe they'll sing it in the Oak Room at the Plaza!"

"From your mouth to God's ears," Robin prayed.

More strobe lights flashed. By now a sizable crowd of gawkers had gathered—even the local pickpockets working the confused gathering were impressed.

It wasn't until the limousines were halfway into Manhattan that Rafe Fallone suddenly remembered there were two more people due to arrive! The couple from New Mexico! Helen would murder him; he was a sure bet to find himself included on the Farewell Committee! Shit, there went another Sunday in the Sack with Robin!

When the limousines pulled up in front of the Plaza Hotel on Central Park South, the stately grandeur of the huge pile of masonry seemed to have a sobering effect on the visitors from Chicago. They piled out of the cars and sailed into the ornate lobby, cold sober and as though to the manor born.

"What happened?" Ferde Ungar snapped at Rafe. "I just counted heads and you're two short. Who's missing?"

"The people from New Mexico."

Ferde's blood pressure soared. Right at the start,

something had to go wrong! Helen Meyer would kill him! "So what happened? Was their plane late? Jesus, you could have waited for their plane!"

Rafe seized at the excuse Ferde had unintentionally offered. "No, Ferde, that would have been bad public relations. These people were all raring to go. We couldn't hold them up just for the sake of two others, could we? Now you've got twenty-three happy people and only two unhappy—instead of the other way around," he finished lamely.

Ferde looked doubtful. "I'm going to call the airport as soon as I get these folks checked in and find out what happened to that plane."

It was too much for Robin. She put them both out of their misery. "Ferde, the truth is this group was such a handful we simply forgot about the others. They're probably on their way here now by taxi. Reimburse them for the cab, send a bottle of champagne to their room, and forget it—before Anyone Else gets wind of it. You know what I mean?"

Ferde knew exactly what Robin meant and ordered the champagne sent to the Hotchleys' room immediately.

But it was warm and flat long before Hilda and Harold caught their first glimpse of the Manhattan skyline.

Angela Dolan was a vision as she made her entrance into the Oak Room on Noel Winston's arm. The assembled group, already seated at their places, burst into spontaneous applause as the distinguished-looking couple appeared.

Noel's dark blue suit, crisp white shirt, silk tie of military stripe, and his rich head of wavy silver hair were a perfect foil for the shimmering impression Angela created. She wore a dinner gown of elegant white lace over peach georgette, edged with faux pearl trim along the deep V neck. The slightly flared skirt was flatteringly drop-waisted, and her svelte figure was complemented by her lush ash-blond hair which she wore tonight in a soignee French twist. An enormous white lace scarf floated after her, and her pearl drop earrings and matching double-strand necklace shimmered softly in the romantic light.

Angela swooped down on the banquet table and passed beguilingly from one bemused fan to the other, showering greetings and good wishes, cooing her appreciation to one and all. Noel trailed along behind, shaking hands and smiling, smiling, smiling. With his deep tan and astonishingly trim body, half the women in the room began to forget they'd ever heard of Rex Reynolds.

When they were finally seated, Angela turned to Noel and whispered between motionless lips, "You've got to help me out. I didn't get a single name."

"I don't think it's going to matter," he murmured back to her. "They love you, every one of them."

"Well, aren't they the sweetest things?" She looked up at the dozens of happily expectant faces and half-turned back to Noel. "My God, do they expect me to make a speech?"

"Why don't you? You've got them eating out of your hand anyway."

Yes, why don't I? Angela thought. This is one time I'm not going to play second fiddle to that pushy redhead! Angela rose to her feet and the group fell silent.

"Dear friends," she began, "and we *do* think of you already as our friends—I don't think I can find the words to tell you what it means to us that you've all come so far to see us and be with us for this wonderful week. You know, when you're working on the business end of the camera—and it *is* work, it isn't all glamor and glitter as you might have thought—when you're working on the business end of the camera, you never know who's looking at you. It's as though there are a million eyes and ears out there behind the camera, but we can't see them and we can't hear them . . . and oh, my dear friends, we do so much want to see you and hear you and get to know you! So you see, when I say it's *we* who honor *you* and not the other way around, it comes from the heart."

Angela fluttered in pretty confusion and sat down again to a burst of enthusiastic applause. There was a mutter of hurried conversation at the far end of the table and then a clearing of throats.

"Yes?" Angela said. "Does someone have a question? Let's all ask each other questions and give answers and get to know each other, shall we? Let's not be so formal."

"Miss Dolan," a quavery voice said, "could I ask you something?"

"Of course, my dear, anything you like. But not until I know your name."

"It's Croydon. Louella Croydon."

"Well, Louella! What a lovely name. What is your question, Louella?"

"Well, maybe it's not the right time or place, but—well, when do we get to meet Nina McFall?"

Noel quickly came to Angela's rescue. "If I might respond, Angela, I'd like to thank our dear friend Louella for reminding us that Nina McFall sent you all a special message this evening." Having gotten himself into a hole, Noel proceeded to dig out. "She said to tell you that she's just . . . dying to meet you, but . . . she's just a little bit under the weather . . ." A quick intake of breath signaled the general consternation at this tragic news. ". . . but she's sure she'll be able to enjoy the pleasure of your company at dinner tomorrow."

"Dinner? You mean we're not going to see her at the studio tomorrow, either?" asked Louella, in evident dismay.

"Alas," Noel intoned, "tomorrow just happens to be one of those days when Melanie Prescott is not scheduled to appear on the show. But meanwhile," he hurried on, hoping Angela hadn't heard the chorus of disappointed sighs, "let us start the evening off in style and help you shake the dust of travel from your parched throats. Champagne for everyone!"

The thought cheered them up considerably, and the actual wine itself went a lot further. After a second glass, Patti Martinus leaned over to Louella Croydon and said, "Louella, I think you hurt Miss Dolan's feelings. Why did you ask about Nina that way?"

And Louella leaned back to explain, "Eddie made me do it."

Patti shot a glance at the glowering Eddie and said, "Louella, I don't think you better have any more of this champagne. Imagine blaming poor Eddie for it. Next thing you'll be saying the devil made you do it!"

"Where's *The Turning Seasons* party?"

The desk clerk looked in disbelief at the bedraggled elderly couple before him. "I beg your pardon?"

"You know, the TV people. We're a little late."

"Ah, the Meyer Productions dinner," he said, the light dawning. "I'm afraid that concluded an hour or so ago."

"Hilda, I—"

"Quiet, Harold, I'll handle it." Hilda turned back to the desk clerk. "Listen, we got a little problem. The bus broke down twice and our food ran out before they got it started the second time. And I'll be dipped if I'm gonna pay those fancy prices at the bus depots. So before we turn in, where's a decent place to get a sandwich around here?"

"A sandwich? At this hour? I doubt you'll find a sandwich. Perhaps room service could be of assistance."

"How much?"

"Beg pardon?"

"I said 'how much?' Don't matter how loud my stomach's rumbling, I'm not paying more than one buck fifty for a sandwich."

"I see. Were you planning to stay with us, madam?"

"Bet your boots!"

"Did you have a reservation?"

"Sure did. Still do."

"I assume you are Mr. and Mrs. Hotchley?"

"Never assume, son. It makes an *ass* of *u* and *me*. Gotcha there!" Hilda cackled.

". . . Indeed. Are you the Hotchley party?"

"I guess we been called worse things."

"And you're also part of the Meyer party."

"Yep, and we're also part of the Republican Party, in case anybody wants to know."

"May we show you to your room? And please feel free to enjoy all the amenities. You are the guests of Meyer Productions in all respects."

"What's that mean?"

"It means all sandwiches are one buck fifty, madam."

"*Now* you're talking my language! Harold, pick up those bags and get moving. Some fancy place, huh?"

The visitors weren't due at the studio until nine-thirty the following morning, a schedule Helen had arranged so that the cast would have a solid hour and a half to get the day's episode under control before the inevitable interruptions began.

So Myrna was somewhat irritated when the guard at the front door phoned to say that two people were there demanding admittance.

"They're not due to arrive until nine-thirty, Hector."

"*I* know that, Miss Rowan, but *they* don't."

"Tell 'em."

"I did, but they don't believe it."

"Who are they? Where are they from?"

"Their name is Hotchley. They're from New Mexico."

"Oh boy, the two we lost yesterday!"

"I think you better come out here, Miss Rowan."

"I think so, too, Hector. Be right there."

When Myrna got to the front desk she was ready to launch into a hastily composed speech of apology for the mix-up at LaGuardia, but it wasn't necessary. The strange-looking little couple in the bright polyester outfits required no apologies.

"Pleased to meet you, dearie. I'm Hilda Hotchley and this is Harold. Now about the plane tickets, don't worry—it's all taken care of. When we got 'em we looked 'em over and called the airline and found it was no mistake, we were supposed to fly first class all right, so we just cashed 'em in right off and went and bought some bus tickets instead. Gonna put the difference right under the mattress, know what I mean? Listen, did you ever go cross country on a bus? You really see some sights, believe you me! And by the way, I'd like to know what you're spending on that fancy hotel, because I've got a pretty good idea we can do better on our own, know what I mean?"

"You're going to put the difference under the mattress, right?"

"That's it. You catch on fast. I think I'm going to like you. Okay, what do we do first? Harold wants to meet Nina McFall real bad."

"No I—"

"Hush up, Harold. You do, too. So where is she?"

"Let me explain the situation. Would you—"

"I *knew* it! She's not here, is she?"

"Not at this very moment, but she will be. Why don't you come inside and have a nice cup of coffee, and—"

"You got Postum? Harold only drinks Postum."

"I'm sure we can find some, if they still make it. Now you see, on soap operas not everyone appears every day. And this happens to be one of the days that Nina is off."

"Well, shoot! She gonna be here tomorrow?"

"Oh yes, definitely."

"See you then. Come on, Harold."

"But the rest of the group will be here at nine-thirty. Don't you want to tour the studio and meet everyone? Then we're going to take you all to lunch and bring you back and you can see how a soap opera is put together. After all, you *are* going to be on the show this week, starting on Wednesday."

"No, I'm not."

"But aren't you one of the three winners?"

"Yep. But I'm giving my spot to Harold."

"Hilda, I don't—"

"See, Harold's the actor in the family. You should have seen him on the Little Theatre stage when they did *You Can't Take It With You*. He was some sight! Weren't you, Harold?"

"Well, it was—"

"Okay, that's enough gab. Let's go, we got to find some place else to hang our hats tonight. See you tomorrow, dear."

And she was out the door, with Harold trailing obediently behind. If this is how the week is starting, Myrna thought, exchanging meaningful looks with the uniformed Hector, I shudder to think how it's going to end.

At nine-thirty the group promptly arrived, led by Mark Viner, who had collected them at the Plaza. They were somewhat more subdued than they had been the day before, owing to Noel's generosity with the Plaza's wine cellar at Helen Meyer's expense. Still, there was a definite air of growing excitement as Myrna explained the day's schedule.

"First we're going to split into two groups and tour you around the studio. I'll take one group, and Mark Viner will take the second. After about half an hour we'll join up at the main rehearsal hall, and you'll meet the cast."

A ripple of excitement surged up; now they were getting down to cases!

"But remember, this is a workday and the actors have to concentrate on getting the show on its feet and ready for final tape by two-thirty. They break for lunch at eleven-fifteen. A lot of them go to a place around the corner, Corrigan's Pub, and that's where you'll be taken. Your hosts for lunch will be Susan Levy and Tom Bell, whom I'm sure you're familiar with."

"Why doesn't Nina McFall take us to lunch?" someone piped up, and several other voices murmured agreement.

"Of course, you want to be with Nina, of course you

do. Well . . ." Myrna thought she'd let someone else take the heat this time. ". . . You *will*. This evening at dinner. Your dinner hosts are Rex Reynolds and Nina McFall! And you're going to Le Perigord, one of the best French restaurants in New York! Won't that be great?"

Before the reaction could go beyond an initial burst of approval, Myrna put the tour in motion and led her contingent into the bowels of Meyer Studios while Mark led the other half in a different direction. Half an hour later, both groups converged exactly on schedule in the main rehearsal hall. The visitors were totally awed at the sight of so many familiar faces in person.

"There's Rex Reynolds!"

"There's Sylvia Kastle!"

"There's Bob Valentine again! And Robin Tally!"

"There's Rick Busacca! Is he ever a doll!"

"There's Noel Winston and Angela Dolan! Yoo-hoo! Oh, they're waving! She looked younger last night, didn't she?"

"So where's Nina?"

"Don't tell me she's not here, either!"

"Come on, girls, let's tell them how we feel!"

And Robin, realizing she was about to get her dying wish, focused happily on Angela Dolan's face as the chorus swelled:

"We want to see Nina! We want to see Nina! She's the only s-s-s-star that we adore! When the sh-show ends, On the b-boob tube, We'll be calling out for m-m-m-m-more!"

Bellamy Carter, who was directing the day's episode, studiously avoided looking in Angela Dolan's direction when the rousing number ended. He jumped to his feet and launched into a rapid-fire brief welcoming speech, made a totally unnecessary mass introduction, explained that Melanie Prescott had been written out of this particular episode, and asked the visitors to take seats at the rear so the rehearsal could proceed.

"All right, people, break's over, back to work; now where were we? Oh yes, Victoria was trying to persuade Harley not to go away with Buffy for the weekend, so

Angela darling, would you pick it up where we left off? And *quiet* please, everyone: now Rick, please give Angela her cue. Action!"

Robin watched the firmly clenched jaw that belonged entirely to Angela Dolan and not at all to Victoria Allender and waited for the expected reaction. But she was disappointed when Angela apparently overcame her rage and resumed the scene.

"It's no use, Mrs. Allender, my mind's made up."

"Harley, you can't! It isn't right!"

"We're going away for the weekend and there's no way you can stop us," Rick said. Then he gave Angela a particularly nasty smile and added, "You wouldn't be jealous by any chance, would you?" And Angela whirled around and smacked him.

"Cut!" Bellamy called out. "Great, but I have one tiny suggestion. Angela dear, the smack lacked conviction. Give it a little more, okay? Once again. Action!"

The visitors were fascinated by their first inside look at how it all really happened.

Rick and Angela went through the scene three more times before Bellamy realized that he just wasn't going to get as much conviction from Angela as he wanted.

Robin felt cheated out of a Dolan explosion, but not for long. When they reached the next break, Rick absentmindedly began to whistle the tune of "K-K-K-Katy," and Angela whirled around and smacked him so hard his teeth rattled.

"Anything to please my director, darling," she purred. "Motivation is all."

If only Nina could have been here, Robin thought, maintaining a totally disinterested mask.

She wasn't the only one in the room thinking along those lines.

Chapter Thirteen

Nina spent her day off in a frenzy of preparations for the coming reception at the penthouse on Saturday evening: bullying Alibi Al, conferring further with the caterer and the musicians, arranging to have a piano delivered and tuned and then removed two days later, checking with the booking agent of the musicians she'd hired. Throughout, she kept her eye on the clock, knowing that she'd have to leave a full two hours to soak in a relaxing bubble bath, take a brief but essential nap, do her hair to perfection, and dress for the evening's festivities.

She considered calling Dino just to chat for a few minutes, but thought better of it. He knew that she had to be escorted this evening by Rex Reynolds for professional reasons, but that didn't mean he had to like it. A call would only remind him, and she'd lose more than she'd gain by it. Of course, if he were to call *her*, that would be another story. Good grief, did all men take so much handling?

At four-thirty Nina eased her way into a warm tubful of luxuriously scented bubbles and groaned aloud as the soothing water went to work on her aching muscles. Mmmmmm. She wondered if it was too late to change her specifications on the master bath in the penthouse and have a Jacuzzi installed.

After soaking for twenty minutes she commanded herself to get out of the tub before her fingers and toes started to turn into prunes. Time for the hair ritual, which could only be done properly in the shower. The shampooing was nothing, but the secret to really gorgeous hair, she'd discovered, was simple—just rinse it thoroughly for a full five minutes under running water. That got all the soap out and left both her hair and scalp tingly clean and highly responsive to styling.

Just as she finished blow-drying her ravishingly beautiful mass of flaming red hair, the phone rang. But it wasn't Dino.

"Nina, it's Rex."

"Hi, what's happening?"

"About the dinner this evening—"

"Don't tell me you can't make it!"

"No, no, everything's fine. I just wondered what time you'd like me to pick you up." She hadn't known he was planning to pick her up at all, and she didn't particularly want him to; it might lead to a run-in with Alibi Al.

"Oh, that's not necessary, Rex. I'll meet you there."

"I don't know—won't it look funny if we don't arrive together? That way we can make a big entrance. Wow the people, give them a thrill."

That wasn't at *all* what Nina had in mind.

"Rex, thanks for the offer but I don't think that's how we should play this scene."

"Oh? What's your idea?"

"I was thinking about it earlier," she said, bending close to the magnifying mirror to search out any eyebrow hairs that were misbehaving, "and it seems to me that the usual star entrance is wrong for this group. After all, *they're* the ones who won the contest, so let's turn the tables and treat *them* like the celebrities."

"And how do we do that? Ask for their autographs?" The sudden cynicism in his voice indicated his negative attitude toward anything but a star turn for himself.

"No, smarty, just by being there ahead of them and

greeting them when they arrive, instead of the other way around."

"Sure, I guess we can do that. What time shall I pick you up?"

Persistent fellow, wasn't he? "Rex, I'll meet you at the restaurant at six forty-five. The group is due at seven, and I'm sure Mark will have them there promptly. That way we'll have time to look over the seating before they walk in."

"Whatever you say. See you later."

She hung up and continued with her hairdo.

The phone rang again just as she finished giving it a light spray, but when she picked up the receiver there wasn't anyone there—or was there? She thought she heard someone breathing. She said "Hello?" a second time, then quickly hung up. Obviously a wrong number. . . .

Nina arrived at Le Perigord before Rex, checked the menu with the maitre d', and inspected the table. The private room at the rear of the elegant establishment had been specially set up for the occasion, with the tables arranged in a squared-off U shape at Nina's request. She wanted to be certain that no one would be too far removed from anyone else, and that she could easily get up from time to time and circulate among the group.

Everything was in perfect order. The soft rose-pink tablecloths and deeper pink napkins were complemented by the vases of white and pink rosebuds that were distributed artfully over the tables. The lighting in the room was soft and glowing, throwing off highlights from the tall crystal stemware, the perfectly polished flatware, and the gleaming white dinnerware. The little private bar off to one side was fully stocked with every type of liquor and mixer imaginable, and there was plenty of space for the guests to have a stand-up drink or two before settling down at the tables.

There didn't seem to be anything to do but wait. As she wandered around the room, Nina found herself wondering if Rex would pull a grandstand play and arrive after everyone else, despite her thinly disguised instructions. Was he that much of an egotist?

Nina was suddenly aware that a pair of eyes was watching her intently, and she had the same creepy feeling she'd experienced when the phone rang and no one was there. All this stress was really getting to her—that vacation was long overdue.

She turned slowly and released a sigh of relief when she saw the bartender, who had come silently into the room to take his place. And even when she caught him staring, he still continued.

"Good evening," she said, breaking the spell.

And a spell it was, for Nina's outfit was one of the simplest and most elegant she had ever assembled. Her dress, perfect for the end of a sizzling August in New York, was a glamorous black peau de soie that left one creamy shoulder totally bare and allowed the delicate diamond necklace she wore to twinkle alluringly on her flawless throat. Sleekly fitted over the hips, the skirt flared in a trumpet shape to the floor, giving the impression of movement even when Nina was standing absolutely still, which she was doing at the moment.

"Good evening, Ms. McFall. Pardon me for staring," the young man said, and then blurted out, "You look great on TV, but in person—you're a knockout!"

Nina laughed and smiled her appreciation. "Thank you, kind sir. I only hope my guests share your opinion."

He grinned, displaying so many perfectly capped teeth that Nina realized she was talking to a would-be actor. It was a good bet; she knew that at any given moment half the waiters in New York were trying to get into the theater, and the other half were trying to get *back* in.

She considered opening the subject with him, but decided against it. If he had talent, he'd find a way to make it known. And if he didn't, it would be unkind to give him false hope. This is a tough business, she reminded herself as Rex Reynolds walked into the room. It was two minutes to seven.

"Nina, hi, sorry, traffic tie-up, you look great, and I could use a drink." Rex covered all the bases in a hurry.

"I'm holding off until everyone is here," Nina said, wrapping the strong suggestion in a sweet smile.

"Oh, Christ, let's get this over with," Rex muttered. "Nice place."

"Have you ever been in the private room before?"

"Are you kidding? I've never even sat at the bar."

"No wonder. They don't have a bar."

At that moment, the ever-efficient Myrna arrived, leading the way for the goggle-eyed group of guests. The first ones into the room were Patti and George Martinus, and they were staggered to find Nina already there. Judging from the comments made during the introductions, the rest of the group had similar reactions; Nina's plan to surprise and flatter them had succeeded, casting an immediate warm glow over what could have been a stiffly formal event.

The stand-up drink or two stretched into four or five, and the evening swam by in a genial haze. Nina was careful to spend time with each and every person in the group, and equally careful to lavish particular attention on the three chief guests: Patti Martinus, Melinda West, and Hilda Hotchley.

With Patti, it was easy. Nina remembered to thank her for the perfume which had finally arrived, and the woman was so thrilled to be face to face with her ideal that she turned into an instant chatterbox, leaving Nina time to wonder if the remote resemblance between Patti's outfit and a dress Melanie Prescott had once worn was entirely coincidental. As for George Martinus, Nina found him to be a surly bore, although no one could have guessed her opinion by observing the scene. Patti chattered on, Nina smiled graciously, and George scowled. He scowled at Nina. He scowled at the bartender. He scowled at Patti. And he scowled particularly long and hard at Rex.

In the case of Hilda Hotchley, Nina had to do a little

more work. Hilda introduced her husband Harold as the real "actor in the family" and then for once in her life retired from the conversation, leaving it to Nina and Harold to toss around the theatrical ball. After a little coaxing, Harold began to understand that Hilda really was going to keep her mouth shut for a while, and he just had time to tell Nina about his participation in the Las Cruces Little Theatre's production of *Desire under the Elms* before dinner was served.

As for the third winner, Nina had to wait until after the first course to chat with Melinda West. Here she finally ran into the heavy sledding she was afraid of; the young woman seemed afraid to open her mouth and couldn't get much beyond "Thank you so much," and "This is all so lovely," and "I didn't deserve to win anything at all." Her husband was the best-looking man in the room, Nina thought—after Rex and the young bartender. But they were actor-handsome, whereas Mike West was the real thing. He stood close to his timid little wife, almost as though steering her by the elbow, and seemed to be every bit as overawed as she was.

But Nina was equal to the situation; she'd carried the conversational ball by herself many times before and in many situations far stickier than this. She found out where the Wests came from and what Mike did, and then chatted easily about public education. Although it rather left Melinda West out of the picture, at least it filled the gaps until the next course was served and it was time for Nina to return to her seat.

As she did so, she glanced across the room at Rex. He was being monopolized at the moment by a middle-aged woman who'd been introduced as Louella Croydon, the one with the odd-looking husband who was looking daggers first at his wife and then at Rex.

Mrs. Croydon was apparently not used to an open bar, and Rex was keeping up with her drink for drink—out of desperation, Nina assumed. Louella Croydon's control seemed to be a thing of the past as she leaned toward Rex, repeatedly touching him on the hands, the arms, and occasionally on the shoulder as she rattled on and on and on. Nina suspected Rex wasn't listening to a single word. His slightly bleary gaze was fastened on the youngest member of the group, a rather pretty little blonde who seemed to be traveling with neither husband nor boyfriend. Watch yourself, sweetie, Nina warned silently; his nickname of "Sexy Rexy" isn't exactly undeserved.

But despite the bumpy spots the evening was a raging success, and at the end the visitors parted from Nina and Rex in a blizzard of boozy good wishes and high-proof sentiments.

Nina didn't give Rex the chance to try to see her home; while he was still bidding his adieus to the clinging Mrs. Croydon, she stepped into a cab and was soon whisked back to the comfort of Primrose Towers, where she had an odd dream about good-looking bartenders, good-looking actors, good-looking schoolteachers, good-looking detectives, and Louella Croydon hanging on to all of them and wearing a necklace with a pendant of intertwined cobras.

Tuesday morning dawned much earlier than Nina considered fair, in view of all her intensive efforts the night before to give the visitors a good time. But the evening had lasted a good hour and a half longer than she'd planned. Fortunately she'd had the foresight to limit her alcohol intake to exactly three glasses of champagne, carefully nursed and spaced throughout the evening. Taken alone, they might have left her with a slight headache, but the delicious dinner had served to avoid that penalty.

So she wasn't in the least hung over, just tired when the radio alarm went off and the gentle music of her favorite station raised her from the deep well of sleep to the surface of reality.

Chessy, of course, was raring to go, exactly as on any other morning. "Poor baby," Nina said, cuddling him in her arms and stroking the soft fur under his chin. "Did

Mommy leave you all alone last night? Ahhhh, what a good guy you are."

As if in reply, the battle-scarred tom opened one eye and gave his mistress a look that said, "Cut the baby talk, just scratch." To compensate for the hours of loneliness she'd foisted on him, Nina carried him straight into the kitchen and opened a can of his favorite flavor catfood. When he smelled it, he stopped wrapping his tail around her legs and gazed up in fascinated confusion.

"I know, I know, this is dinner food, not breakfast. But you deserve a treat today. And tonight, I'll bring home some cantaloupe and really let you go wild."

Nina had discovered that her adopted stray had a few very peculiar culinary preferences—he wouldn't walk across the room for a dish of tuna fish and he didn't really give a damn for milk, but he'd risk his neck for a piece of cantaloupe or a piece of fresh asparagus.

After Chessy had hunkered down to his morning supper, Nina made herself a cup of eye-opening coffee. She usually drank tea, and herbal tea at that, because she was convinced that coffee was bad for her complexion, but this morning she needed the extra jolt from the caffeine.

As it turned out, the jolt that propelled her into full wakefulness came from a totally different source.

The phone rang just as she was stirring the coffee. She was immediately on guard; people who made phone calls at six forty-five A.M. were usually not calling with good news.

"Hello?"

"Hello, babe."

"Dino? What's wrong? You sound strange. Is something wrong with Peter?"

"No, he's fine. I've been here since about five this morning."

"Where are you?"

"At the station. Listen, I have something to tell you. One of your dinner partners didn't make it home last night."

"Tell me who you're talking about." Nina's head swam with images of the pretty little blonde waking up in a strange bed in a strange part of the city, but she wasn't alert enough to wonder why that would have brought Dino to the police station at five in the morning.

"It's Rex Reynolds."

A chill went through her as the world came sharply into focus.

"What about him?"

"They pulled him out of the river early this morning. Dead."

Chapter Fourteen

When she'd hung up the receiver, Nina sat in the kitchen, frozen, her untouched coffee rapidly cooling. Echoes of the call she'd just had from Dino swam in her mind. Rex was dead . . . pulled out of the Hudson early this morning . . . apparently drowned . . . official cause of death to be determined . . .

She'd had the presence of mind to ask Dino who had been notified and he'd told her no one had because they didn't know whom to notify. The only thing Nina knew about him was that he was unmarried and lived alone; she hadn't a clue as to his family, or even where he came from. They'd have to look into his personnel file at the studio to discover his next of kin.

"Dino," Nina had said, "this couldn't have happened at a worse time."

"Especially for Reynolds," he remarked dryly.

"You know what I mean. The show—all these people here from out of town. And my God, the publicity! Helen will go berserk. What are you going to do next?"

"Depends. What times does the studio open?"

"The guards arrive at seven o'clock, but there's usually no one there but staff technicians until eight o'clock, when we have the first call."

"So that means someone's going to start wondering where the hell Reynolds is at eight o'clock."

"Not today. Chandler is written out today."

"Who's Chandler?"

"Rex's character. Oh God, Dave and Sally will be frantic if the part isn't recast."

"When do Mrs. Meyer and Krueger show up?"

"It varies. They're usually in by ten o'clock if they're coming in—some days they don't come to the studio at all. But it's a safe bet they'll be there every day this week, because of the contest winners' visit."

"Okay, I'll be by at about nine-thirty to let them know what's happened."

"Dino? Do the papers have this yet, or the TV news people?"

"No. I knew you'd want me to sit on it."

"Thank God! Please, I know this is stretching regulations, but can you keep it quiet a while longer, until we can figure out what to do?"

"'We'? Are you on the team already?"

"You know what I mean—'we' at Meyer Studios. You have no idea how much is riding on this week. If this got out now, the news could ruin it."

"Nina, you're losing your perspective. I know the contest promotion is a big deal for all of you, but a man is *dead*, you know."

"Yes, I know. I'm starting to sound like Helen. Oh, this is crazy! Rex didn't have all that much to drink! I'm sure he wasn't drunk—he was too busy fighting off Mrs. Croydon and flirting with a cute little blonde, one of the guests. How could he have fallen into the river and drowned?"

"You're getting ahead of yourself. First, no one said he was drunk; it'll take some blood work by the lab to tell us that. And second, no one said he *fell* into the river. There are other ways of getting wet, you know. And third, we don't know that he drowned. All we know for sure is that he was found floating in the river and he's dead. Now what's this about a blonde?"

Nina filled him in on the events of the night before

and made him promise not to go public with news of Rex's death until after he'd met with Helen and Horst Krueger. She also extracted his promise to keep her fully informed.

Now she sat there stunned, thinking over the evening and sipping her coffee, not even noticing that it was stone cold.

When Nina arrived at the studio just before eight, she realized she had no recollection of her movements after Dino's phone call. Somehow, functioning on automatic pilot, she'd showered, dressed, gathered her things, locked the apartment, and hailed a cab. "Muscle memory," they called it. And all the while she was concentrating on everything she'd seen and heard the night before, seeking some clue that would help throw light on Rex's untimely death.

She passed through the studio's front door and was on her way to her dressing room when a voice stopped her in her tracks.

"Nina! Good morning, darling! Tell me all about last night, quickly, before you're needed at first reading."

It was Helen. Why, dear God, *why* was she there so early this morning of all mornings?

"Helen. What a surprise. It was wonderful. Wonderful. Everyone had a really wonderful time."

Helen's eyes narrowed.

"What's wrong?"

"Nothing's wrong," Nina chirped blithely.

"Stop trying to fool me! I've been watching that face for too many years offscreen and on not to know when you're lying."

"I swear, Helen, nothing's—"

"If you don't tell me, I'll get it from Rex. Or if necessary, from one of our guests."

Nina gave up. How could she stall this insistent woman until Dino was due at nine-thirty? Why hadn't she suggested he come to the studio early, just in case? What could she say?

"Nina, you're getting paler by the second. You must have something really terrible to tell me. Come on, out with it! What did you do?"

"Helen, can we go into your office? And is Horst here yet? Or Ken?"

Both producers were just arrivng, and Helen herded them all into her office, leaving word for Bellamy Carter to start the first reading of the script without Nina. As soon as the door closed, Helen wheeled on Nina.

"I can scarcely believe, Nina, that somehow you've managed to louse up your first meeting with these people! You know how important this whole week is to us! You're not an amateur! What are you trying to do? Sabotage the whole promotion?"

Ken looked distressed; Horst heaved a sigh and asked quietly, "Helen, what are you talking about?"

"I don't know yet!" Helen spat out. "I'm waiting to find out!"

Horst turned to a very nervous Nina. "Nina? Can you tell us what Helen is talking about?"

"It seems I have no choice," Nina said. "But it would be so much better if we could wait until later."

"How much later?" Helen snapped.

"Only an hour or so, until Di—Detective Rossi gets here," she finished lamely.

"*Rossi!*" Helen exploded. "You mean the *police* are involved again? I do not *believe* this is happening!"

Now Horst was getting as perturbed as Helen. "Nina, I don't think we can wait for anything. What's going on?"

"All right. It isn't anything anybody did—but it's very, very bad news. Early this morning, I don't know what time exactly, the police discovered that Rex had fallen into the river last night, after the dinner party . . ."

"Good God, is that all? So he drank too much. I was expecting that," Helen said with smug satisfaction. "That's why I scheduled him as co-host on a night before he had a day off. Hah! *I* know who drinks around here and who doesn't."

But Horst knew there was something more to the story.

"Nina, what else?"

"And . . ." she took a deep breath, "he's dead."

There was a long silence while it sank in. Before they could start to ask a million questions she couldn't answer, Nina told them how she'd learned the news and assured them that the information had not yet been leaked to the press—at least, not as of six-forty-five that morning.

"Detective Rossi is coming here to tell you what he knows, and to look at Rex's personnel file. The police don't know anything—who his next of kin is, or whom to notify. . . ." For the first time Nina felt the shock wearing off, and her vision blurred as the awfulness of Rex's death began to sink in. "I feel so terrible for him. . . ."

Horst's arms went around her comfortingly, and she put her head down on his shoulder for a few minutes while the tears flowed.

"And I suppose he wants to ask questions. The 'few questions' bit again! Oh, this place is cursed!" Helen muttered—and then an awful thought struck her.

"He's going to want to question our visitors! Oh, my God, he *can't* do that! They come to New York to do guest shots on a soap opera and they wind up being questioned by the goddamned police! We'll be the laughing stock of the industry! This *cannot* be allowed to happen!" she declaimed with even more fervor than Nina had ever seen her summon up before.

For once the producers and Helen Meyer were in accord. Under no circumstances were the police to be allowed to question the visitors. Rossi would have to get all his information about events at the dinner party from Nina. And the whole thing would have to be kept out of the news at least until after the visitors had left.

"But I don't think you can get the police to agree to that," Nina warned. "I know how important this is, but . . ."

"*We* aren't going to get the police to agree to that, *you* are!" Helen declared with unshakable finality.

By the time Dino had arrived, Helen, with the aid of Horst and Ken, had concocted a cover story: Rex had been suddenly called to his family's home, out west somewhere—Denver to be specific, because someone—all right, his mother—was seriously ill. No one knew how long he'd be away. He'd just have to be written out for the duration. . . . That would have to suffice until next Saturday, after the visitors were gone. Then they'd just have to make the best of it.

Nina didn't think Dino would be exactly crazy about the idea.

And she was right.

The fans and Dino arrived at the same time, exactly on schedule at nine-thirty. Nina greeted Dino and signaled him toward Helen's office while a shaky Ken Frost put on his best face to greet the group and steer them into the rehearsal hall. Observing his performance, Nina realized the producer had acting abilities no one had ever suspected; as he shook hands and joked with the visitors he seemed the very personification of carefree geniality.

"What's going on?" Dino asked Nina privately, outside Helen's office.

"Helen and Horst Krueger know about Rex. Ken Frost, too," she said.

"How did they find out? Did *you* tell them?" His irritation was evident.

"I had to, Dino." Nina related the conversation she'd been trapped into with the three executives, and Dino's anger subsided.

"Okay, I guess there wasn't anything else you could do. Except steer clear of everyone until I got here."

"That's what I *meant* to do," she said, becoming irritated herself. "But I ran smack into Helen. It was just a case of bad luck; she's never been here this early."

"Hey, cool down. We're on the same side, remember?"

Nina looked into his big dark eyes and smiled back at him.

"Okay, coach. Let's go get 'em."

"Before we talk to your boss lady, there's one thing I don't want her to know." Nina waited expectantly, certain she wasn't going to like what Dino was about to say. "The cause of death was definitely drowning, but there were some marks on his body that might indicate he was in a fight, or at least a struggle, before he went into the river."

"You mean somebody pushed him in?"

"I don't know. It's possible. We're still waiting for the lab report on the alcohol level in his blood. Do you remember anything happening last night that could have led to a fight later on?"

"No, nothing specific. Unless . . ."

"What is it?"

"I can't believe this is important, but Rex was doing the usual flirting bit with a few women in the group, and some of their husbands weren't too happy about it."

"Was anything said?"

"No, nothing. I'm just remembering some of the looks Rex was getting from the men."

"Which ones? Be specific."

"Well, two in particular. George Martinus, the husband of the president of the fan club. But that can't be important—he looks as though he hates everyone. Particularly me," she added ruefully.

"Who else?"

"The funny-looking little guy. His name is Croydon. Not that Rex was flirting with his wife, but because *she* was all over Rex. Literally couldn't keep her hands off him. Poor thing, I felt so sorry for her. It reminded me of the way Helen was gaga over that creep Rob Bryant. . . ." The memory of Bryant and the two young women he killed earlier in the year crowded into Nina's mind momentarily, until she forced herself to focus on the matter at hand. "Anyway, that's it. I don't remember anything else happening that might lead someone to . . ."

"Nina?" Helen Meyer's tense voice called out from her office, stabbing into their hushed conversation. "Is that Lieutenant Rossi with you out there?"

He quickly put a finger across his lips and then threw her a brief pantomimed kiss as he stepped into the office.

"Good morning, Mrs. Meyer. Mr. Krueger."

"Good morning to you," Helen said coldly and then addressed Nina. "Bellamy just called from the rehearsal hall; they need you. *Now*."

"As soon as I—"

"They cannot go one word further without you. On the other hand, I'm sure Lieutenant Rossi is capable of doing exactly that. Surely he'll fill you in later," Helen added with heavy sarcasm.

Nina glanced at Dino, but he was concentrating on Helen and Horst, so she left the office and went toward the rehearsal hall. Step by step, she forced herself to cast off all thoughts of Rex Reynolds's death and concentrate exclusively on Melanie Prescott's problems.

When she stepped into the large room, she waved cheerfully to the group of visitors who were seated at the side, trying not to lock eyes with any of them but aware that every one of them was avidly watching every move she made.

Careful now, she told herself. This is their first glimpse of Nina McFall at work, and they're going to talk about it when they get back home. So make it good, baby. Make it *very* good.

She did, and it was.

When the midday break arrived at an uncivilized eleven-fifteen A.M., Sylvia Kastle and Mary Kennerly assumed their assigned hostess chores and shepherded the visitors off to lunch. Nevertheless, a few of them managed to maneuver themselves close to Nina before departing, to repeat their effusive thanks for the previous evening. Some of the women expressed disappointment that Rex wasn't at rehearsal, which was when Nina noted that the Croydons weren't in evidence.

Had they already left the rehearsal hall, and she'd simply not seen them? Or hadn't they been there at all—and if not, why not?

Nina returned to her dressing room to put her feet up and try to relax before even thinking about lunch. And, as she hoped, Dino was there waiting for her. Maybe he'd have the time to take her to lunch.

She closed the door and went to him for a long, gentle kiss before either of them spoke.

"What happened?" she asked, pulling out of his embrace.

"Not much. I told them only the minimum—that Reynolds was found dead at about four A.M., victim of an apparent drowning, probably accidental, after drinking too much. They seemed to buy it, but they didn't relax until I agreed to keep the whole thing under wraps while this fan club thing is going on."

"Oh, Dino, thank you! You are truly a wonderful man! I know how grateful they must be!"

"I'm not doing it for them, you loonybird, I'm doing it for you. And it's strictly against my better judgment. But I told them this much: If anything crops up that suggests there's good reason to question anybody, including these visitors, nothing's going to stop me."

"Well, I've thought of somebody you might question."

"Who?"

"Alibi Al."

"The contractor? What's the connection?"

Damn, now she'd have to tell him that she'd enlisted Rex's aid in getting Alibi Al into line. Taking a deep breath, she got it over with as quickly as possible, making note of Dino's nerve-wrackingly steady gaze as she did so.

"For the moment we'll skip over your reasons for not asking me to intercede on your behalf," he said slowly and evenly. "But you can be sure we'll come back to that part later." She nodded miserably. "But for now, are you suggesting that this guy Al was so ticked off at Rex that he'd lie in wait for him outside a restaurant, follow him, pick a fight, and then shove him into the river?"

"It does sound rather farfetched," Nina admitted.

"You said it. But I'll have Charley Harper check up on the guy anyway. You never know."

"What did you find in Rex's personnel file?"

"Damn little. He didn't list anyone as next of kin, and his insurance beneficiary is his former wife."

"I didn't know he had one. Who is she?"

Dino consulted his notepad. "Beatrice McMillian Felice. Lives in Jamestown, New York. Someplace near Buffalo, I think. We'll check that out, too. Otherwise, that's it."

"Not much to go on, is it?"

"Nope. But if we find out Reynolds was soused and there's no reason to investigate further, it'll be listed as accidental drowning and that'll be the end of it."

"But what about the bruises? You said he was bruised."

"Nina, drunks fall down. Maybe he took four or five tumbles before going into the river."

"Yes, maybe. But there are bruises and there are bruises. I mean, doesn't it depend on where the bruises are? And what kind of bruises they are? I'm sure a bruise from a fall is one thing and a bruise from a punch is another. And that reminds me, if he fell down so much, his clothes would somehow show it, wouldn't they? Were the knees of his trousers—"

"Whoa! Whoa! Put it on hold. Believe it or not, the police have handled just a few similar cases in the past, and we really do know what to look for."

Her face registered the resentment she felt at his rebuke.

"Unless you'd like to switch jobs. How about it? You do the investigating and I'll go on television. Melanie could have a sex-change operation, and I could turn up as Mel Prescott. Mel? As in Melvin?"

"Ha ha. As in don't make me laugh."

"I'll make you laugh. Come here, you goof." He put

his hands on her hips and suddenly tensed his fingers just enough to start her giggling at the mere possibility of being tickled.

"Dino, don't! Stop!"

"Until I met you, I never knew anybody who was ticklish on the hips. Those other places, yeah. But the hips?"

She reached under his suit jacket and wrapped her arms around him, feeling the heat that radiated from his skin right through his broadcloth shirt. In a moment he forgot about her ticklish hips and concentrated on her tingling lips.

"Mmm, that was good. Just for that, I'm going to let you take me to lunch."

"Can't do it, babe. Got to get back to the station. I'll talk to you later, okay?"

"Okay, but first . . ."

"Mmmmmmmm."

After Dino left, Nina checked with the front desk to find out where Sylvia and Mary had taken the visitors. Assured they'd gone out of the neighborhood, she trotted around to Corrigan's for a quick bite. She loved her fans, but at the moment she was simply not in the mood to be with them. There'd be plenty of that as the week wore on. Besides, she wanted to think more about what had happened to poor Rex. For a change, there was no one from Meyer Studios in Corrigan's, so she was able to concentrate. She kept coming back to Eddie Croydon and his peculiarly unpleasant attitude.

At twelve-twenty-five, Nina entered the studio and found Nick Galano, apparently waiting to take his charges in tow as scheduled.

"Nick, hi. Are you on duty this afternoon?"

"Yep. First the three winners go to wardrobe so we can find something for them to wear on the show. Then it's off to makeup for a coiffure and a complete facial."

"Helen certainly ordered the full treatment. That's nice, it'll give them a real thrill. But I don't think you're going to have to do a coiffure job on Mr. Hotchley, and I doubt if he'd accept a facial."

"Mr.? What happened to the Mrs.?"

"The Mrs. told me she's stepping out of the spotlight in favor of the Mr. 'He's the actor in the family.'"

"No kidding. That's kind of sweet, isn't it?"

"It really is. I can't imagine any of the others refusing a role in a soap opera just because their husands do amateur theater."

"Well, I wouldn't go so far as to call these 'roles.' In the first scene, they're just going to walk into a restaurant, sit down, look at menus, and order some food. All in the background, of course. In pantomime, no lines."

"And in the foreground?"

"You know. That's the scene where you're having a clandestine lunch with Rex."

"Oh, of course. I'd forgotten about that scene. . . ."

"Are you okay? You looked funny there for a second."

"Touch of indigestion, probably. I think I ate too quickly. See you later, Nick. I want to lie down for a while before we start the runthrough."

"Yeah. Uh-oh. Here they come."

Nina hurried down the hall. The restaurant scene! She'd forgotten. It was mainly Melanie's scene, but Norman Chandler was definitely in it. Now how in hell would they get around *that* tomorrow, she wondered, going into her dressing room.

Flowers! A beautiful little bouquet awaited her on the dressing table. Dino must have come back and left them here, to apologize for not taking me to lunch, she thought, burying her nose in the fragrant blossoms. What a romantic softie he was turning out to be. Flowers in the middle of the day weren't really his style. And a card . . .

"For Melanie, my angel of love, from your Secret Lover."

She dropped the bouquet as though it had turned into a living snake. Of course! She should have recognized that damned handwriting immediately. This has gone far enough, she thought. Whoever this man is, he's definitely lost touch with reality. I'm going to ask Dino to find him and call him off. That'll make up for not asking for his help with Alibi Al. But how *can* Dino find him?

Then she remembered the unopened letter, the one she'd shoved into a drawer. She knew the other letters had lacked a return address, but a letter always offered some clues, didn't it? There had to be a postmark.

Nina took the envelope out and stared at it for a moment. It was postmarked New York. She tore it open and began to read:

"Dearest Angel Melanie. Within only a few days now we will be together and our new life will begin. But you tease me so by not wearing my gift, the symbol of our love. I was disappointed at first, and even angry, but now I realize you are waiting to wear it when we are alone at last, when we will submit to each other and become one. All this will begin to happen in only a few short days. But no, not short—time away from you drags so slowly. And your Secret Lover wants you so very much. Your own one."

Her knees suddenly gave way and Nina sank down onto her dressing table chair, her heart pounding with fright as she tried to figure out when this letter had arrived, and what he meant by "within only a few days. . . ."

Oh, dear God, that postmark means he's *here*. Whoever Melanie's "Secret Lover" is, he's here. And he didn't send these flowers—he probably walked in and left them!

Her hands trembled as she reached into her purse for change. She'd have to call Dino immediately and tell him what had happened! He'd be angry that she hadn't told him about these letters sooner, but how could she have known this lunatic was serious? And what had she done with that damned cobra pendant, the "symbol of our love"? The thought of it sickened her.

Nina opened the dressing-room door just a crack and cringed when she caught a blurry glimpse of a male back just disappearing around a bend in the corridor. My God, was that the man? She had a momentary impulse to run after him, but reason prevailed. If it was, he could be truly insane. He could have a knife, a gun. He could go berserk and attack her on the spot, drag her into an empty dressing room and tear at her clothing and . . .

Footsteps. Was he coming back for her?

She withdrew into the dressing room and closed the door, locking it with shaking hands. Then she waited, listening. The footsteps drew closer and stopped on the other side of the door.

She nearly jumped out of her skin when someone abruptly knocked on the door. Should she answer? She could always scream without even opening the door. The walls were so thin she'd be heard all the way to the guard's desk out front . . .

"Who is it?" she quavered.

"Nina, it's me."

Robin! Oh, thank God!

Nina unlocked the door to admit Robin and then quickly shut it and locked it again. Robin looked at her oddly.

"What's the bit with the lock?"

"Oh, did I lock it? Just a habit."

"And a good one. Did you hear what happened?"

"No, what?"

"Somebody broke into Horst's office while he was out to lunch."

"A robbery?"

"No, that's the weird part. Nothing was taken."

Nina had a flash that told her exactly what had been taken—a dressing-room key. Taken, used, and then returned. She knew because she'd done exactly the same thing herself not too many months earlier, when she'd had to get into Rob Bryant's desk to search for the evidence that helped convict him. Robin knew that, too, of course, since she'd stood guard while Nina pulled off that little caper. But it didn't seem to occur to Robin now that that might be the explanation. Just as well.

"Probably a prank. Somebody suffering from midsummer madness. Let's get down to the main hall before they start yelling for us."

Robin laughed. "Nina, if I didn't know better, I'd swear you were afraid to go alone."

"Well, aren't you just bursting with silly notions! Let's go."

The call to Dino would have to wait.

"So how's it going?" Nina asked as they walked along the corridor. Even inane conversation would be better than silence right now.

"Pretty smoothly. But I'm *very* glad Rex is written out today."

Oh, Lord. "Why do you say that?"

"Rafe is on the warpath again. We had a big fight last night about the same old thing, and he stormed out on me. Stayed out all night this time, the jerk."

That was what Nina had been about to tell Dino earlier, when Helen had interrupted their conversation in the hall—Rafe and Rex. Not that Rafe could possibly be responsible for Rex's death, yet . . .

"Listen, I have to make a quick phone call," Nina said. "Give Bellamy some excuse; I won't be long."

"Sounds urgent."

"Oh, it's just a little detail I forgot to arrange for the party Saturday."

"You know, Bellamy was very ticked that you were so late this morning. Can't it wait?"

"Not really. You never know which details are going to prove important in the long run."

Chapter Fifteen

Nina's hurried phone call to Dino proved to be a disappointment—Bruno Reichert answered the call and told her that Dino was out on a case and wasn't expected back until late afternoon. Was there something he could do for her?

"No, I'm afraid not. Just ask him to call me whenever he can." She was sure Dino would understand the urgency.

But either he *hadn't* understood the urgency or he hadn't gotten the message. All through the afternoon, Nina kept hoping to be called to the phone, but when the whirlpool of dress rehearsal and last-minute fix-ups began, leading to the inviolability of "final tape," she knew she'd have to wait until she got home to talk to him.

As soon as the final tape was ended, Nina tore out of Melanie's clothing, into her own, and bolted from the studio. She didn't care if anyone thought she was rude or cuckoo, there was no way she was going to stay in that place one second longer than necessary, particularly when it was emptying out for the night.

But again a knot of fans was waiting for her on the broiling sidewalk, and Nina's rapid exit was delayed. How can I brush past them? she thought. It's still over ninety degrees and who knows how long they've been out here waiting?

So she hastily signed autographs, smiling and mumbling about having to rush to an appointment. Then she had a sudden inspiration and announced that if anyone could flag her a cab, she'd be eternally grateful. Even as she uttered the simple request she hated herself for sounding like a third-rate Scarlett O'Hara at her simpering worst.

"You don't need a cab, Miss McFall. If you're in a hurry, I can drop you somewhere."

She looked up and to her surprise saw Mike West, but no Melinda.

"That would be wonderful. But I thought you and your wife flew into New York."

"We did. I rented a car as soon as we got here. Not that it's been of much use. I guess when you live in a town like Rutland you just get so used to driving yourself everywhere that you can't be without a car."

"I know exactly what you mean; I keep a car in the garage under my apartment building, though I really could do without one. It's just a habit. Anyway, a lift would be greatly appreciated." She turned to the group of fans, who were apparently mesmerized at this unexpected opportunity to listen in on a real moment with a celebrity. "I have to run now. Bye-bye. And thank you all *so* much for coming!"

Mike's car was at the corner. Nina told him the best route to Primrose Towers and they were soon embroiled in the sluggish stream of afternoon traffic that was making its laborious way up the West Side.

"It's been really fascinating to see how the show is put together," Mike said. "There's a lot more to it than I would've guessed."

"Oh, it probably looks a lot more complicated than it is," Nina said, enjoying the feeling of security that had settled over her as soon as the studio was behind them. "And when you've been doing it as long as I have, it gets to be a routine. But at first, it's murder."

"How do you mean?"

"Until I got used to the rhythm of production, I never thought I'd be able to handle the pace. The constant memorization, the endless changes—most of all, the concentration that's needed to pull the whole thing off and create a believable characterization."

"Yours is totally believable, or so they tell me."

She laughed. "I wasn't fishing for compliments. By the way, what have you done with your wife?"

"She wasn't feeling very well and went back to the hotel about two hours ago. Miss Kastle and Miss Kennerly treated us to an enormous lunch. We're not used to all this rich food. Do you people eat this way all the time?"

"Lord, no! We'd be big as blimps. Lunch is usually a version of rabbit food, or sometimes pasta, and dinner is most often a very small piece of lean meat or fish. As for alcohol, the less the better, particularly during the week."

"Pasta? I thought that was fattening."

"It can be, if you eat a ton of it and wash it down with gallons of vino. But we eat small portions, and the calories get burned up right away because of all the energy we expend on the afternoon's taping."

"I wonder what Mrs. Meyer is going to feed us tonight," he said.

"That's right, you're dining at Leatherwing. Believe me, you're in for a treat. Helen doesn't entertain much since her husband died, but when she does it, she really *does* it." She laughed again. "Tell your wife not to wear anything tight."

"How long will it take me to drive up there?"

"About an hour from midtown. But aren't you going in a limo? I'm sure Helen has arranged first-class transportation."

"No, I'd rather drive and see some other parts of the city. We haven't been to New York in a long time, and who knows when we'll get back?"

They chatted on easily until he pulled up in front of Nina's building.

"Well, thank you again for the ride. That was so much more enjoyable than a taxicab."

"My pleasure, Miss McFall. Any time."

Nina smiled. "I think we can safely get onto a first-name basis, don't you?" She was touched to see that he blushed slightly. When was the last time she'd seen a man blush?

"Well, thank you. I'd be honored, Miss—Nina."

"See you tomorrow, Mike," she said, getting out of the car.

"Let me help you." He jumped out and ran around to her side of the car to hold the door for her. "Nina?" She half-expected to see him bow. "I meant what I said about 'any time.' If you'd like, I could pick you up in the morning and take you to the studio. We Vermonters are early risers, so it'd be no trouble."

Nina was charmed by the generous offer, but turned him down just the same. "How lovely of you to offer, but you're going to be here for only a few more days, and I'd get spoiled rotten by such service. Enjoy your evening, Mike!"

As she went into the building she turned to wave and saw him standing exactly as she'd left him, still holding the car door and smiling that marvelously engaging grin.

They don't grow 'em like that in li'l ole New York, she mused as the elevator carried her upward. Melinda was a lucky girl. . . .

The phone was ringing when Nina entered her apartment, and she rushed to grab it, totally ignoring the noisy greeting Chessy was offering.

"Later, Chessy," she said, reaching for the receiver. "Hello?"

"Hi, babe. Got your message just now. Anything new?"

She told him about the flowers, the letter, the pendant, and all the rest of it, but he didn't seem particularly alarmed. "The poor guy is bananas about you—not that I blame him. If we locked up every man who ever dreamed of spending some time alone with you, we'd have to lease the World Trade Center to hold them all."

"But the flowers! He must have gotten into my dressing room with the spare keys from Horst's office."

"Nina, I bet you're not even sure you locked the door when you went out to lunch."

"That's true."

"Your imagination is working overtime, babe. Relax, enjoy the flattery, and don't get paranoid."

Nina sighed. "Maybe you're right. This business about Rex is making me very jumpy. And that's the other thing I have to tell you about . . ."

She described the altercations between Rafe and Rex Reynolds, ending with Robin's description of what had happened between her and Rafe the night Rex died.

"Nina, now you've got your teeth into something! You should have told me this sooner!" Dino sounded jubilant.

"It just didn't register until the talk I had with Robin today. I felt I had to tell you about it, but I'm sure Rafe has a perfectly innocent explanation of where he went last night."

"*You* may be sure, but I'm not. He had motive and opportunity. I'll be interested in hearing his alibi for his whereabouts when Rex took a swim."

"Dino, please!"

"Sorry, babe. I know how you feel about fingering your pals."

"Robin *is* a good friend, and so is Rafe. I don't really believe this is the answer. In fact, I didn't even want to mention it to you, but . . ."

"But what?"

"But I thought that if, just on the barest, remotest, least likely farfetched hare-brained possibility . . ."

"I get your meaning. Go on."

"If Rafe did have something to do with it, and I hadn't told you something that might have helped, well . . ."

"Now you're thinking like a cop. You can't let personal feelings get in the way, and you rule out nothing until it's been gone over from every possible angle. And then you go over it a few more times, just to be sure."

"So what are you going to do?"

"You know what I'm going to do. Check up on Mr. Rafe Fallone."

Nina's heart sank. If Robin found out how Dino had gotten on Rafe's trail, she'd never forgive her former friend.

"Dino? Keep me posted?"

"Hey, don't worry about it. We have a deal, remember?"

She remembered. They each told each other everything, no exceptions, nothing held back. So why didn't she tell him she was planning to do a little snooping on her own regarding the threatened happy-ever-after with her "Secret Lover"? Dino would have scoffed at her, and he was probably right. All the same, she just wanted to put her suspicions to rest.

"Come on, Chessy, let's get reacquainted," she said, patting the sofa cushion and holding out her hands to receive the flying ball of orange fur.

Rehearsal on Wednesday morning went at a perfectly normal pace until the fans arrived, when it immediately became apparent that they were all in a state of high excitement. This was the first of the really big days, when the lucky ones would actually put on costumes and makeup and rehearse with the pros. Then they'd go on camera, and in just about three weeks, when these episodes of *The Turning Seasons* aired, they'd wind up on view in living rooms all across the country!

"Okay, next up is the restaurant scene," Nick Galano called out. Since it was Bellamy's day to be good shepherd, Nick was taking care of the directing chores.

He turned to the keyed-up group of visitors and

called out, "Mrs. Martinus, Mrs. West, Mrs. Hotchley, if you please."

"*Mr.* Hotchley is taking my place," Hilda reminded him curtly. "He's the actor in the family."

Nina glanced around to see if there would be any cheeky reactions to Hilda's statement from the professional cast, as it had already become a catch-phrase. But they were all on their best behavior. She also wondered when it would be revealed to the new "actors" that Rex would not be showing up.

Patti practically fell over her feet in her eagerness to get into the rehearsal group, whereas Harold walked across the floor with great dignity and seriousness. Melinda came last, showing signs of extreme nervousness and hesitancy.

Nick explained the scene to them. On their cue, which would be a hand signal, they were to enter the restaurant set, be shown to a table, take their seats, and open their menus. They were to read the bill of fare, talk about what to order, and then when the waitress came to their table, place their orders. After the waitress left, taking their menus, they were to chat among themselves.

"And of course, you won't actually be saying anything. Just mouth your words in silence. Our sound equipment is highly sensitive, and all we want to pick up is the conversation between Melanie and Norman . . . Yes, Mr. Hotchley?"

"Who are we?"

"Why, you're restaurant customers."

"I mean, what brings us to this restaurant together?"

"*Hunger,* Mr. Hotchley. You're all hungry. For lunch."

Nina thought she heard a smothered giggle coming from Robin's direction, and cast her a severe look. It was a perfectly acceptable question for an actor to ask, but dear Harold Hotchley couldn't know that in the fast-paced world of daily television production there was barely time for even the principal characters to discuss motivation, let alone extras.

"Naturally," Harold persisted. "But are we three related? And if so . . ."

"Yes, you're related," Nick said quickly, since the only way was through the middle. "You are Mrs. West's father, and Mrs. Martinus is your niece. You're here to celebrate Mrs. West's birthday. Her twenty-seventh birthday. You're a retired plumber, she's a secretary in a law firm, and Mrs. Martinus is a brain surgeon. *Places!*"

The strangled gurgles that came from some of the principals were mercifully lost in the hustle and bustle as everyone shuffled around and got into position for the scene. Nina went to the front table and took her seat in the "downstage" position, where the cameras would catch her from both the full-front and side angles. Then Gary Johnson came in and sat opposite Nina, with his back to the cameras.

"That's not Norman Chandler," Nina heard Louella Croydon whisper loudly. "Where's Rex Reynolds?"

Without looking up from the script he was consulting, Nick repeated what he'd told the cast earlier, at the first read-through. "Mr. Reynolds was suddenly called out of town—illness in his family. Until he comes back we're using Gary Johnson, whom you all know, of course. We're not recasting, you understand. We're shooting 'Norman' from the back and keeping him off camera as much as possible. He has very few lines in this scene, and Gary does an incredible job of impersonating Rex's voice. Now can we *please* get started?"

The balance of the morning proceeded smoothly, but Nina had the nagging feeling that someone was watching her steadily. As an actress she was used to being looked at, of course, but this was different; this time she felt that she was being closely *observed*, and she didn't like it. The creepy feeling became so uncomfortable that it was interfering with her concentration, and she decided to do something about it.

She began to violate one of her strictest rehearsal rules—never to look directly at anyone except the other characters in the scene. Every time she had the chance, her eyes flickered toward the visitors' group, and by the process of elimination she soon discovered who was watching her so intently. Then she had to figure out what to do about it.

At the next break, she saw that her surreptitious observer was standing apart from the others, so she took the bull by the proverbial horns and walked casually in his direction.

"Enjoying all this?" she asked in the friendliest tone she could manage.

"Oh, sure. It's really interesting. You've got a good show."

"May I say something to you? You don't strike me as a soap-opera fan."

"All kinds of people watch soap operas."

"Yes, I know. But somehow you still don't seem the type. Frankly I'm delighted, because I was getting the impression that you were sort of uncomfortable here. How long have you been watching *The Turning Seasons?*"

It was an unwelcome question. She could sense the alarm bells going off in Eddie Croydon's mind.

"Quite a while now."

"What got you started?"

There was a long pause before the almost inaudible answer came out. "Time hangs heavy in prison."

Nina emitted an involuntary gasp; she was getting more information than she'd expected. For once she was stymied; what's the appropriate small talk for an ex-convict: "What were you in for?" "How much time did you do?" "How are things in Dannamorra?"

She was spared the trouble of deciding as Eddie said, "I don't try to hide it anymore because I'm not ashamed of it. It was a mistaken conviction. I served three years for armed robbery because of a wrong identification."

She wondered if she was hearing the truth. The statement sounded completely sincere, but Nina knew that not all the good actors in the world were found on stage.

"How terrible for you," she said, hoping that she sounded sympathetic rather than skeptical.

"The worst part is that not everyone believes me. Even people in my old neighborhood, people I've known most of my life—a lot of them still believe I really did it. It's tough to live with that kind of stuff hanging over your head. Hard on the wife, too. Sometimes I think even she . . ." His voice trailed off.

"Why don't you and Louella move? Go live somewhere else. Make a fresh start, as they say."

"At my age?"

"If it's important enough to you, your age won't stop you. Besides, you can't be all that old. I'd say you're just about the right age for one of those typical midcareer switches. A lot of people—whoops, the break's over. Got to run. We'll talk more later."

As Nina eased back into Melanie Prescott's psyche, she realized she still didn't know why Eddie Croydon had been staring at her so intently. Well, it would have to wait.

The smoothness of the morning's rehearsal provided an ironic contrast to the bumpiness of the afternoon's final taping. Nick Galano wasn't happy that there were so many outsiders watching the taping; he was afraid they'd make noise or somehow foul up the proceedings. The goal was to get the entire show onto tape with no interruptions unless something truly unacceptable happened, such as someone failing to make an entrance, or tripping over a piece of furniture, or belching into the microphone. But such events were few and far between. Usually.

All went well until the last scene in the day's episode, the restaurant scene. The three cameo guests entered nearly on cue, walked to their appointed table fairly naturally, and took their seats with acceptable grace. But as the actress playing their waitress handed them the menus, Melinda West sneezed loudly and Patti Martinus promptly declared, "Gesundheit!" and began to rummage in her purse for a tissue, in the process knocking over a full water glass.

"Cut," Nick Galano said quietly. "Okay, accidents happen, don't worry about it. Let's get a dry tablecloth and take it again. Somebody empty those water glasses, please?"

On the second take, they didn't get far enough for the water glasses to matter. As soon as the trio entered the restaurant, Patti Martinus dropped her purse and in bending to retrieve it knocked heads sharply with Harold Hotchley, who was also reaching for the bag. Harold recovered nicely, but Patti ricocheted backward into the restaurant wall, which swayed as though an earthquake had struck directly beneath the restaurant.

"Cut. Mrs. uh, if you put your arm *through* the strap, the purse won't—that's right—good. Now, from the top. And if anybody drops anything, we have a rule about that: Whoever drops it picks it up. Okay, once again."

On the third take, just as the waitress returned to take their orders, Nick broke in again.

"Cut. Mrs. uh, please don't look into the camera." Melinda went deathly white. "Don't even look anywhere *near* it."

"I'm so sorry," she whispered. "I didn't mean to."

Before the eighth and final take, Nick adroitly restaged the background action: The retired plumber, the legal secretary, and the brain surgeon were already seated at the table when the scene began. The waitress would bring them their menus immediately, and they were to study them intently throughout the proceedings.

When this new piece of direction was pronounced, Harold Hotchley opened his mouth for the first time since the morning rehearsal.

"Why . . ."

"Because you're on a low-salt diet, your daughter is allergic to shellfish, and your niece is too constipated to eat. *Action!*"

When they finally got through the scene, Nina felt that a brief word might go a long way toward soothing the cameo trio's wounded or embarassed feelings, but all three were engaged: Harold was deep in consultation with Hilda, probably discussing the personal thoughts of a retired plumber; Patti was drying her tears on a handkerchief provided by a glowering George; and Melinda was being led away by Mike, whose easy smile suggested that he was able to provide all the comforting and encouragement his wife could possibly need.

Good. Nina had no time to spare anyway; there was still so much to do in preparation for Saturday. She whipped through her dressing room, changed in record time, and flew out of the studio. Luckily there was an empty cab just rounding the corner and not a fan in sight.

At Primrose Towers, Nina went directly up to the penthouse, looking at her checklist in the elevator. By now the downstairs rooms should be ready for the painters on Thursday morning. The painters had to start and finish on schedule so the man could come and hang the drapes, and *he* had to be in and out promptly so the floor man could get in and do his thing and get out so it could dry before the rented furniture and the piano were delivered on Saturday and Oh, Lord, help me live through this week, Nina prayed.

Amazingly, the rigid schedule she'd delivered to Alibi Al was actually being observed, if you overlooked a few peculiarities here and there, such as the light switches that were installed upside down and the cold water tap that was on the left instead of the right. . . .

Nina went down to her old apartment much relieved. Maybe, just maybe, the party wouldn't be a disaster after all. Despite her irritation with Helen Meyer and her resentment at the blackmailing aspects of the party, Nina really did want to give the visitors a grand finale to their week in New York, and she was beginning to think it might actually happen. The only uncontrollable element was the appalling death of Rex Reynolds, but that information was still under wraps—at least so far.

She let herself into the apartment and found Chessy playing with an envelope that had apparently been pushed under the door.

"Hey, Chess. What've you got there, fella?"

Chessy abandoned his new toy and came to Nina for the ritual greeting. She bent down to pick him up and at the same time she picked up the long white envelope he'd been batting around, wondering why she was getting a rent statement under her door instead of in her mailbox downstairs as usual.

But it wasn't a rent statement.

"My Sweet One," she read in fascinated horror. "Now that I've seen to it that Norman no longer stands between us, we can be together. Unless there is someone else, someone I don't know about. Not to worry, I can resolve that, too. Give me the sign I have been waiting for and I will come to you, my adorable angel of love."

Nina was on the phone in a flash, and Dino was on his way instantly.

By the time he arrived, Nina had checked with the doorman and found out that the envelope had been delivered in the midafternoon by a boy of about nine or ten. Probably some child off the street who was thrilled to earn a few dollars from a stranger, Nina supposed, and Dino agreed.

"Let me see this necklace he sent you," Dino requested grimly.

Nina brought the pendant out of her bedroom, where she had tucked it away weeks ago, still in its original box and wrappings. When she held it out to him, Dino whistled softly and reached for it.

"It's just a piece of costume jewelry, isn't it?" Nina asked.

"You didn't look at it very thoroughly."

He turned it over and held it under a strong light so she could see the tiny hallmarks on the back of the pendant.

"My God, it's *real!*"

"I'll have it checked by my friend Manny the jeweler, but I think I know what he's going to say."

"It's gold, isn't it?" Nina whispered.

"Real and solid. And I bet those pretty little stones are genuine emeralds."

"Dino, this must be worth thousands of dollars!"

"Yeah. Obviously this Secret Lover of yours isn't kidding around, if he meant what he said about eliminating Norman. He's deadly serious."

Chapter Sixteen

After Dino left with the gold and emerald pendant, a very worried Nina gathered Chessy in her arms and curled up with him on the sofa for a session of very deep thought. The tough old tom was a good companion at such moments; he agreed with everything and never interrupted her train of thought except to burrow his warm, flat head under her chin or nudge her hand gently with a paw in case she forgot to keep scratching his belly.

So he was rudely surprised and justifiably indignant when she suddenly dumped him on the floor and sprang up from the sofa, a determined glint in her green eyes.

"I'm going to do it!" she told him, burrowing in her purse and a moment later running her finger down her copy of the list of scheduled events for the fans. There it was: "Wednesday—seven P.M., Dinner at 21. Hosts, Ferde Ungar and Doris Kinling."

Exactly an hour and a half later, a transformed Nina stepped into a cab in front of Primrose Towers and told the driver to take her to 21 West 52nd Street. The cabbie was disappointed—not because it would be a relatively short hop, but because he liked to have good-looking women in his cab, and this was the best-looking woman he'd ever picked up.

During the time between Chessy hitting the floor and Nina closing the door, she'd worked like a fury, and the results were spectacular. She wore one of the splashiest numbers in her wardrobe, a daringly snug emerald-green taffeta dress with a deep sweetheart neckline, shirred bodice, and a hemline a good three inches above the knee. Her arms were bare and the dress was scooped very deeply in the back, but the thin straps that went over her shoulders were covered in a burst of frothy white petal-shaped flouncing. Her brilliant red hair was piled high on her head for maximum coolness in the sultry summer heat, so her long drop earrings of seed pearls showed her elegant neck to best advantage.

"Hey, lady, I gotta say something," the driver said as he pulled up in front of the restaurant. "You look good enough to drink."

Well, at least he was original. "To *drink*?"

"Yeah. You look like a walking mint ice cream soda. With a cherry onna top."

For that, she doubled the usual tip.

When Nina burst into the private dining room that had been reserved at 21, she created exactly the effect she'd hoped for—a sensation.

"Can you make room for one more?" she cheerily asked the amazed group.

"What are *you* doing here, Nina?" Ferde Ungar said. "You're not scheduled to host tonight."

"So what? I happened to have a free evening, and I wanted to be with people I like, and I like these people. Come on, gang, let's *party!*"

At that moment Nina could have asked the group to chip in, buy 21 for her, and gift wrap it, and they would have done their damnedest.

She planned to start with the obvious ones, and then work the room very carefully. She'd see to it that the champagne flowed freely, and that no one's glass was ever empty. What faster way to loosen a few tongues? No one would ever guess why she was really there, or what she hoped to learn.

Ready?
Action!

"Well, Patti, this is your big day! You did it! You made your debut! You, too, Melinda. And Harold. Do you know, when you made Nick come up with a personal relationship for the three of you to play, I wanted to cheer! That's *exactly* what background actors need, but does anyone ever give it to them? Noooo. Drink up, you've earned it. And that's why the people in the background often look so *lifeless*—they have nothing to *think* about. Now I have a suggestion for tomorrow's scene, but I want to get *your* ideas on it. . . ."

Nina's cab deposited her in front of Primrose Towers just before midnight. She'd pay for the lack of sleep tomorrow, but it was worth it. When she told Dino what she'd . . .

"Dino! What are you doing here?" she gasped, as he got out of an unmarked car.

"Waiting for you. Thanks, Jack, that's it for tonight," he said to the cabbie.

The driver threw a quasi-salute in Dino's direction and drove away.

"But I didn't pay him!"

"That's right, you didn't pay him. *I'll* pay him. Later."

Then it sunk in.

"You mean he's a *policeman*? What's going on here?"

"Let's get upstairs and we'll go into it."

The elevator ride was ominously quiet, and they walked down the corridor to Nina's door in silence. Obviously Dino was steamed.

"So you're up to your old tricks again!" he said the minute Nina's apartment door closed behind them.

"All I did was . . ."

"All you did was put yourself in danger. There's a nut running around loose and he seems to be very, *very* fond of you! Fond enough to send you a piece of antique jewelry conservatively valued at nearly two thousand dollars."

Nina tried to speak, but Dino cut her off.

"Shut up and listen to me! I have to give the damn thing back to you, because there's no official reason for the police to hold onto it. It's not stolen property, as far as we can tell, and there are no prints on it except yours and mine, so it's not evidence." He took a small package encased in plastic out of his pocket and shoved it into Nina's hand. "Put it somewhere safe for the time being. Do you have a safe-deposit box?"

"Y-yes," Nina stammered. "But I keep all my really valuable jewelry in a wall safe behind that painting over there." She indicated an original Georgia O'Keeffe which was probably worth more than all her jewelry put together. To Dino, it was just a picture of a flower.

"Good," he growled. "Stick it in there. Right now!"

Nina did.

"Now keep listening. We don't know who he is or where he is. We don't know anything except that he's here and he's implied that he knocked off Rex Reynolds because he thought Reynolds stood in his way. And you take it into your fluffy little birdbrain to get rigged up like a high-class hooker and go out *alone*? What the hell did you think you were doing?"

"I only went to Twenty One. And this 'hooker outfit,' as you so charmingly refer to it, cost over four hundred dollars!" Nina snapped.

"I don't give a damn how much your dress cost and I know where you went. How else do you think you were picked up and brought home by a plainclothes policeman?"

"How did you arrange that? That was very clever," Nina said, hoping to mollify him. "I'm royally ticked off at your attitude, but I have to admit I admire your technique."

Dino grabbed her by the shoulders and stared hard into her eyes. Then he crushed her in an embrace that left her breathless and ended in a long, deep, passionate kiss.

"Babe, don't you realize you may have been in the same room with a *murderer?* That's why we had the place staked out. When they called and told me you were there, I had a fit! I almost barged in, just to be sure you were all right. Oh, Christ, Nina, if anything happened to you, I don't know what I'd do. I'd go out of my mind. I'd want to die!"

How many times did she need him to prove how he felt about her? But each time he did it, it was like the first time all over again—thrilling and wonderful.

"Dino, you darling," Nina purred. "Now come on, let's calm down and talk. I have so much to tell you, I don't know where to start! Let me give you the headlines up front. First, Melinda West is a fake. It took about thirty seconds to find out she doesn't know beans about *The Turning Seasons*. She must have sent in somebody else's answers, or maybe there was a foul-up in the tabulation. Anyway, she's terrified she's going to be found out. She seems terrified of everything and everybody. Okay, headline number two: George Martinus really hates his life and everyone in it. He doesn't just *look* angry, he *is* angry—especially at his wife. He's threatened to leave her if she doesn't straighten out, by which he means stop spending all her time watching soap operas. And number three," she said, saving the best for last, "is this: you know Eddie Croydon? The strange little guy who looks like an ex-con? He *is* an ex-con!" Nina sat back to savor the moment as Dino's eyebrows shot up.

"He did three years for armed robbery, but he says he was framed. He also admits that a lot of people don't believe him—possibly and probably including his wife. Frankly, I don't know whether *I* believe him or not, either, but if I were married to him, you can bet I'd know the truth. Anyway, I think he wants to move to a new city and do the fresh-start bit, but from what he told me tonight, I gather good old Louella isn't too crazy about that notion. In fact, Louella Croydon isn't very crazy about anything except handsome strangers. She was the one who clamped onto poor Rex at Le Perigord. And you should have seen her tonight, ogling some of those waiters!"

"Never mind her. Let's get back to Eddie Croydon.

Tell me everything you know about him, and tomorrow I'll run down his background. Mr. Croydon is starting to fascinate me."

Nina was even rockier the next morning than she'd feared; if she'd gone straight to sleep after returning from 21 it wouldn't have been too bad, but she and Dino had talked far into the night and when he finally left, it was after two o'clock.

Definitely a coffee morning, and a two-cup one at that.

But she knew she was fully alert when she started to wonder if the cabbie who was driving her to the studio was really a cop. And when she got out of the taxi and looked around to see if she could spot any unmarked police cars, she decided there were two.

When she found Dino already inside the studio, she knew he was truly concerned. The cast and crew by this time were getting used to Dino's presence, considering how many times in the past fourteen months he'd been involved in cases that revolved around Meyer Productions. But this time no one seemed to know why he was there; the news about Rex Reynolds hadn't leaked yet, and no one but Nina and Dino knew about the mysterious Secret Lover.

She decided to play it cool. "Good morning, Lieutenant Rossi," she said brightly, for the benefit of Patti Martinus and several of her fan-club members who were giving Dino a thorough and appreciative once-over with their eyes.

"How do, Ms. McFall?"

"To what do we owe the honor of your company today?"

"Why, I thought you knew. They asked me to act as technical consultant on a scene that's coming up involving police work."

"Oh, Nina," Patti said, clinging to the palsy-walsy mood that Nina had established the night before, "come off it! We know who he is, and we can sure guess why he's here. Can't we, girls?"

The "girls" certainly did and could; they'd been devouring scraps of information about Nina long enough to know a few surprisingly intimate details about her personal life, and they were thrilled to be in the company of the man who was rumored to be her current boyfriend.

"I guess I can't fool you," Nina said idiotically. "Yes, there *is* truth to the rumors; we are definitely good friends." The fountain of giggles that greeted this inane statement gave Dino a chance to make a fast exit in the direction of Helen Meyer's office.

"Nina, he is di-*voon!*" Patti squeaked. "If only he could act, wouldn't he be great opposite you on the show!"

"Somehow I doubt if Lieutenant Rossi is interested in an acting career," Nina said, suppressing the impulse to titillate them with a reference to the heartfelt performances he gave offstage.

"Let's go, folks. This is a work day here at old Meyer Saltmines," Spence Sprague purred. "Nina, the darned old line rehearsal is about to start, and I'll just bet my boots they'd be gosh-darned pleased to have you join them. What say?"

Nina cast Spence a withering look and mentally forgave him for making her nauseous so early in the morning; he was developing a folksy persona for his role as today's group guide. She was beginning to wish it were next Monday, when things would hopefully be back to what passed for normal on the set of TTS.

But then she remembered—she'd be on vacation next Monday. Or would she? Better let Melanie take over for a while; Nina's pooped.

The morning rehearsal was uneventful, so much so that Nina had to restrain herself from dozing when she wasn't actually in the scene. It would have been better if she were heavy on lines today; the additional activity would have forced her system to pump adrenaline.

At one point in the proceedings, Nina noticed that Dino was still there, observing things from the back of the main rehearsal hall. But the attention he was drawing from the ladies in the visitors' group was too much; he told her during a break that he was going back to the station house.

"But don't worry, I've put somebody in here. He'll be close by if you need him."

"Who is he?"

"He's dressed as a handyman, blue coveralls with Empire Cleaning on the back. He's a good man—you'll be all right. Call me when you're ready to leave and I'll have you picked up."

"That's not—"

"Call me." It was definitely not a casual suggestion.

"Yes, sir. Uh-oh, here she comes again."

"And tell your writers that the scene will be fine with just a few alterations," Dino said smoothly, raising his voice for Patti Martinus's benefit. "I'll send this copy back tomorrow," he added, patting his breast pocket so convincingly that Nina caught herself wondering why he was carrying a script around.

Maybe he could be an actor after all, Nina thought, watching his broad-shouldered figure as he walked away and wishing she could go with him.

When the lunch break finally arrived, in what seemed like several weeks later, Nina seized the chance to go into her dressing room and flake out on the sofa. If she could only doze for a few . . . She was sound asleep before she could finish the thought.

She slept deeply, so deeply that she didn't hear the soft sound of her wardrobe door being opened from the inside or the sound of light breathing as a man's figure silently approached and then stood over her. Nor did she hear the whisper of fabric as he slowly raised his arm and then swiftly clamped his hand over her mouth.

Her eyes flew open, and she tried to scream but couldn't. She could only stare into Eddie Croydon's terrifying and disturbed eyes.

Chapter Seventeen

"Be quiet, be real quiet. Don't make any noise. All right?"

She nodded in frightened agreement, and he relaxed his grip on her jaw. "I'm sorry. Don't get mad, but I had to see you. Alone."

"Why didn't you just ask?" she said, matching his hushed whisper.

"There's always too many people around. I found out where your dressing room was and I was going to leave you a note, but then I heard somebody coming and jumped into the closet."

A note? Nina suddenly had a desperate need to see his handwriting.

"How did you get in? The door was locked."

"You're kidding. These locks are easier to open than a tube of toothpaste," he scoffed.

"I see. Anyway . . . where's the note?"

"Forget that. It only asks if I could talk to you, and now we're talking."

"Yes, we certainly are." Nina tried to keep her voice calm. "Why did you want to see me alone, Eddie?"

"Because I got to thinking about what I told you. You know, the stretch I did, all that stuff. I thought, how come I told that to *her*, of all people? I don't know, but there's something about you that just makes people say things easier. You look like a nice lady who can be trusted. So I decided to go all the way and ask you for a favor."

Nina tried her best to assess the situation accurately. Eddie Croydon sounded sincere, and he looked sincere. But his behavior was decidedly peculiar. Hiding in a wardrobe? Dino would probably find that alone enough reason to drag him in for questioning. She looked at Eddie, and then glanced surreptitiously toward the door, estimating whether or not she could get it open and run into the hallway before he could stop her.

She decided against it; he'd probably beat her to the door, and heaven only knew what he'd do to her if he decided he couldn't trust her after all.

Half an hour later, with only twenty minutes left of the lunch period, Eddie stood up and thanked Nina for the hundredth time for listening to him and for agreeing to help him. His favor had been relatively simple; he still insisted that he'd been jailed in error and had been thinking about her suggestion that he go away somewhere to make a fresh start. New York City seemed a good place to go—he and Louella could get lost in the crowds for a while—but he needed some contacts. Could Nina direct him to someone, anyone, who might help him get a job?

Nina's best thought was for Eddie to go see her friend Scotty Lane. As a retired newspaperman, Scotty had more contacts than anyone she could think of, and he was always eager to do her a favor. Besides, now that she was over her fright, she suspected the two men would get along famously.

She wrote Scotty's name and phone number on a slip of paper. "Don't call him for a few hours yet; it'll be better if I have a chance to speak to him first." She hesitated to ask the next question, but took a chance. "Are you going to tell him everything?"

"Would you?"

"Yes."

"Okay, I will."

"Good," she said, going to the door casually and noting that he made no move to stop her. She opened the door wide, smiling. "Now I've got to arrange for some food before the lunch break is over. You know, it isn't every day that I entertain a gentleman in my dressing room."

"Yeah? Well, it isn't every day that somebody calls me a gentleman. You're a sweetheart, you know that?"

"Could I get some lunch for you?" said a voice from the corridor.

Nina jumped, startled, and turned to see Mike West.

"Oh, Mike! You surprised me. I didn't expect to see anyone."

"I was just wandering around and I heard what you said about lunch. Let me run down to the corner and bring you back something."

"You don't have to do that. I can phone for it."

He grinned. "I can get it here faster."

She smiled back. "You probably can. All right, and I really owe you one. *Another* one!"

"I'll see you later, Nina," Eddie said. "And thanks again. You're special. I mean it."

"So are you, Eddie, and I mean it, too. Take care."

The day's final tape was a subdued repeat of the day before. Patti had difficulty walking alone across the background on cue, and finally Nick Galano told her to take the arm of one of the professional extras. Melinda West followed her cues all right, but she looked absolutely terrified every moment despite the fact that she was supposed to be on her way to a bridal shower. Harold Hotchley, as a doctor in the hospital scene, did everything to perfection, even avoiding a near disaster; as Angela Dolan was about to collide with an IV stand on wheels, he smoothly grabbed it and rolled it out of her path. Nina recalled that scene at the end of the day as she changed into her own clothing, and realized she was beginning to view the odd little man with new respect.

Well, thank God she had no official duties this evening regarding the visitors. As a change of pace, the ladies were being taken to Windows on the World by Angela and Mary Kennerly, while the much smaller men's group was offered a pub-crawling tour guided by Rafe Fallone and Bob Valentine. The split arrangement had caused Dino Rossi a minor headache, since he had to arrange for surveillance of both groups.

As for Nina, she could accomplish everything on her schedule via telephone; she firmly intended to crash into bed as early as possible. When she got home, she collected her mail and a package that had been delivered, and then looked in on the penthouse again. Relieved to see that the painting had been finished on schedule and delighted to find that the new oriental rug had arrived, she went down to her old apartment and called the furniture rental firm for a final confirmation of the arrangements she had made. She could hardly wait to get at the huge oriental beauty, to unwrap it, unroll it, and drool over it, but that would have to wait until later.

Next there was a call to the caterer; the weather prediction was for an unseasonal dip in temperature on Saturday, and she wanted to be certain there were several hot selections on the menu in addition to the cold meats and salads. She added tortellini casserole, stuffed baked ham, and cheese fondue to the already lavish menu and checked another item off her list. When it came to parties, Nina's motto was "something for everyone." Finished with the confirmation calls, Nina telephoned Scotty Lane and told him the highlights of her talk with Eddie Croydon, and Scotty promised to do whatever he could.

Finally she eyed the package she'd brought up from the lobby, admitting to herself that she was definitely apprehensive about opening it. Maybe she should wait until Dino was there, just in case . . .

Just in case what, dummy? She tore off the wrapping and a moment later was beaming with delight. It was a framed photograph of herself and Dino that Peter had taken that unusually warm day they'd all spent at the beach. The little devil had caught them in an unguarded moment, standing close with Dino's arm around her shoulders, looking into each other's eyes. The love in both their expressions was unmistakable. It was a lovely picture, and a beautiful gift. She hugged the frame to her chest while she read the note Peter had tucked inside.

"Dear Nina, I took this that day we all went to the beach. It was the start of the best summer ever, and I know you're the one I have to thank for it. Love, Peter."

She wiped away a tear that spilled down her cheek. Now *there* was a guy who really knew how to write a lady a mash note! He could give Secret Lover a lesson or two!

She looked around for a prominent spot to display the photograph, and suddenly realized that she'd totally forgotten about scattering the penthouse with personal possessions. It was supposed to look as though she already lived there, wasn't it? That meant an assortment of knickknacks, objets d'art, pictures, ashtrays, vases, books, magazines, and on and on and on.

Groaning to herself, she started through the apartment, selecting items to take upstairs for Saturday's festivities. Better not leave it for later; experience had taught her that even when *nothing* was left "for later," there was always a last-minute crisis or two to resolve before a party. Well, at least it answered the question of where to display Peter's photograph.

She giggled at the thought of the reaction that would come from Patti Martinus and "the girls" when they saw a picture of Dino Rossi in his swim trunks!

"Nina, have you seen Louella's husband today?" Patti Martinus asked as soon as she arrived at Meyer Studios on Friday morning.

This was the last day the visitors would spend at the studio, and Nina expected it would bring its share of professional problems, but she wasn't about to get involved in any personal entanglements.

"No, I haven't. Why?"

"Louella told me he's missing. He never came back to the hotel last night."

"Are the other men all present or accounted for?"

"Far's I know."

Nina didn't like the sound of this. "Where is Louella?" she asked.

Patti hesitated, then said, "Back at the hotel, packing. She said she doesn't care where he is and she's glad to be rid of him."

"What a sweetheart," Nina said dryly. "Listen, do me a favor, Patti. Call Louella and tell her *not* to check out of the hotel. Tell her Lieutenant Rossi wants to see her."

"Does he?" Patti asked, her eyes popping.

"It's a safe bet," Nina said, going to the phone to call Dino.

It was a very safe bet. Dina ordered all airports, train stations, and bus terminals checked, and then arranged to have the Croydons' hotel suite placed under surveillance in case Eddie showed up there.

Nina also related to Dino her conversation with Eddie of the day before, suggesting that Dino check with Scotty Lane to find out if Eddie had contacted him.

Then it was time to turn into Melanie Prescott again.

As Nina expected, Helen had arranged with Spence Sprague and the assistant directors for the cameo guests to do something extra special on this last day. She could see Nick grinding his teeth as he explained the scene to Patti, Melinda, and Harold. They were to be customers in a department store—and they would have lines to speak! Well, a few words anyway. A special arrangement had been made with the Screen Actors' Guild, and there'd be no problems as long as they didn't exceed five words each.

"Now, Mrs. uh, you're returning a sweater, and Mr. uh, you're the salesman. Mrs. uh, you walk up to the counter with a shopping bag, put it on the counter, take out the sweater, and Mr. uh, you ask, 'Is something wrong?' Then Mrs. uh, you say, 'It doesn't fit me.' Then the camera will pan over to this counter where Melanie is helping Buffy decide what to buy for Gregg's birthday—but actually Melanie is trying to break them up, as you know. After Melanie and Buffy leave, the camera will pan back to the counter where *you*, Mr. uh, are showing a purple umbrella to *you*, Mrs. uh. You say to her, 'Beautiful color,' and she shakes her head and says, 'Not for me.' And you begin to show her a yellow one as we fade out."

Patti looked hopeful, Melinda looked terrified, and Harold's expression was unreadable.

"Let's try it," Nick said, without a shred of hope in his voice.

But to everyone's amazement, it all went fairly smoothly. Patti didn't drop the package more than twice the entire morning, and Melinda only forgot her line once during the dress rehearsal. As for Harold, he was perfection personified.

The final taping, however, was a different story.

Patti entered on cue, walked up to the counter looking as though she were about to gun down the salesman and rob the store, slammed the shopping bag loudly onto the counter, and responded to Harold's inquiry with, "It doesn't fit me *at all*!"

"*Cut.* Mrs. uh, that was six words. You're limited to five," Nick said quietly. "We have to stick to that or the union will give us trouble. All right? Let's do it again, and this time just say, 'It doesn't fit.' Places!"

"Is something wrong?" Harold asked politely.

"It doesn't fart. *Fit.*"

"*Cut.*"

That was where they lost it. No one was totally unaffected by the blooper, but Robin nearly fell on the floor.

"Is something wrong?" Harold said as though he'd never uttered those words before in his life.

"This is a terrible fit," Patti declaimed, and Nick's sigh of resignation was almost picked up on the soundtrack.

After Melanie had failed for the umpteenth time to

make Buffy see that Gregg was wrong for her, the camera picked up Melinda and Harold.

"Beautiful color," he murmured encouragingly.

"I'll take it," Melinda said.

Nick closed his eyes, expecting Harold to be thrown for a loop. But there was silence, and he peered through slitted eyelids to see Harold calmly putting the purple umbrella in a bag that had been lying on the counter.

"Fade . . . and cut. It's a wrap!"

Cameo guest week was over at last.

When Dino phoned Nina later that evening, he was very irritated at his squad's inability to find Eddie Croydon.

"The guy's disappeared," he grumbled. "By now he could be anywhere in the country."

"Or right under our noses," Nina said. It didn't make any sense to her that Eddie would vanish just when he had a contact like Scotty who might help him find a job.

But Dino had discovered that Eddie Croydon hadn't called Scotty Lane at all. It didn't add up, unless Eddie had been lying to her. But why would he do that— unless he needed a convincing story to cover his presence in her dressing room?

As for Louella, despite the promise of a private interview with the devastating Dino Rossi, she'd checked out of the hotel anyway. Like Eddie, she seemed to have vanished.

Well, there was nothing Nina could do about any of it now. The rest of the visitors were at that very moment enjoying the first act of *The Phantom of the Opera*, and were scheduled to go afterward to Sardi's for a late supper. As for Nina herself, all she wanted was a long soak in a warm tub and a blissful, uninterrupted ten-hour sleep.

He gazed at the commotion with unseeing eyes. He should have guessed that Norman wasn't the only one standing between him and Melanie. A roar of laughter went up from the people around him, and at the same moment, his somber expression changed into a satisfied smile. That one had been so easy to take care of. They'd probably never find the second one. And if they did, so what? That fool had been in the way! He'd gotten what he deserved, the same as Norman got. The same as anyone would get if they tried to keep him away from his angel of love. And he was so close now. Just one more day . . .

Chapter Eighteen

For once, the weather prediction was right on the money. Saturday dawned cool and crisp, a hint of the autumn to come, and although by midday the temperature was back up in the high seventies, it was still a far cry from the usual steambath that was normal for New York in late August. Just as well, Nina thought, as she raced about the penthouse living room, distributing the personal objects she'd selected from her apartment the day before. It'll be wonderfully cool again this evening, and we can dance on the terrace without sweltering.

It had already been a long day. The first thing she'd done on arising was to rush up to the penthouse to make sure the refinished floors were dry. Despite her best efforts, the schedule had slipped by half a day, which meant that the drapery people would be hanging drapes at the same time the furniture was being delivered, and the piano tuner would still be clinking away when the caterers arrived, and the florist would tangle with the "staff" who of course weren't waiters and bartenders at all but policemen in disguise. . . . Never mind, Nina told herself, as long as the drinks are cold and the music is hot. She was grateful for the unusual lack of humidity which meant that the floors had dried almost instantly—otherwise, she'd have had the whole affair down in her old apartment. Nina shuddered at the thought.

Amazingly, things fell into place. The floors, beautifully refinished and smooth as a bowling alley, were bone dry and sparkling. The drapery people were only two hours late, but the furniture arrived an hour early. The piano was rolled in exactly on schedule, closely followed by the tuner. The florist came with a small army of artists, and the caterer wheeled in his carts on schedule, took over the kitchen, and began to set up a bar.

Finally it was time to unveil her precious oriental rug. When it was spread in all its expensive glory, it glittered like a carpet of jewels. She made a special request to the caterer to be sure his people were ultracareful about not spilling anything on it, and then supervised the placement of furniture. With the draperies going up over every window, framed artwork being hung on the walls, and personal items casually dressing tables and bookcases, it was beginning to look downright homey.

At first Nina had selected a particularly prominent spot for the picture of herself and Dino, then changed her mind. She removed it from the top of the etagère and placed it instead on a bookcase, along with some flowers, a crystal candy dish, and a small lamp. There. Now it looked less like a stage setting and more like an inviting corner in a real room. Which, in a few months, it actually would be.

With two hours left until the guests were due, Nina prepared to make her escape and begin her transformation from frazzled party giver to relaxed and glamorous hostess. Before going downstairs, she motioned Charley Harper out onto the terrace for a private moment. The policeman looked completely convincing in his barman's outfit. Dino himself wasn't due to arrive until just before the guests, but he was clearly taking no chances.

"Charley, that suit fits you perfectly. Have you ever actually tended bar?"

In response he smiled and pulled a little bartender's

guide out of his pocket. "As long as nobody orders any really weird drinks, this'll get me through."

"Good. Look, I'm going to disappear now and get myself ready. If anything pops, you know how to reach me." Just then somebody came to the door with another delivery and Nina's attention was drawn to the foyer. "Now what? I thought everything was already here."

But this particular delivery was nothing Nina had ordered, and as she began to look through the assortment of boxes and cards, she realized what they were: the *Turning Seasons* fans must have gotten together and arranged to send farewell gifts. She opened one of the cards and read, "Dear Nina. I just wanted to tell you what a wonderful time you've given us this week. If I live to be a hundred . . ." They were all individual notes and presents! What a sweet thing to do!

"Charley, would you ask somebody to put these in the living room? I'm going to open them at the party and make a fuss over every single one. The fans will love it!"

Then she zoomed downstairs to feed Chessy and jump into the tub. There was time for a brief nap before dressing, but it was no use. All day the endless details of the party had kept Nina's mind off the more ominous questions seething in the back of her mind, but now she couldn't stop thinking about Rex Reynolds and the missing Eddie Croydon—not to mention her anonymous, steadily approaching, and possibly homicidally insane Secret Lover.

At five-fifteen Nina gave Chessy a final hug for the evening and went back upstairs to the penthouse. The Nina McFall who let herself into the foyer was quite a different creature than the harried young woman who'd left earlier, and the caterer's helper who happened to be in the foyer when she arrived almost dropped the tray of canapes he was carrying.

Nina was understatedly elegant in a white pique floor-length sheath softened by a black bow and a huge pink silk rose at the bustier top. The skirt was highlighted with a double peplum, lined in black and curved very low at the back. Her shoulders were bare, and she wore a necklace and earrings of glittering black jet. It was cool enough not to have to sweep her hair up, so the famous red mane fell in glowing waves to her shoulders, framing her lovely face and emphasizing the sparkling green of her eyes. The effect was hypnotic.

As she moved into the living room, Charley Harper gave her the "all's well" sign and a large grin of approval. She checked the bar and the buffet table, noting the chafing dishes and the fondue pot and mentally congratulating herself on her decision to add some hot food to the menu, for the temperature was dipping noticeably.

Only one thing was missing: Dino. Don't start to fret, she told herself. If he's really delayed, he'll call. Concentrate on your guests.

Moments later the doorbell rang and Nina gave the three-piece combo the signal to begin.

"Nina, you did not exaggerate," Helen Meyer said, casting reluctantly admiring glances in all directions. "The place has fantastic possibilities. It's going to be quite livable."

Refusing to rise to the bait, Nina smiled sweetly and showed Helen to the bar, where Horst and Ken were already placing their orders. The first group of *Turning Seasons* regulars was quickly followed by a second, and a third, and then it seemed the door might as well have been left standing open. Within twenty minutes the entire Meyer party had arrived and were straining the bartenders' ability to pour fast. Their work week was so tense that they didn't allow themselves to indulge much between Sunday night and Friday afternoon. But on the two weekend nights it was a completely different script.

By the time the fans began to arrive in small groups, the Meyer contingent was well on its way to a full-fledged blast. Nina noted with pleasure that everyone seemed to be having a wonderful time, which was exactly what she had in mind.

Gary Johnson, who proved to be as bad at holding his liquor as he was good at imitating Rex Reynolds's voice, was holding forth to anyone who cared to listen on the foolishness of not casting him as Norman Chandler in the first place, the stupidity of not casting him in the role when Reynolds was called out of town in the second place, and the goddamn idiocy of not writing a role especially tailored for his talents in the third place. No one paid much attention, nor did anyone observe that a truly unpleasant mean streak was coming to the surface as the alcohol surged through Gary's brain.

Nina, oblivious to Gary Johnson, was busy with her guests of honor. Harold Hotchley, with his unexpected display of solid professionalism, had proved to be the surprise star among the three cameo guests, and Nina wondered why Hilda seemed to be so mad at him. She'd reverted to her initial overbearing control of him, for no apparent reason.

With the help of a few Singapore Slings—which sent Charley Harper into the kitchen to consult his bartender's guide—Patti Martinus was confiding to Nina that George really meant it this time, he really was going to leave her unless . . . unless . . . She looked utterly miserable as her voice trailed off.

"Unless what, Patti?" Nina asked with real concern.

"Unless I stop trying to look and act like you!" Patti blurted out.

Nina was dumbfounded. It was the ultimate compliment one woman could pay another, but she said, "Patti, if that's so, then you should listen to him. After all, it's *Patti* he married, not Nina. If he wanted a Nina, he'd have gone after a Nina . . ."

Or a Melanie? a voice inside her head said, but she brushed aside the notion. That was too ridiculous—wasn't it?

Melinda West was still behaving like a child who has been constantly chastised, and Nina was beginning to believe that the relationship between the Wests left something to be desired. One of them had probably married the other for the wrong reason, but which one?

And for what reason? And what earthly business was it of hers, anyway?

More important, what was keeping Dino? She glanced at the photograph on the bookcase, wondering if any of the women had spotted it yet. Apparently not, or she would have heard about it, she was sure.

But Nina was wrong—the photograph had been noticed. Noticed, stared at briefly, and then used as the focal point of a blazing surge of hatred that was even now raging to find expression. The pressure was building rapidly now, and there was no safety valve. As soon as it found its target, it would explode.

Half an hour after the visitors were assembled, Helen Meyer took it upon herself to assume her standard leadership role and asked for a moment of quiet so she could say a few words.

"Oh, no, not the few words bit!" Myrna grumbled, edging toward the bar and at the same time away from the persistent Mark Viner, who was finding fascination in recounting to Myrna the intricacies of the plots of the *Thin Man* series one by one, in chronological order.

Helen droned on and on about "wonderful" and "marvelous" and "touching" and "talented" and "loyal" and blah, blah, blah. . . . When it was evident that she was capable of talking until midnight, Nina whispered a suggestion to Rick Busacca, who didn't need a second nudge.

Rick steered Bob Valentine and Rafe Fallone to the far end of the living room where the three of them quickly built a low murmur of fake conversation into a burst of laughter. Instantly those nearest to them sidled over to find out what was so funny, and the fake conversation became quite real. A moment later someone called out, "Where's Angela? Come on, Angela, do some numbers!" and Helen's moment at center stage was abruptly ended. Gracious in defeat, she sailed over the bar, smiling but looking around slit-eyed as she tried to figure out who had made the intrusive request.

Angela was already on her way to the piano. Even stone sober, she could be counted on to sing at parties. It was her way of venting her frustration at failing to carve out a career for herself on the musical stage. The first time Nina had been present when Angela stood up to entertain, she had been amazed as the older woman's strong, clear voice filled the room with her standard opening number, "I Got a Right to Sing the Blues." Nina had wondered why Angela hadn't found a place for herself in musical comedy, but she soon knew the answer: Angela could sing only torch songs, a fact that she obviously didn't realize herself. No matter what she sang, it came out like the blues. "Put On a Happy Face" sounded like "Moanin' Low"; "Blue Skies" came across like "Stormy Weather"; and when Angela launched into "I've Got You Under My Skin," she seemed to be seeking a cure for psoriasis.

When Angela had finished her performance, several voices called out, "Now Nina! Come on, Nina, you're next!" Oh, what the hell, she thought. When else will these people have a chance to be part of a real theatrical party in a Manhattan penthouse? Besides, she made no bones about it—she loved to sing.

After a brief conference with the piano player, she gave them a trio of "you" songs: "It Had to be You," followed by "You Are My Lucky Star" and "You, Wonderful You." And then, feeling devilish, she performed her special impression of Julie Andrews singing a few verses of "My Favorite Things" that had not been written by Oscar Hammerstein:

> Bendel's and Bonwit's and Bergdorf's and Bloomie's, There's nothing like shopping for chasing the gloomies. Altman's and Macy's from basement to tops, These are a few of my favorite shops. . . .

Despite the enthusiastic applause and calls for more, Nina felt she was taking too much of the spotlight, and decided it was the right moment to shift attention back to the guests by opening their cards and packages. Otherwise it would have to wait until after the buffet supper was served, and by then, she suspected, it might be too late to focus on anything but the bar. So instead of an encore, she said, "Listen, I want to share something nice with all of you. All these lovely things arrived this afternoon, but there was no time to open them, so I'd like to do it now. Patti, as fan-club president, would you read the cards while I open the packages?"

Patti nearly died of happiness at the thought of sharing center stage with her idol. As she came forward, Nina noted that George was headed for the bar, a look of total fury on his face.

The first note Patti picked out of the pile was gushy but brief. "Dearest Nina," she read. "We will never forget this week with you and the rest of the wonderful people on *The Turning Seasons*. Please use this once in a while and think of us back home watching you every day and remembering what it was like. Love, Martha Wilson." Nina had opened the package and was holding up a cosmetic case covered in a lurid orange floral print.

"Martha, where are you?" Nina called, looking around the room and waving when the thrilled and furiously blushing Martha waved back. "Thank you, Martha, it's lovely!"

"Dear Nina," Patti read from the next card. "A great big hug and a thank you from somebody who thinks you're the greatest! Love, Jill Simpson."

"Thank you, Jill, I love it!" Nina called, throwing a kiss in Jill's direction and holding up a stuffed teddy bear. "Next, Patti?"

"Dear Angel of Love," Patti began, and Nina's blood froze. "Finally I can—"

Nina snatched the note from her hand. "Patti," she said quickly, "I don't want to wear these nice people out. Maybe we should take a break and have supper. Then we can get back to these later, okay? All right, folks, that's enough for—"

"Why don't you read that one now?" a voice demanded. Nina looked up and saw George Martinus

210

staring at her. "What was that about an angel of love? Sounds pretty hot to me. Right?" he asked the room in general and was rewarded with encouraging applause and several calls of agreement.

But Nina knew she couldn't read the rest out loud. Dino, she thought frantically, where are you? Her eyes wandered to the bookcase where she'd placed the photograph of the two of them, and with a jolt she realized it was gone.

Suddenly things began to fall into place. In a flash, she knew that whoever had removed that picture took it not out of love for her, but out of hatred for Dino. Whoever he was, Secret Lover saw the photograph as proof that Dino stood between him and his beloved—and Dino had to be removed!

Oh Dino, stay away! Don't show up here! Wherever you are, stay there!

People were waiting for her to continue. Keep going, just fake it, she told herself. There's only one person who's going to know I'm not really reading the words in this note. She glanced around to find Charley Harper, and saw that he was busy at the bar.

"Dear Angel of Love," she began slowly, her mind racing madly while she paused for the catcalls and whistles that greeted the effusive salutation. "Finally I can tell you the reason I call you that. . . ." Nina looked up and smiled idiotically, stalling for time while she groped about wildly for a reason. "It's because you have made me understand that you truly love your work . . ." Smile! ". . . and also everyone you work with . . ." Smile, smile! ". . . and only an angel like you could play a devil like Melanie . . . and put up with some of the nonsense they put you through." Oh, God, that was *awful*! "It's unsigned," Nina added.

This unusual sentiment was greeted with a mixture of snorts, gasps, barely suppressed giggles, and raised eyebrows. Helen was thoroughly miffed and stalked out onto the terrace while Robin regarded Nina with more than a little suspicion. Obviously she knew Nina was up to something, but couldn't figure out what.

Nina looked desperately from face to face, trying to find the expression she was looking for, the one that would give away the game and tell her what she needed to know. But there was nothing to go on. Either the writer wasn't there, or he was the best actor in the room.

Who was the best actor in the room?

Harold Hotchley? Nina wondered if she was going completely mad.

Then she had an inspiration. There was only one way to smoke out her Secret Lover, and Nina knew what it was. He'd mentioned waiting for a "sign" in his last letter, a sign from her. Well, she'd give him that sign. She knew it was dangerous, but she'd alert Charley Harper and hope for the best. She'd do anything to expose the maniac before Dino showed up!

"We're going to serve dinner in a few minutes," she called out to her guests. "Help yourself to the bar, and you can dance on the terrace, if anyone's in the mood."

After a whispered word to Charley, she took advantage of the moment to slip out of the penthouse and hurry down to her apartment, unclasping the jet necklace as she went. As she took the pendant from her wall safe and hung it around her neck, she noticed the message light flashing on her answering machine, and she turned it on, dreading what she might hear.

"Couldn't get through to the penthouse phone," Dino's somber voice said. "Bad news, babe. Your friend Eddie turned up in the river, just like Reynolds. But we don't need to wait for lab tests this time. There was a knife sticking out of his back. Still no sign of Louella. I'm on my way."

On his way! Oh, no! How old was the message? He hadn't left the time!

In a few minutes she was going back up in the elevator, willing it to travel faster. Why were elevators always so slow when you were in a hurry? As the elevator doors parted on the top level, Nina gasped as she saw the front door of the penthouse closing on a pair of unmistakable broad shoulders.

"Dino! Wait!" she cried.

But the music and the babble of conversation covered her voice. Nina raced across the elevator lobby and hurled herself into the penthouse foyer. She had to stop him, before . . .

"Well, here she is! Here's our angel of love now!"

"Rafe, where's Dino?"

"Haven't seen him."

"He just came in!"

"Search me, love," Rafe said, giving her a dopey grin.

Nina hurried into the living room, sweeping the scene with her eyes. Where could he have gone so quickly?

"Hi, Nina! Some letter, huh?"

"Bob, have you seen Dino Rossi?"

"Nope. Sorry. Hey, great food, Nina."

"Sylvia, I'm looking for Dino."

"Haven't seen him, Nina. What's that marvelous thing around your neck? Another gift?"

"Angela, did you see Dino? Helen, did you?"

"Not this evening. What a fantastic piece of jewelry!"

"Hilda, have you seen Lieutenant Rossi?"

"That cop of yours? No. Listen, Nina, that thing you're wearing doesn't go with the rest of your outfit. Do yourself a favor and take it off."

"Patti, I'm trying to find . . ."

Nina's question was cut short by a crash of glass and a long piercing scream as someone frantically pushed through the crowd in the living room. Confusion reigned as the figure shoved its way through the French doors and onto the terrace, colliding with the couples who were dancing in the moonlight. The music stopped abruptly as the babble of excited voices rose louder and louder.

"What's wrong?"

"Charley, where are you?"

"Stop her!"

"She's going to jump!"

"Who's screaming?"

"Somebody *stop her!*"

Everyone in the living room was surging toward the

doors to the terrace to see what was happening, and Nina was confronted by a solid wall of backs.

Unguarded, unprotected backs.

Nina finally found what she was seeking. One of those backs belonged to Dino Rossi, and a pistol was pointed directly at it.

"*Dino!*" she screamed.

Acting purely on reflex, Nina picked up the first thing she could reach. Seizing a bubbling fondue pot from a mesmerized waiter and scorching her hands badly, she flung the fondue at Mike West.

He roared in agony as the sizzling hot cheese liquid splashed over him, but it was too late—the pistol went off.

The bullet missed Dino by inches, burying itself in the piano casing. Mike writhed on the floor, bellowing in agony, clawing at his face and rolling in rapidly congealing cheese.

The crowd surged back into the living room, Charley Harper keeping a tight grip on a sobbing Melinda as Nina hugged Dino in a fierce embrace.

"Nina," Helen Meyer remarked frostily, looking down her nose at Mike, "That's no way to treat a fine oriental rug."

Chapter Nineteen

It was just past midnight, and Nina and Dino were finally alone on the terrace of the penthouse. The party broke up soon after Charley Harper and his disguised assistants took the Wests away. Mike would be booked for the murders of Rex Reynolds and Eddie Croydon, and Melinda would undergo pyschiatric evaluation before any decisions could be made.

Dino was just opening a fresh bottle of champagne, and Nina lay on the rented chaise longue, admiring his tall, graceful figure.

"I think you deserve this," he said, handing her the brimming glass.

She took it gingerly in a bandaged hand. The burns from the fondue pot were less severe than they had seemed at first. Dino had minimized the damage by plunging her hands into an ice bucket and then gently rubbing the melting cubes over her throbbing fingertips.

"And you also deserve a spanking," he added, "for putting your adorable neck in danger again."

"It wasn't deliberate, believe me. After I realized someone was after you, everything happened so fast . . ."

"All in all, quite a week. When you show-biz people

put on an event, you don't kid around, do you?" he said, sitting down beside her.

"Poor Melinda! Do you think she knew he was insane?"

"I doubt it. She must have realized something was wrong, but how could she guess it was that serious?"

"I said she was a phony, remember, about the contest answers? He must have filled out the entry forms and mailed them in her name. And when all those earrings didn't make any impression, he sent the pendant."

"Yes. But he sent it to *Melanie*, not Nina. And he wanted to see Melanie wear it, not Nina," Dino reminded her.

"After a while, I don't think he could make the distinction," she said, pitying him in spite of herself. "But he seemed so *normal*! So polite—always ready to hold a door, or offer a ride. I suppose he rented that car just so he could do that, get a few minutes alone with his Melanie. That should have struck me as odd at the time. To rent a car for a week when you never have to move farther than midtown Manhattan was a very peculiar thing to do."

Dino raised one eyebrow. "I believe you had a few other things to think about at the time."

"Yes—like poor Rex. It's horrible to think that Mike would have gone after anyone who played the romantic interest in Melanie's life. And Gary Johnson was so disappointed that he didn't get the role! Little did he know! Did Mike tell you how he actually killed Rex?"

"It was pathetically simple. After the dinner at Le Perigord, Mike whisked Melinda back to the hotel, then returned to the restaurant, where Rex was just leaving. He offered him a lift, drove to the West Side docks, picked a fight, and decked him. Rex apparently wasn't very good at defending himself. And then Mike just rolled him into the river and he drowned."

"Horrible! I didn't much care for Rex, but he didn't deserve that."

They sat on the terrace in the moonlight, sipping

champagne in silence for a while and gazing out at the darkened Jersey shore across the river.

"The thing that bothers me," Dino said, "is why West decided that Eddie Croydon was a rival, too."

Nina sighed. "I think I know why. The day Eddie was in my dressing room, when I opened the door for him to leave, I found Mike right there in the corridor. He could have been watching the dressing room all along, and knowing that Eddie was in there with me for at least twenty minutes, he probably came to the conclusion that we were carrying on a torrid affair."

"If that's all it took," Dino said, "it shows you what a psycho the guy really is. Anyone who looks twice at you gets it in the neck."

"Not at me—at *Melanie*," she reminded him. "So on Thursday, after 'Boys' Night Out' he must have pulled the same stunt with Eddie that he did with Rex. Then he probably imagined he could move right in and claim his prize. I guess the sight of the photograph of us on the bookcase drove him over the edge. Where did he get that gun?"

"He could have had it with him all along. Who knows? He might have brought it with him from Vermont. And even if he didn't, guns aren't too hard to find in this crazy town, I hate to admit."

"Funny what an obvious trail he was leaving with that pendant," Nina mused. "If I'd had any idea it was a family heirloom or that he'd told Melinda it was lost, I would never have put it on."

"Probably the shock of seeing it around your gorgeous neck was what made her snap."

"Do you think she was really trying to kill herself?" Nina asked.

"Not really. I think she was just trying to get away from him."

Sounds from inside the apartment reminded her that the musicians were still there.

"I guess you'd better tell them they can go home," Dino said, but Nina had a better idea. She rose and went inside for a moment, then came back out as the soft strains of a romantic ballad floated out onto the terrace.

"After all, they're engaged for another half hour yet," she said, holding out her arms.

"That's my goofball," Dino murmured, taking her into his arms and leading her into a slow dance.

They shuffled slowly around the flagstone surface for a while without speaking, enjoying the closeness of each other's bodies, the cool breezes, and the beauty of the night scene that stretched into the distance in all directions.

"You know," Dino whispered into her ear, "a guy could get used to this kind of life."

That's the idea, you dope, she thought.

Nina decided to let the musicians depart early after all. The oriental carpet had been christened, but suddenly, accidentally, and in a most bizarre fashion.

There was still the rest of the apartment to go, and Nina thought she just might be able to persuade Dino to join her in a more time-honored ritual. . . .

In Book Five of Eileen Fulton's Take One for Murder . . .

Nina's wild about the beautiful antique wedding gown she will wear on an upcoming episode of *The Turning Seasons*. But she experiences an inexplicable aversion to the brooch the costume department has supplied to go with it—the red jewels remind her of drops of blood.

Her uneasiness is confirmed after Angela Dolan "borrows" the brooch without Nina's knowledge, and the body of Evan Greer, Angela's new love interest, is discovered in her living room. Angela had just learned that Evan was cheating on her with a younger woman, and Dino Rossi immediately casts her as the prime suspect in the murder case.

But Horst Krueger, whose off-again-on-again romance with Angela had been abruptly terminated by her affair with Evan, had a strong motive for eliminating the competition as well. While Dino and his squad concentrate on Horst and Angela, Nina as usual trusts her instincts, following a convoluted trail of clues that lead her to a host of suspects.

Nina finally narrows things down to a bizarre situation involving the brooch, and decides to use the wedding gown in a segment of *The Turning Seasons*'s new plotline to flush the killer into the open. But in the process, she unwittingly places both herself and Dino in deadly danger. . . .